Advance Praise f

"A moving and magical story about the things we hold most dear, *Wish* will grab hold of your heart."

JASON WRIGHT,
New York Times bestselling author of *The Wednesday Letters*

"*Wish* pulled at my heartstrings like few books ever have. Baseball fan or not, you'll find something to love. This story is a poignant reminder that life, like any great game, is less about the final score and more about how we play."

KEVIN ALAN MILNE,
author of *The One Good Thing*

"*Wish* grabs ahold of your hand and beautifully walks you through baseball's greatest potential. As a father who loves the game, I came away from the story realizing I have not wished enough in my life."

DOUG GLANVILLE,
ESPN baseball analyst, author of *The Game from Where I Stand*,
and former MLB player

"Your one wish after finishing this novel will be that it had never ended. Jake Smith has written a heartbreaking—yet uplifting and totally enthralling—novel about fathers and sons and families. It's a triumphant tale of the mysteries and wonder of our own humanity."

DOUG STANTON,
New York Times bestselling author

"A delightful, remarkable debut novel, *Wish* reveals the power of faith and love in the most difficult of times. But it is more a story of hope than heartbreak. I recommend it highly."

DAN WALSH,
bestselling author of *The Unfinished Gift*

WISH

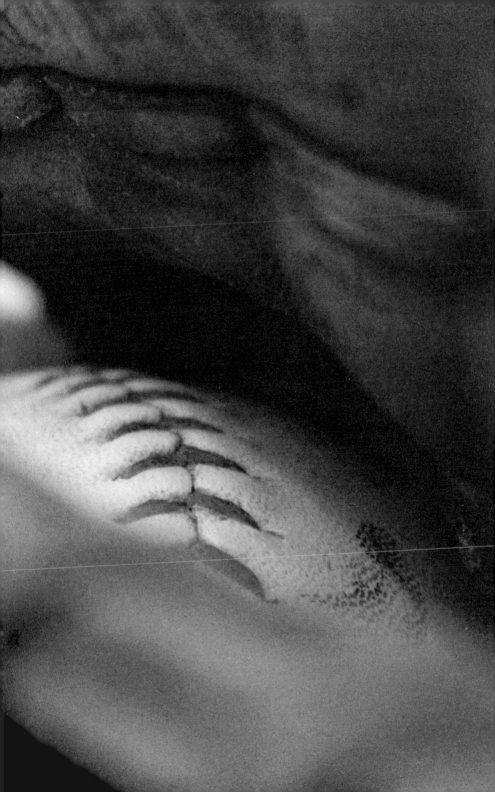

WISH

— a novel —

JAKE SMITH

Tyndale House Publishers, Inc.
Carol Stream, Illinois

Visit Tyndale online at www.tyndale.com.

Visit Jake Smith's website at www.jakesmithbooks.com.

TYNDALE and Tyndale's quill logo are registered trademarks of Tyndale House Publishers, Inc.

Wish

Designed by Daniel Farrell

Edited by Caleb Sjogren

Published in association with Folio Literary Management, LLC, 630 9th Avenue, Suite 1101, New York, NY 10036.

Scripture taken from the New King James Version.® Copyright © 1982 by Thomas Nelson, Inc. Used by permission. All rights reserved.

Wish is a work of fiction. Where real people, events, establishments, organizations, or locales appear, they are used fictitiously. There is no connection with the MLB, MiLB, or their affiliates, nor have they endorsed this novel in any way. All other elements of the novel are drawn from the author's imagination.

Library of Congress Cataloging-in-Publication Data

Smith, Jake, date.
  Wish / Jake Smith.
    pages cm.
  ISBN 978-1-4143-9156-4 (hc)
  ISBN 978-1-4143-9154-0 (sc)
  1. Detroit Tigers (Baseball team)—Fiction.   2. Fathers and sons—Fiction.   3. Sons—Death—Fiction.   4. Last words—Fiction.   5. Baseball stories.   I. Title.
  PS3619.M58828W57 2014
  813'.6—dc23   2013042320

Printed in the United States of America

20   19   18   17   16   15   14

7   6   5   4   3

For those who fight every day, the families who
fight alongside, and the memory of those who fought
so bravely . . . past, present, and future:
I wish you strength.
I wish you health.
I wish you laughter.
I wish you perseverance.
I wish you peace.

For Vickie, Pete, Mark, and Madeline:
Forever and always, my love and my life.

1

JAMES McCONNELL LOVED THIS MOMENT, when the sinking, early May sun transformed the high school baseball field into Yankee Stadium, gilding the pitcher's mound and bases and each blade of moistening grass. With a golden brush, it painted over the field's blemishes, smoothed the pockmarks around third base, greened the scrubby grass in shallow center field, and refilled the crater consuming the right-handed batter's box. Everything softened and melted together in that evening glow, and the high school's small field, carved out of a northern Michigan swamp, became a place where professionals played.

The slanting sun sharpened his concentration. In the first base coach's box, he bent forward and rested his hands on his knees, legs spread wide, and studied the opposing left-handed pitcher. The teenager had just walked the leadoff batter in the bottom of the fourth inning on four straight pitches, and James recognized the pressure clenching in the pitcher's jaw. For most seventeen-year-olds, pressure meant mistakes. And James spotted one brewing in how the kid, lips mashed together in frustration, took far too long getting the sign from the catcher. James figured a wild pitch was coming. That, or a medium fastball right down the middle, a perfect pitch to hit. Either way, he told the runner on first to be ready. Sure enough, the next pitch skipped in the dirt, low and away to the left-handed batter, but the catcher blocked it, keeping the runner at first base.

James straightened, and in the few seconds between pitches, he marveled again at the evening sunshine and how it always seemed to make his baseball career feel complete—from high school star at eighteen, to promising college standout at twenty, to part-time assistant high school coach at thirty-four. It created a moment that, unlike many others in his life, felt perfect.

The moment shattered.

The runner, shuffling back to first base after the pitch in the dirt, said, "Hey, Coach Mac," and flicked his head toward the first base dugout.

A burgundy SUV streaked down a paved No Vehicles Allowed footpath that wound down from the school and around the track and softball diamonds. Greg's car. A hand shot out the driver's window with a frantic wave. The SUV dipped, threatening to veer down the grassy slope toward the baseball diamond, but the driver fought back, straightened it out, and jammed the brakes. Tires screeched.

James sprinted off the field.

He knew why Greg, the school's athletic director, was there, and that perfect moment he treasured vanished. The golden light, the performance of his team, the eternal hope of an unlikely state title, his love of baseball—none of it mattered. Not anymore.

The cancer was back.

2

JAMES PLUNGED HIS SHOULDER into the stubborn gate near the first base dugout. The gate never budged without a battle. It didn't have a prayer of winning this time.

"Grab your stuff!" Greg shouted from his SUV. He slammed the vehicle through a three-point turn and aimed it back up the path. James snatched his backpack from a utility closet behind the dugout, and his cleats kicked up mud and just-greening grass as he dashed up the slope.

"Where is he?" James asked when he jumped in. He dug his cell phone out of the backpack—ten missed calls, two voice mails, and one text from Emily that simply said, Call me!

"At the hospital." Greg steered carefully down the path, which rimmed a high embankment alongside a wetland behind the softball field. When it straightened out, he nudged the engine faster.

"I talked to Emily between games, and he was fine, sleeping," James said.

In the first message, he deciphered "911" through his wife's crying; in the second, she said, with more composure, "The ambulance is here. Your parents have Lizzie. I called Greg, and he's on his way to get you." The ten missed calls and the text had come between the two voice mails. James removed his navy cap and wadded a handful of his thinning brown hair.

Greg maneuvered through an S-curve at a gate and back into the school's parking lot. "She just told me that Aaron woke up disoriented and then collapsed. An ambulance took them to North Mercy."

James pointed at his tan truck. "I'm over there." He pulled his hat back on and searched for his keys in the backpack, but Greg sped past the truck.

"I'm driving you."

"But I'm—"

"You're in no condition to drive across town."

"I'm not in any condition. I'm fine."

"You're shaking." Greg nodded at James's trembling hands clutching the backpack. "Look, I'm sure Aaron's fine, but your family won't be if you kill yourself driving like a lunatic. Now buckle up." At the school's entrance, Greg glanced left, right, then rolled the stop, darting out in front of a minivan; at the first intersection, he tramped on the gas through a yellow light.

"You know he's not fine," James said after a few minutes of staring out the windshield. "None of it's fine. And it's never going to be *fine*." The SUV devoured the cars in front and spit them out behind. "It came back."

"You don't know—" Greg's phone jumped to life with the University of Michigan fight song, and he answered it before the Victors were fully hailed. "Hey, Tom. Yeah, it's Aaron; he's back in the hospital. Hang on." He handed the phone to James. "Here."

"Figured you'd be on the line, and I didn't want to beep

in," said Tom, the head coach, calling from the dugout. "Look, don't worry about us, okay? We got this covered without you. You focus on that boy of yours. Keep me posted, all right?"

"Yeah, okay. Thanks." James ended the call.

With nothing to do except fret, he rested his elbow on the passenger door, massaged his forehead, closed his eyes, and thought of his nine-year-old son.

His blond-haired, blue-eyed boy.

An all-American kid.

No, that's not right. He's never been an all-American kid.
He's never really been a kid at all.

Aaron had suffered through so much—*too* much—the last four years. They all had. But things had turned around. Aaron had pulled through. And just when it looked like he'd be able to play baseball for the first time, even if only in the backyard, to catch a pop-up or field a grounder or hit a ball *for the first time*, as he rebuilt his strength with the intense physical therapy sessions . . . the fever . . . the aches . . . the fatigue . . . all like before . . . all in a matter of days. And now . . . *this*.

His mind burned with snapshots of Aaron. In his arms as he rocked him and sang him a lullaby. Crying in his crib. Blowing out three birthday candles. Going to preschool. Wearing a Detroit Tigers baseball cap with a shock of blond hair escaping from the sides. The two of them tossing a plastic ball back and forth in the living room. Bald and smiling in a hospital gown during a chemotherapy session. Thrilled at the first signs of fuzzy hair. A Christmas, this past Christmas, a *real Christmas*, no pain, no needles, in complete remission. Feebly clutching a baseball while falling asleep on the couch in front of the Tigers game a couple of weeks ago. Their special good-bye handshake routine earlier in the day, the one they always did whenever James coached.

Something coiled around James's chest. A python. Squeezing. Tightening. Crushing. Dragging him to a place—

He opened his eyes and yanked off his navy-and-gold team jacket, tangling himself in the sleeves and seat belt. Snarling, he finally peeled it off and flung it into the backseat.

The city blurred past as Greg hit almost every green light and ran two reds, and before more images tortured James, the North Michigan Mercy Hospital complex appeared beyond the rooftops of downtown homes. The tires squealed again when Greg hit the brakes under the covered emergency room entrance. James burst out of the SUV without a word.

The lobby rattled with the sound of his cleats as he hustled to the check-in desk, packed at least ten deep. No one moved particularly fast on the other side, either. He fidgeted; he looked around for someone else. "C'mon; c'mon. . . ." The few seconds took too long, and he bullied past the line to the desk.

A young receptionist glared at the interruption. "Sir, I'll have to ask you—"

"My son is Aaron McConnell. An ambulance brought him in a little while ago. He's a . . ." James swallowed. "He's a cancer patient. Where is he?"

"Sir, I will help you when it's your turn, so please—"

"My turn's right now, young lady. Tell me where Aaron McConnell is. Nine-year-old boy. Came in here with his mom by ambulance."

"I'm with another patient right now." She motioned for the person James had elbowed aside to come forward again.

James's shaking hands grabbed the edge of the desk and squeezed in a last, desperate hope of keeping it together. "Just tell me where my son is, what room he's in." Her eyes flicked to her computer monitor. "You've got it right in front of you!"

"Is there a problem here?" a husky voice called from behind.

A hulking security guard wearing a uniform that looked two sizes too small covered the lobby in three strides.

"No," James said, taking a step back.

"Yes!" the receptionist cried.

"I'm just—"

"This guy barged in here and started yelling at me!"

"I'm not—" James clenched his teeth behind a fake, faltering smile. "I'm not yelling," he said to the guard. "I just want to find out where they took my son. He's nine. With cancer. They rushed him in here about a half hour ago." He turned back to the receptionist. "Please, tell me where he is, and then you can get back to saving the rest of the world."

"Sir, I think you'd better come with me," the guard said, grabbing James by the elbow.

James wrenched it free and demanded Aaron's room number again. And again. And again. The guard shouted, the receptionist shouted, James shouted; the emergency room crowd took a sudden interest in the latest celebrity gossip in their magazines.

"Hey!" A woman's bark from down the hall pierced the commotion. "Whoever's disturbing my peaceful environment of calm and healing is gonna get popped in the nose! And I just got a manicure! Now who's causing all . . . ?" The short woman with a black beehive of hair and flushed cheeks matching her scrubs spotted James over the top of her thick, silver-rimmed glasses. Her lips pursed.

"Listen, Deena," James said, "I don't know where you found this candy striper, but she won't tell me where Aaron is. And I'm trying to explain to the nice big officer here that—"

"Save it," Deena said, cutting him off. Her cheeks faded to the same color white as her lab coat. "They're back here." She flicked her head down the hall and held up a hand to the guard. "He's fine, Trevor; I got him."

"You sure?" The guard inflated, ready to pounce if the head ER nurse gave the order.

"Yes, I'm sure. But I'll call you if there's a problem." Deena raised one black eyebrow and scowled at James as he approached. "Won't I, Mr. McConnell?"

His plastic cleats left a trail of baseball field dirt for the guard to follow. He was in no mood for a reprimand. "Just tell me where he is."

3

"YOU DON'T HAVE TO GO BALLISTIC ON MY PEOPLE," Deena said, leading James down the emergency room's main corridor. "Everybody in here's got problems. They're all someone's son or daughter."

James's cleats clacked through the hall. "Yeah, but not with a cancer that should be in remission." Examination rooms sprouted off every ten feet, and he held his breath at each doorway, praying the nurse would stop.

"No, some of them have broken legs or are bleeding out or need their chests pounded on." Deena stopped and looked up at James, a full six inches taller. Her black hair glistened under the fluorescent lights. "Look, you don't know that it's back, and even if it is, God forbid, you can't control it."

His head lowered. "That's the problem. So what happened?"

"He got severely anemic, so we started a blood transfusion. He's a tough kid. But you—" she gently poked him in the chest—"have to learn to be a little softer."

James nodded and gazed at the ceiling, his eyes burning.

"I know you think the cancer's back, but there's a whole process for this. One step at a time, then another, then another. We've known each other a long time, and you guys have always taken that next step. You'll take this one, too. But if the cancer is back, it's going to involve a lot of people again, like last time, and that starts with—"

"I know; I know," James said, sniffing once. "I'll apologize to the candy striper—"

Deena cleared her throat and stiffened; the pursed lips returned.

"I mean, the, uh, nice young lady trying to help people."

Deena smiled. "There, not so hard, right? Right." She patted him on the shoulder and continued walking. Finally, at a closed door near the end of the hall, she whispered over her shoulder, "Remember: softer."

At the sight of his wife, James knew something was terribly wrong. Emily McConnell battled the tears, but some dripped from her puffy eyes. She dashed a wadded tissue across her cheek.

Aaron, however, simply appeared sleepy. Although pale and obviously weak—and with a bag of blood draining into his right arm—he comforted his mom. He held her hand, his face calm and consoling, hers twisted in helpless consternation. He patted her on the shoulder, muttering that he'd be fine; she nodded, breathing into the fist-clenched tissue. Her chest seized at stifled sobs bubbling from somewhere deep down, a place James knew she'd often visited early on in Aaron's first cancer fight years ago.

He knew that place. *The Place*, to him, with two great big ugly capital letters. Unlike Emily, he'd visited it every single day while enduring the nearly four-year ordeal of Aaron's fight against acute lymphoblastic leukemia. Watching his five-year-old son identified as a "cancer patient" and subjected to a treatment regimen that no child should have to bear, sitting powerless and horrified as something so minuscule and intangible dictated that this particular child would in fact have no childhood at all. . . . When James couldn't fight the situation with stubbornness, he wallowed in The Place. The Place where pictures of life without his son filled the walls. The Place where he sat in the corner wondering what he could've done differently. The Place where he grew old staring out a smudged window, imagining who his little boy would have become had his life not been stolen.

Since the completion of Aaron's final phase of treatment in December—and with the most recent tests all clear—James hadn't visited The Place. He thought it had been gutted and remodeled to house the normal, everyday fears of a typical parent, one who worried about his child climbing a tree or taking the car out for the first time or going off to college. The *cancer patient* era had ended, and Aaron and his family graduated into a different class of people, those defined by tenacity and perseverance and luck and faithfulness and hard work—all summed up in two words: *cancer survivor*. It immunized him, mentally and emotionally, to everything else with a vaccine of "No matter how bad it is, we've gone through worse."

But now was worse. Now, the *patient* was back. *The Place* was back. And it was an examination room in North Michigan Mercy Hospital's ER.

James feigned a smile. He didn't feel softer.

"See, I told you it was him," Aaron said to his mom. "I heard his cleats."

James's heart skipped at how far away the boy sounded. Emily rose and melted into her husband's embrace. But he studied Aaron.

"You heard his cleats but not the ruckus?" Deena said, raising one eyebrow. "Thought they would've heard that up on the tenth floor."

"You caused a ruckus?" Emily said, dabbing her eyes.

"It wasn't a ruckus."

"It got Trevor involved," Deena said.

"Who's Trevor?"

"One of our security guards."

"*What?* Which one?"

"The *big* one." Deena's other eyebrow rose.

"Whoa, that guy's huge," Aaron said, his voice still distant.

"Yeah, well, Trev and I are on a first-name basis now, and he said he'd stop down later to see how you're doing." James ruffled Aaron's thin blond hair and kissed him on top of his head.

"You're lyin'," Aaron said. His eyes fell to slits. James felt the boy's comfort at having both of his parents nearby.

"Oh yeah? Then how would I know he's got an anchor tattoo right here?" James pointed to his forearm.

"Because he almost put it through your mouth," Deena said. Emily laughed, and a feeble but toothy grin spread across Aaron's face.

James tried to match the boy's smile as he sat down and crossed his arms on the bed railing. "How ya doin', buster?"

"I'm okay, Dad. And you don't have to fake it. I know you wanna freak out right now."

"Me? Freak out?" James waved it off. "Took care of that already. How do you think Trev and I got to be so tight?"

"I'm going to leave you three while I go find the doctor," Deena said. "I'll tell *Trev* you said thanks for not cramming your ball cap down your throat." She closed the door behind her.

"All right, what happened?" James said.

"How's the game going?" Aaron asked, his voice not quite strong enough to change the subject.

"Nice try." James turned to his wife. "Last I heard from you, he was sleeping."

Emily sat next to James and laid a hand on Aaron's leg, causing him to stiffen and wince. She yanked her hand back, apologizing. "He kept complaining of a really bad headache, and then he started thrashing while he slept—"

"He does that a lot."

"But he doesn't moan. When he did that, I looked in, and he was white as a sheet. I mean, I know he's been pale for a few days, but this . . ." Emily's lips curled, and she took a deep breath. Only a sudden welling in her eyes leaked through. "I woke him up, and he staggered around and then collapsed."

"I just tripped on a shoe or something."

"No, you collapsed. You didn't know where you were," Emily said. "I called 911, called you about a million times, called Greg, got your parents to come get Lizzie. When we got here, they said he was severely anemic and started the transfusion right away."

Aaron attempted to shrug off the bag of blood hanging above his arm, but a stern look from his father set him straight.

"Has the doctor checked . . . everything?" James asked.

"I don't think so," Emily said. "We're just waiting now."

James sat back and inspected the all-too-familiar monitors surrounding Aaron—one measuring his heart rate and another the oxygen streaming through the nasal cannula's prongs inside the boy's nostrils. They beeped steady and normal, though the heart rate monitor's cadence remained high.

He put an arm around his wife and pulled her close. "Good job getting him here," he whispered. Emily rested comfortably in his arm, her brown, shoulder-length hair enveloping him with its familiar aroma of vanilla-scented shampoo and hair spray. After several minutes, Aaron asked again about the doubleheader.

"We lost the first game, eight to one," James said.

"Danny pitch?" Aaron asked.

"No, Justin. The other team had their ace going in the second game, so we flipped them. We were up five-zip in the second game—" he turned to Emily—"before Greg came tearing down the path like some deranged NASCAR driver."

"Deranged?" Aaron's pallid face scrunched.

"It means crazy," Emily said. "Mr. Fitzpatrick and your father both drive a little deranged."

Aaron snickered, muttering, "Deranged . . . cool." He leaned his head back into a mushy pillow and closed his eyes, breathing deeply through his nose.

"Anyway—" James leaned on the railing again—"through four innings, Danny had ten strikeouts already. He was blowin' it by them."

"Don't forget to get the scorebook," Aaron said, his voice still weak. He looked ready to fall asleep any second.

"I know; I know. I'll snag it for you."

The door opened. Deena and the doctor walked in. James wondered how much longer the short young man in pale-blue scrubs, white coat, and rimless glasses had left on his ER rotation. He shook hands with James and introduced himself as Dr. Toby. "All right, folks, here's what's going on. I gave Aaron's doctor at West Mercy a call and went over everything with her, and I want to make sure I didn't miss anything." He opened a chart and, pushing up his glasses, reviewed Aaron's cancer history time line and the recent events, from when he complained of flu-like symptoms over a week ago, to the fatigue, to the terrible drama of the previous few hours.

It's so much faster, James thought.

"Is there anything you remember that your wife might have forgotten?" Dr. Toby asked James.

James shook his head, still stuck on hearing, again, the details of the day and the retelling of Aaron's cancer history. It sounded like his entire life. The Place called, inviting him back in. Back home.

"Okay," Dr. Toby continued, "I communicated all of that to Dr. Adams. She's due up here at the clinic next week, but she doesn't want to wait to see you until then." He closed the chart. "How'd you like to take a trip tonight, young man?"

Aaron opened his eyes and lifted his head off the pillow. He stared at Dr. Toby. "In the helicopter?"

Dr. Toby threw his head back and laughed. "Y'know, I asked already, and the pilot lost the keys. Sorry. Ambulance."

"Sirens?"

Dr. Toby crossed his arms. "Perhaps."

"Can they go fast?"

"What good are the sirens if you don't go fast?"

Aaron mumbled, "Awesome," and rested back on the pillow.

"Dr. Adams wants to get a look at him before any tests," he told James and Emily. "And since she's got the book on his treatment, I thought it best to turn it over to her."

"Is there anything you can tell us right now?" Emily asked.

"At this point, no."

"But if this is something serious, we need to get some things together."

"Well, it's serious enough that I want Dr. Adams to take over down there, but that's more of a precautionary step than anything else."

Emily's hands fidgeted with each other. "But he's been fine for five months. Why would this anemia come on all of a sudden? You must have some idea what's going on."

"Nothing I'd feel comfortable discussing without—"

"Just tell us!" James yelled. Aaron jumped, and James apologized to him with soft eyes and a weak smile. He settled himself with a measured breath. "Just tell us if it's back," he said in a calmer tone. "It is, isn't it? The leukemia."

The air went stale at the word. Unbreathable. Even the monitors seemed to pause their beeping, waiting for an answer. James didn't care. He didn't want to fool around playing a guessing game for the next several hours.

But Dr. Toby forced them to endure a bit longer. "Look, I know that's what you're thinking, but really, we won't know for sure until—"

"Until they poke the heck out of me," Aaron said. "Wish they could do it with a lightsaber or something. I wouldn't even feel it; it'd just be *vvvmmmmmm-vvmmm*." He made a weak stabbing and slicing motion like a Jedi master. "I'd at least get a cool scar." The vacuum in the exam room pressurized again.

Dr. Toby chuckled. "Yeah, they'll have to do some lumbar punctures and bone marrow tests to be certain and cover everything. And last I heard, their lightsaber needed repairs."

"When does the ambulance leave?" Emily asked.

"Well—" the doctor reviewed Aaron's monitors and the progress of the transfusion and flipped through his chart again—"this is all going smoothly. It won't be long before the transfusion's complete, and he should feel good after that. Plus we can give him some Tylenol for any pain. I'll round up a crew so they can get gassed up. Who wants to ride with him?"

"I do," James and Emily said together.

"Why don't you go home and change your clothes and then come down behind us," Emily said. "You can be home and back before the transfusion is even done."

"Greg drove me here; I don't have my truck. And besides—"

"Besides, Mom, you know how much Dad likes to wear his uniform and spikes," Aaron said.

James looked down at his home-white jersey, pants, and black cleats, then at his son. He shook his head and sighed. The anxiety of having to wait for results disappeared at the sight of the boy's grin.

"Sorry, folks, our rule is that only one parent—" Dr. Toby began.

"We're both going," James interrupted. "You said he'll be feeling good, and we can squeeze in."

"But—"

"I'm going down in the ambulance with my family tonight, Doctor."

"If you thought he threw a ruckus before . . . ," Deena said.

"I'll call your parents, let them know Lizzie's spending the night," Emily said. She slipped out of the room while pulling a cell phone from her pocket.

Dr. Toby opened his mouth to argue, but Deena shook her head not to bother. "Okay, then, a packed crew." He gently squeezed Aaron's toes. "If I don't see you again before I leave, you take care, okay? And let me know how their lightsaber's coming." He handed the chart to Deena, who told James and Aaron that she'd be back in a minute.

"Did the Tigers start yet?" Aaron asked. He leaned back and closed his eyes again.

"I wasn't exactly paying attention. Had some other things on my mind," James said. "Besides, it's a late game. Aren't they in Kansas City?"

"No, Cleveland. They're starting a four-game series. First pitch at 7:05." Aaron's voice, strong a moment ago when things were tense, relaxed.

James glanced at the clock. Almost six thirty.

"You think they'll turn the game on in the ambulance?"

"I'm sure you'll ask," James said.

The ambulance ride that night was one of the most uncomfortable in James's life, surpassing even the endless bus odysseys of his collegiate baseball days. With his knees in his chest and his polyester uniform constricting in all the wrong places, James either sat straight up without support or hunched forward. Emily leaned on her husband, using his shoulder and arm for a lumpy pillow, while James rested a reassuring hand on Aaron's knee. James needed the touch. *He's right here. I've got him right here.*

Emily squeezed James's elbow and kissed him on the cheek. "I'm glad you're with us and not following behind."

James wriggled an arm free and pulled her even closer. The added discomfort was worth it.

Twenty minutes into the ride, Aaron—now as "normal" as they could've hoped for with the transfusion, and wide-awake after sleeping most of the day—found out the EMT was from Minneapolis and a die-hard Minnesota Twins fan. The debate raged. Starting pitchers, cleanup hitters, base stealers, infield defense, double-play combinations—every facet of both teams dissected and argued. Eventually, after nearly an hour and a half, they discovered common ground in their loathing of the Chicago White Sox.

"If my Twins don't make the play-offs and your Tigers don't either, then it better not be because of the Sox," the EMT said. James laughed at Aaron's enthusiastic agreement and litany of statistics about the various bullpen pitchers in the American League Central division.

As they approached the northern edge of Grand Rapids, everyone sat straighter. The baseball banter stopped, and the ambulance's sirens, dormant for most of the trip, pierced the darkness. Cars still streamed on the interstate even at the late hour, and James watched out the windshield, providing Aaron a play-by-play of traffic peeling away to either side.

"It's like the Red Sea," the EMT added. He held out his hands and then spread them wide. "Like Moses, ya know?"

"Except for that one coming up," James said. A Pontiac Vibe scuttled along at the speed limit, oblivious to the hulking, flashing, wailing vehicle barreling down on it.

"We got something for that," the ambulance driver said. He raced up behind the Vibe and blasted a fire engine–like horn. The Vibe fishtailed, dove to the shoulder, and skidded to a stop, dirt and stones engulfing the car.

"Someone's gonna need a new pair of shorts," the EMT said. Aaron snorted so hard that the nasal cannula flew out of his nose, and he laughed—and then cringed from laughing.

Well, he hasn't stopped laughing at underwear jokes yet, James thought.

The McConnells could've navigated the circuitous entries and exits surrounding West Michigan Mercy Hospital's complex in their sleep, but they never had the benefit of ambulance sirens. Brake lights lit up, and cars cleared a path to the emergency room entrance, where a cluster of medical staff waited outside, all dressed in pale-blue scrubs. They removed Aaron on the gurney, and a nurse helped Emily out while James jumped down.

Inside, Emily groaned when she saw Dr. Meg Adams in jeans and a zip sweatshirt. Her auburn hair was pulled tightly into a high ponytail. "You didn't have to come in this late," Emily said, hugging the doctor. "I'm so sorry. I never thought they'd send us down here. But seeing you now . . ."

"Oh, don't be silly," Dr. Adams said, rubbing Emily's shoulders. "But I am going to need a hug from this big guy with the brand-new blood." She leaned over Aaron; he reached up and lightly wrapped his arms around the oncologist's neck. "You hanging in there, tough guy?"

"Yeah."

"Hey, these nurses are going to take you to a room and get you settled for the night. I wanna chat with Mom and Dad. Okay?"

Aaron nodded, received a kiss from both parents, before two nurses wheeled him off down the hall. The EMT followed and struck up another baseball argument.

Dr. Adams led James and Emily to a tiny family waiting room lit by low amber lights, devoid of reading material. James took two steps inside and froze. It was a "death room," as he called it, a space where families were sequestered to comfort one another during their first moments of grief. Four broad paintings filled the cream-colored walls, all showing the same forested path but each in a different season: budding and muddy in spring; green and dense in summer; rippling with color in fall; bare, white, and bleak in winter. James assumed they represented some sort of "circle of life" theme. He wanted nothing to do with it.

Emily saw his reluctance and took his hand, guiding him to an overly cushy love seat. They sat down across from the doctor who had already brought Aaron through years of treatment and into remission.

Or what they thought was remission.

James began by asking the same question he asked Dr. Toby at North Mercy.

"And I'll give you the same answer," Dr. Adams said. "We've all known one another a long time, and you guys know I won't be cagey with answers. But the fact is, we simply don't know."

"And you should know that you can give us your opinion and we won't take it for an official diagnosis," James said.

"We've been through so much together, Meg," Emily said. "Please."

Dr. Adams nodded. "To me, his anemia aside, I'd be prepared for this to be a relapse of the leukemia."

James felt a fist in his gut, official diagnosis or not.

"I don't like the speed with which it hit him."

"That's what's freaking me out," James muttered.

"And that's why he's not staying here."

Emily straightened and looked at her husband and then back to the woman a few years older than them. "But this is where he was treated before. Everyone knows his case around here. He's—"

"—going to another hospital," Dr. Adams said.

"But you're his doctor." Emily's face flushed. "You're *Aaron's doctor*. You got him through the first time. You can—"

"There's a pediatric cancer research hospital a couple hours away, near Ann Arbor, sort of out in the middle of nowhere. It's called St. Francis. Have you heard of it?"

"Yes, but—"

"They're doing some amazing things there," Dr. Adams said. "And they're much better equipped to deal with relapses, if that's what this is. The doctor there, Dr. Charin Barna, he knows Aaron's case inside and out. Actually, the two of us developed his previous treatment plan. He'll love meeting Aaron in person. I'm not ashamed to say that he's probably done more for your son than I have. We talked constantly. St. Francis really is the best place for him now."

James and Emily sat in silence, blindsided, like a lifeline had been cut, casting them off into the unknown.

"Better equipped to deal with relapses. . . . The best place for him now."

"The best place . . ."

"Relapses . . ."

No. Nothing's for sure. Not yet.

James cleared his throat and shifted gears. "The doctor at North Mercy said we won't know for sure until they check his bone marrow. Is that true?" He kept his tone professional, businesslike, just as he'd done before during Aaron's long cancer treatment. Asking questions was the only way he could remember all of the details and maintain a clear head.

The hard part was dealing with the answers. That's when The Place's bony fingers would crawl up his legs, dig in its nails, and pull him under.

"That's true," Dr. Adams said. "And if it is, everything starts over again, right back to induction therapy, then consolidation/ intensification, and finally maintenance. It'll be harder on him, too, and it's even more important that we find a bone marrow match."

Emily leaned into James. They had been through the bone marrow searches before, both within the family and in the general registry. Always futile. "He seemed so much better," Emily said. She concentrated through deliberate breaths when James let her go. "I know he was really looking forward to this summer, when he could get outside and . . ." She glanced at James and then gazed at the painting of the forest path in autumn.

James's lips tightened, and he took over the conversation. "So what's next?"

Professional. Businesslike. Questions.

"He'll spend the night here," Dr. Adams said.

"When do we leave?"

"First thing in the morning."

"How long will we have to wait for a bed?"

"I already called them on my way in and told Dr. Barna you were coming. They always keep some rooms open for an emergency, so they're prepping one for you now."

Emergency.

"What about the first tests?"

"There's no sense putting him through those here. I want him to get as good of a night's sleep as he can. They'll do the tests as soon as you're checked in, and they get results same day down there. Actually, that's where we send our samples."

"Where will we stay?"

"St. Francis is state-of-the-art. The rooms are actually small hotel rooms, like suites but without the hot tub." She smiled. James stayed focused. "You'll stay right in the same room with him. With all of the same precautions as last time, of course. The entire hospital is HEPA filtered."

"For how long?"

"For as long as Dr. Barna wants you there. But I'd guess until Aaron gets into remission."

"Lizzie?"

"Certainly."

"Schooling?"

"They'll go over all of that with you down there. Their child life counselors and assistants are from all over the world, top-notch."

"How are we getting there?"

"Another ambulance ride, I'm afraid. But not as long as what you already did."

"And what should we do tonight?"

"Get some sleep," Dr. Adams said. "You'll leave in the morning, but only one of you can go with him. Now that he's going to St. Francis, we've got protocols to follow, and that means the patient, an EMT, a nurse, and one family member."

"I'll go," Emily said softly.

"But—"

"You rent a car. Go home; get the bags. Give Lizzie lots of kisses for me."

James and Emily had told their six-year-old daughter good night on the phone while in the ambulance—Aaron even talked to her for a minute. Now, at the mention of her name, Emily teared up, her fingers twisting together. James knew she wanted to hold the girl.

"Okay, but I'll leave in the morning. I want to be here tonight."

Dr. Adams led them down the hall, and James pulled off his white jersey along the way, pushing the sleeves of his dark-blue undershirt to his elbows. After spending so much time over the past few years in hospitals, especially West Mercy, he thought the sterile smell wouldn't bother him anymore. His nose grew so accustomed to West Mercy's particular mixture of bleach water and orange freshener that he smelled it every-where. But over the past five months, since their last lengthy stay, the desensitization gradually reversed. Now the aroma pierced his nostrils and slapped him with a furious headache. It brought back every sharp, painful memory of their previous life in West Mercy's halls.

Aaron's room lay quiet and dark, and when they entered, he grinned—weakly, but from fatigue, not pain. A cot lay open on one side of the half-raised bed, a thick chair on the other. ESPN's *Baseball Tonight* flashed game recaps on the small TV.

"Hey, tough guy," Dr. Adams said, sitting on the edge of his bed. "You're going to a new place tomorrow, one for kids just like you." Aaron's eyes peeled back. "Once you meet Dr. Barna, you'll forget all about me." The boy's smile returned, but his eyes darted elsewhere. "Your mom's riding with you. Dad's going to go home and pack some bags." Aaron nodded that he understood, but he didn't say anything. "Don't worry; they'll figure out what's going on." She patted his foot good night, told everyone she'd see them off in the morning, and left the McConnell family behind a quietly closing door.

Emily took the cot, laying a hand on Aaron's arm. Sleep consumed her in a matter of minutes. James propped his dirty-socked feet onto Aaron's bed and watched the highlights from the Cincinnati Reds and Atlanta Braves game with him.

"Tigers won," Aaron said. "Nine to three. Boz hit two homers."

"Who pitched?"

"Franke. He went seven innings and gave up four hits."

"That's, what, his fourth win of the season already?" James asked.

"Fifth. And it's only early May."

"Been a while since a Tiger pitcher won more than twenty games. Who won the most in the league last year?"

"Parsons, with the Phillies," Aaron said. "Twenty-two games. He won his last twelve starts in a row, too."

"Man, what a streak. Didn't someone have a long hitting streak last year? Davis? Davidson?"

"Davies. From the Rockies. Thirty-two games. Nobody'll touch DiMaggio's fifty-six games, though."

They sat in silence through more highlights. Eventually, the recap of the Tigers game played again, but Aaron didn't stir. James turned off the TV and faced him. A sliver of fluorescent light leaked from the bathroom and cut across Aaron's steadily rising and falling chest, and James basked in the presence of a sleeping child who, for at least this moment, wasn't in pain.

Tomorrow's going to change everything, he thought.

But he leaned back, stared at the ceiling, and found a bit of refuge in his ignorance of the situation. The answers he wanted so desperately earlier in the evening could wait.

For right now, Aaron wasn't a *cancer patient* again.

For right now, he was still a survivor.

4

JAMES HEDGED ON HIS PROMISE TO EMILY: he set the
cruise control in the rental car at eighty, not seventy-five.
Aaron's perkiness in the morning helped James vow to keep his
"deranged driving" under control on his way home to northern
Michigan and back down to the new hospital. Emily didn't
believe him, so he mocked holding one hand on an invisible
Bible, raising the other, and swearing an oath. She swore herself
and slapped him on the arm.

He had left the hospital at dawn in a cab, waving out the
back window to his wife. His stomach soured at the thought of
leaving her to shoulder the transfer and admission to a new hospital, Dr. Adams's assurances aside. And then there were Aaron's
tests as soon as he checked in. The nurses and doctors would
take over for those, but Emily would have to hold Aaron's hand,
help him through the recovery, and then sit alone while he most
likely slept. James had asked for his own promise from his wife—
that she wait for him before hearing the test results.

But that would happen only if he stepped on it, so he

accelerated the cruise control a touch more. The crisp May morning left a stubborn fog on the windshield, but the defroster, cranked to high, cleared two gaping holes, one in front of the driver, the other in front of the empty passenger seat. The dawning sun would burn off the rest as soon as the highway snaked its way out of the heavily forested chunk of western Michigan.

A half hour north of Grand Rapids, his cell phone rang.

"You make it out okay?" Emily asked.

"Yep, clear sailing, no traffic. You guys?"

"We're almost ready to leave. Meg said it's an hour and a half, but the ambulance driver said he'd be fired if it took him that long. Did you call your folks yet?"

"Thought I'd let them sleep in a bit, if that's even possible with Lizzie," James said. "You know they're keeping her home from school today, right? They want to spend some time with her."

"What about work?"

"I'll call them in a little bit. No one's really in yet anyway."

"Oh, can you call Nikki at the school and let her know what's going on?"

"In case Greg hasn't already."

"Yeah." They shared a half mile of silence, the distance between them growing by the second: one car heading north, one ambulance soon heading south.

"You hanging in there?" James asked.

"I think so. I've got a big guy right here helping me." James could tell Aaron was smiling at his mom. "What about you?"

"I won't kid you, this is going to be a lonely drive. Might have to nudge it past seventy-five."

"Like you haven't already." Another quarter mile in silence. "Okay, well, I'll let you go. Don't forget to call your mom . . . and oh, Aaron wants you to bring down his laptop and the scorebook from last night's games."

"Ten-four. Anything for you?"

"Just the ready bag."

"Would've been nice to have been done with that, wouldn't it?"

"Well, we can't help that now. Only one choice to make," Emily said.

"Easier for some than others."

"I know, but it's not about what's easy for us."

"I'll take an IV of whatever it is you're having," James said, snickering.

"Love you. Drive safe."

"Love you guys, too. See you soon." James waited for her to hang up, the way he had ever since their first date in college, and lingered with the phone to his ear, the silence an expanding, deepening chasm. With a difficult gulp, he dropped the phone into the open console.

He drove another twenty minutes before calling his parents. His mom answered with an anxious voice and, after being filled in on the details, put Lizzie on the phone.

Lizzie.

Through Aaron's tests and treatments and hospital stays, the girl had spent her toddler years bouncing back and forth between home and James's parents, and his heart shattered during those rare times a phone call to check on her overflowed with her crying. But she eventually outgrew the meltdowns. Staying with her grandparents provided some valuable stability for her. A routine. Until the last five months. No hospital stays for Aaron, and no overnights in the Disney princesses guest room for Lizzie.

Now, the routine again, at least for a little while.

James choked up at the sound of her chirpy voice and mustered, "Hey, Lizard." It didn't matter that he couldn't talk because she launched into the plot for whatever cartoon she happened to be watching. In midsentence, she erupted in bubbly giggles, rattled off what she found so hilarious, and then said she loved him and passed the phone back to her grandma. James's "Love you, too; see you soon!" disappeared into the void in the exchange. He knew it would be a day of cartoons, movies, and coloring at his parents' house; his mom suggested, rather loudly, that they might spend the entire day in their pajamas, and a cheer pierced the background.

"I'll stop by on my way out of town," James said. "I've got to get home, make a few phone calls, and pack some bags. I'll pack one for Liz, too, so you've got some things for her this weekend."

"You don't have to worry about that, Jimmy. We can always go over there if we need something. You know I've got clothes for her here, too."

"I know. Okay, Mom, kiss Lizard for me."

"Hang in there," she said. "We've got those prayers going. He's in good hands."

"I hope you're right. See you in a bit."

James debated about making his other phone calls while on the road—the school, the team's head coach, his boss at work—but he opted for silence. Maybe Emily would call in the interim with news he could pass on other than the stiff-upper-lip, chin-up platitudes of "Aaron's in a new hospital, but the doctors are top-notch.". . . "No, we don't know what's happening, but I'm sure they'll figure something out.". . . "Thanks for your well-wishes; I'll pass them on.". . . "We'll fight it just like last time.". . . "Yeah, he's a tough kid; he'll come through this stronger than before."

The clichés already sounded hollow. Over the previous years of Aaron's treatment, James had used them so often and for so long that they grew to taste like rotten fruit. It had been easier to let Emily do all the talking. Going beyond those clichés meant delving into the answers of all the medical-related questions James was robotically efficient at asking. And that meant diving into his emotions. Those he reserved for himself and for his family. As much as people tried to make themselves available to him and Emily and Lizzie, they only suffocated him, barging in on their private lives, robbing him of the last remaining days with his son.

That was the effect of The Place. It was a cell. A prison echoing one powerful, spiteful word: *why?*

Aaron's room, untouched, frozen under a burial shroud of dust.

Two years ago, in the middle of Aaron's treatment, James teetered on the brink of a nervous breakdown. Until Emily brought him back. And it wasn't some miraculous progression in Aaron's treatment, nor a catchy, inspirational speech or quote she passed on to him. It wasn't even his meditating in West Michigan Mercy's chapel while Aaron fought off a serious infection.

While they were home during a "good spell," Emily simply suggested that he take Aaron to the high school baseball field during one of the summer workouts. "Push him around the bases. Be with him in a place both of you love," she had said.

Although he'd been to the field many times before, Aaron had never seen his father hit, and he begged James to stand in against the pitching machine, hooked up on the mound with a pitching screen in front of it. The head coach fed balls into the machine, and James took his cuts while Aaron sat in the dugout in his wheelchair, still needed because of his fatigue, with two incoming seniors who treated him like one of the guys. James missed . . . then fouled a couple off . . . then hit a handful of dribblers . . . then some pop-ups . . . and then a line drive right back at the pitching screen. Then another. Then one in the gap. Then a two-hopper to the fence. The muscle memory returned, the groove, the eye-hand coordination that had made James a college star for one glorious season. Aaron and the two players clapped and cheered and *woot*ed from the dugout.

And for a little while, the seven-year-old boy and his dad—one a player and one a spectator, the way it had always been—forgot everything except their love of baseball.

With one aluminum *tink* after another, James drove away the ugly depression that had threatened to swallow him whole and spit out his bones. He'd forgotten how much he loved the game. It rejuvenated him, but it also made him painfully aware that it might be a long time before Aaron would be strong enough—if he were ever well enough—to actually play himself. And if the boy could still show that kind of passion while watching the game he loved, then James could bring that same passion to the cancer fight.

From that point, he told people honestly how tough the battle was, how they were coping, and the clichés weren't tired old sayings anymore. Now he believed them. And Aaron's treatment began working. Perhaps it had always been working, but James had been too bitter to see it. Then he did. And all from one showdown with a pitching machine.

A showdown that now seemed like it had taken place in a dream. Another life.

The miles raced by in silence, and James knew that another showdown against a pitching machine wouldn't work this time.

Without Emily by his side to help him analyze the current situation, or change the subject, the loneliness and frustration gnawed at him. *This wasn't supposed to happen.* The same old wounds, which had never fully healed but at least scarred over, were being rubbed raw, over and over, mile after mile, his images darkening as he saw his boy becoming frailer and frailer. . . . He pounded the steering wheel. Again. *They said Aaron had beaten this.* Another slam, a fist to the horn. *We all were supposed to have beaten this.*

The Place lulled like a Siren. And he sailed right for it with open arms.

Tears dripped down his cheeks.

"I just wanted to play catch with my boy," he whispered to the empty car, to the highway, to the dawning sun, to God. "We were finally there. We'd finally made it."

No one answered.

Only the car hissing over pavement. Static.

"Maybe things would've been different if . . ." He shook his head.

A half hour passed, staring down the highway. Finally James looked at his uniform—the unbuttoned, untucked white jersey with the navy-and-gold numbers and emblem, the bit-too-tight white pants with the navy stripe down the leg. He settled on a decision, which had nothing to do with helping Aaron get better.

He reached into his bag on the passenger seat and withdrew a graying baseball. At one time brand-new and white, the ball had become his stress ball, which he rubbed in the dugout during games he helped coach. Now he brought it to his nose and drank in the distinctive aroma of leather worn smooth from his hands. His eyes spent a few seconds poring over the individual red stitches curving around the ball. He slowly spun it in his fingers.

"If this doesn't go well and it ends without Aaron ever having learned how to catch or throw or hit—to *really* throw or catch or hit," he threatened the ball and any of the baseball gods who were listening, perhaps even threatening God

Himself, "if he can't have any of it, then neither will I. You hear me?" His eyes peeled from the ball and back to the expressway. "I'm done. When all this is over, and if he's . . . I'm just done."

He shoved the ball back in his pack.

He needed company. He found a sports radio station, picking up a signal out of Detroit gabbing about the Tigers and their decent start to the young season. He changed it to a country music station, ticked the cruise control faster, and sank into the seat.

A shuttle from a sister rental car company took James to his truck, and from there, he didn't waste any time getting home. The lawn surrounding the McConnell house in the tiny subdivision glistened from the morning sprinklers, and the new understory emerging in the woodlot behind the home cast a light-green glow in the forest.

James kicked off his cleats into the coat closet and tossed his pack on the dining room table. Evidence of Emily's frantic departure lay strewn throughout the house: toys, books on the couch and floor, dishes from the previous night's dinner on the table, a stack of unopened mail on the counter. He didn't touch a thing and hustled up the half-dozen steps of the tri-level to the master bedroom and bathroom. As in years past, it already felt like more of a hotel than a home.

From under their queen bed, James fished out the packed black ready bags Emily had asked for. After growing weary of unpacking and repacking whenever Aaron had an extended hospital stay, she gave up and bought double of everything—toiletries, clothes, shoes—and left it all in a suitcase for each person underneath his or her bed. They still hadn't unpacked their ready bags, unwilling to tempt fate. Now James wondered if maybe leaving them packed had been the jinx. Holding his breath, he unzipped their duffels and crammed in a few more changes of clothes for both of them. After flinging his uniform in the general direction of the hamper, he headed for the bathroom.

He didn't want to look in the mirror while he brushed his teeth, terrified to see if the brown eyes gazing back at him had already changed from the proud ones of the day before, the eyes of a man with a cancer survivor for a son. Too early in the process to give up, he nevertheless felt the change setting in, the weariness of entering another long fight, a losing fight. Seeing it would be acknowledging it. Accepting it. With his head down, he stepped into a very hot shower.

He yanked on a white T-shirt and brown long-sleeved pullover and started making his calls while threading a belt through his jeans. First, the team's head coach—Tom was eager for news. James filled him in about the hospital transfers and Aaron's request for the stats from the previous night's double-header. Tom laughed. He explained that the second game got dicey after James left—the opposing team pulled to within one run only to strike out with the tying run on third to end the game.

"The boys were all a little concerned for you and Aaron, I think," Tom said.

"I appreciate it. Look, I don't know what's going to come of all this. I might not be at many more games. If at all."

"Don't sweat it. I'm fairly certain we can manage. It's not like we're gonna make it out of districts. You've got more important things to worry about now. We always knew this was a possibility."

James bit his lip.

"I know this is hard right now, but you'll get through it."

Frustration bubbled.

"We're here for you, okay?"

"Um-hmm."

"I already e-mailed Aaron the stats from last night, and I'll keep doing it. He can run his programs and send them back to me."

"He'll like that."

"You take care of yourself, you hear? Emily and Lizzie will need you to be strong."

Hearing the clichés was even worse than saying them. He mumbled a good-bye and hung up.

His boss acted much the same, as if Aaron's doom approached and how they all "feared this was coming" and how it "must be so hard on everyone." James clenched his teeth through it.

"If you want to check your e-mails from down there, fine," his boss said. Then he sighed. "But I suppose we'll just get a temp to cover for you."

"Oh . . . uh, are you sure? I can stay in tou—"

"No, no, it's fine. If I remember from last month's report, you didn't have a whole lot in the fire right now anyway."

"Um . . . okay, I guess."

"And, James?"

"Yeah?"

"I'm sorry."

James almost quit, but he couldn't, not now. The health benefits the insurance agency provided dented the previous medical bills, at least somewhat, and he had no clue where this next bout would lead. Instead, he hung up without a good-bye and vented his wrath with a choke hold on the phone and a slam on the dresser. Three calm, focused breaths helped him concentrate on the next number, the Catholic school's office.

Greg had already filled in Nikki, the school secretary, and she assured James that she'd mail Aaron and Lizzie's work as soon as she had an address for the St. Francis education coordinator.

"We'll round up the prayer warriors again for you guys," she said.

"Thanks. I'm sure we'll need 'em."

In Lizzie's bedroom, on the same upper level as the master bedroom, James snagged her ready bag and replaced some of the winter items with pink and purple shorts, skirts, T-shirts, and light pants. Rifling through the pile of stuffed animals on her bed, he found a squishy, dirty pink pig and a bushy-maned lion wearing a polka-dot bow tie. He stuffed them into her bejeweled duffel.

He shuffled down to Aaron's room on the lower level and paused at the closed door, graffitied with warning signs: *Stay Back! You Can Come In If You Have Cookies! Home of a Detroit Tigers Fan! No White Sox Allowed!* The placard displaying the Detroit Tigers Kids Club logo, along with *Keep Out! Members Only!*, tipped to one side on weakening tape. He pushed it open gently, as if Aaron were sleeping inside.

In the Tiger den, posters of star players, baseballs, and pennants from the Tigers and their minor league affiliates— the Triple-A Toledo Mud Hens, Double-A Erie SeaWolves, Class A-Advanced Lakeland Flying Tigers, and Class A West Michigan Whitecaps—crowded the dark-blue walls with narrow orange stripes near the ceiling. Foam fingers and tiger claws resided on scattered shelves, and Aaron's laptop, decorated with one Old English *D* sticker on the top, lay closed on a desk lined with player bobbleheads like toy soldiers. James yanked the computer's power cord out of the wall and coiled it around itself. Several baseball books stood in a short bookcase, its four shelves painted alternately blue and white: novels, short story collections, nonfiction references, a massive copy of the *Baseball Encyclopedia*, and player biographies, with Matt Christopher and Mike Lupica Aaron's favorite authors.

On the bookshelf's navy-blue top sat a row of baseball mitts—the pocket of each containing a ball, ranging from a squishy one perfect for a toddler to a hard "official league" baseball. James remembered tucking the first mitt—tiny, foam, and light blue—up against Aaron's legs in the bassinet after he was born. Next in line, a brown glove made of neoprene, a little bigger, and the only one in the line that had ever seen any use. Warmed by the memories of his three-year-old's awkward pitches in the living room, James touched the plastic ball nestled inside and closed his eyes.

But he wouldn't touch the next glove. Its black imitation leather shone as brightly as it had in the store, and the spongier ball, tucked inside the pocket, gleamed. Not a smudge of dirt or a single grass stain streak. Brand-new. The mitt—the one James had bought for Aaron's fifth birthday, a month before he was diagnosed with cancer—hadn't moved from that position in years.

He willed himself to rest his hand on the next mitt in line, a real, honest-to-goodness, take-care-of-it-and-you'll-use-it-in-high-school dark-tan leather baseball glove. The one he bought Aaron last Christmas as a gift for achieving complete remission. This was the glove he would use when they played catch together in the backyard for the first time. This was the glove he would wear when he felt that first wonderful sting in his palm when a baseball smacked into it.

James almost picked it up to take with him, but he couldn't. Not right now. Maybe later, when things progressed, it would be a good talisman to have around. But not right now.

When he turned, thoughts of the time he'd missed playing catch with his son disappeared. He froze. Aaron's Detroit Tigers bedspread lay crumpled and heaped. James's mind played images of the boy thrashing and moaning in bed. He saw his son stagger and collapse on the floor, right where he now stood, saw the medics listening to his heart, strapping him to a gurney, wheeling him out of the room, Emily crying as she followed.

Then he pictured himself and Emily coming home, sitting together on his bed, sobbing because Aaron would never again . . .

The Place's spindly fingers slithered up his legs again. But this time they wormed through his stomach and into his chest, squeezing in time with his heartbeat, wringing the air from his lungs. James's eyes dizzied, and before he suffocated, he snatched the ready bag and let the door close on its own in a rush of wind.

He made it all the way back up to the master bathroom before he breathed again, slowly pushing out several gulps of air, each carrying a horrifying image. Cold water on his face helped, too, and after drying himself, he faced the brown eyes looking back at him in the mirror.

This time, he didn't turn away. He forced the stare, searching for the resolute, cancer-patient father from the last two years, the one born from the pitching-machine showdown.

C'mon. You're in there somewhere.

The fifteen-minute drive to his parents' house took ten. He parked the family SUV at the curb, and James's mom and dad embraced him at the door. Lizzie shrieked and scampered to him, leaping into his open arms, and he swung her around before pressing her tight to his chest. He knelt when he set her down, wiping his brimming eyes as she squirmed away. To her sudden frown, he said, "I'm fine, sweetie. They're happy tears because I'm so happy to see you."

He held her at arm's length. So . . . *normal* looking. An ordinary kid. An average, healthy, ordinary kid.

"Are Mommy and Aaron okay?" she asked. As Grandma had suggested on the phone, she was still in her pink-and-green fleece pajamas. Green barrettes held the wild bangs of her short, mussy brown hair out of her eyes.

"They're doin' okay, Lizard. Aaron's going to a new hospital this time." Her brown eyes lowered to the floor, but James gently lifted her chin. "But you know what? This new hospital? There's lots to do there. And best of all, *you*—" he tapped her lightly freckled nose—"and me and Mommy can all stay right in the same room with him."

"You mean I get to go this time?"

"Sure do. It'll be just like we're in a hotel. But not right now. Let me and Mom get Aaron settled in first and through some of his tests. Then we'll get a place squared away for you, okay? You think you can hang out here for a couple days?"

She didn't react one way or the other; instead, she scuffed away without a word and returned with a colored page. "Here, this one's for Aaron," she said, handing him a purple-colored Yoda holding a pink lightsaber. "Do you think Mommy would like one, too?"

"I bet she would," James said.

She ran away again, returning with a Strawberry Shortcake coloring page covered in every shade of red. "I was going to give this to Grandma, but you can give it to Mommy instead." The girl fixed a serious stare on her grandma. "I have lots of time to color you another one."

Grandma straightened up like a soldier. "Oh, most certainly, yes, ma'am."

"Dad, we already watched *Tinker Bell* this morning, and Grandma said that later we're going to the store to get a

VeggieTales movie, too. Or maybe a Barbie one. And then Grandpa said we're having McDonald's for dinner!"

"That's great, darlin'."

She cocked her head. "Did you bring my baby and stroller from home?"

James snapped his fingers. "Sorry, goofball, I was in such a hurry, I ran right out of the house without them."

Her shoulders slumped.

"That's okay, honey," Grandma said. "We'll stop by your house when we're out today and pick them up."

"And Grandma's got lots here; you know that," James said. "But I did pack Curly and Leo." He unzipped the duffel at his feet, and she yanked out the stuffed pig and lion and squeezed them into a pair of headlocks.

"Do they have Uno?"

"Huh?" James said.

"At the new hospital where Aaron's going, do they have Uno? And Monopoly Junior? Or should we bring ours?" Lizzie asked.

"Uh, yeah, I'm sure they do. Probably lots of other games, too."

"Good. I'm going to let Aaron win at Monopoly Junior. Do you think that would make him feel better?"

James rested a hand on her shoulder. "Absolutely, Lizard."

She smiled. "Okay, then I'll let him win." Her face turned stern again. "But *not* at Uno."

James held up his hands. "He's on his own there; you got it."

She smiled and skipped back to another coloring project on the dining room table.

James's parents pulled him into the kitchen and, in whispers, quizzed him about the situation. He filled them in with as much as he knew. They had already heard from Emily that St. Francis was "something else."

"She wants you to call her when you're back on the road," his mom said. "And she's only briefly met this Dr. Barna."

"We can get your truck down there if you need it. Is there anyone you need us to call?" his dad asked.

James shook his head and gnashed his teeth, remembering the conversations he'd already had. "I think I got everyone."

"But . . . ?"

"Oh, nothing, just . . . nothing."

"C'mon, Jimmy; what is it?" his mom asked.

James paused, not wanting to get back into it, but his mom's touch on his shoulder opened the gates. "It's just . . . they're all so . . . I don't know; they were all 'so sorry' and 'we're there for you' and all grief stricken, like they knew this was going to happen." The frustration erupted. "It ticks me off. We don't even know what's happening, or what's going to happen, and they're acting like Aaron just died! It's like they're already treating me like I'm 'the guy who lost his son.' It's how they've always treated me, like they're mourning."

His mom's eyes widened and flicked toward the dining room. Lizzie stood there, clasping a piece of paper and a green marker, her face white. Her eyes welled, and as they did, her trembling lips curled into a deep frown.

James reached her in two long strides and knelt down, wrapping her up. "Oh, honey, I'm sorry. I shouldn't have yelled. Aaron's fine; the doctors will take care of him, okay?"

She snuffled on his shoulder and nodded. Pushing the paper into his hands, she ran for the couch, pulled a blanket up to her chin, and stared at the TV.

James looked at the picture: a rainbow and a single, crooked yellow daisy, and in green marker scrawled across the top: *I LOEV YOU DADY!* He cursed himself under his breath. Joining her on the couch, he hugged her again and thanked her over and over for the picture, raising her spirits by simply sitting and watching the rest of a cartoon snuggled together. But it only sharpened his guilt.

When the credits flickered across the screen and Lizzie appeared fine, he kissed her on one cheek and pecked extra smooches on the other that he said were from Mommy and Aaron. With a mischievous grin turning up a corner of her mouth, she wiped off the ones from Aaron.

His parents walked him out. "I called the school for Lizzie already," he said as he hugged them. When he got in the SUV, he rolled down the window. "Thanks for watching her. Again. Have fun with her this weekend, but you might want to take her to school on Monday so she can gather up some stuff, maybe have one normal day. Come down after that. Lord knows we'll need her, especially Em." He buckled his seat belt, then stared blankly out the windshield for a few seconds. "I don't know; we might even call you before that."

"Don't worry about her," his mom said. "She'll be fine. Just let us know."

"And drive safely, okay?" his dad added, patting James's arm, which hung out the window.

"I'll call you when I get down there and let you know directions." After a final wave, he pulled into the street and sped off with two good-bye beeps on the horn.

5

A FAST-FOOD BURGER AND FRIES were not the best travel-
ing companions. They began a groaning, rumbling argument
in James's stomach like a couple of petulant kids in the backseat, and thirty-two ounces of Coke did nothing to drown their
bickering. Hosts on various sports radio talk shows contributed
their nagging by relentlessly analyzing, nitpicking, and obsess-
ing about the NBA play-offs. James finally silenced them all
with a push of the radio dial and a few antacids. Save for the
occasional whimper from his stomach, he spent the second half
of the trip to the lake-dotted region east of Jackson, Michigan,
in silence.

He maneuvered easily around the relatively light, Friday
afternoon traffic on eastbound Interstate 94. When city buildings shrank behind him and farmland and trees sprang up
along the highway, James straightened in his seat and set the
directions on the console. "Exit 150, exit 150," he muttered.
He passed exit 145, accelerated around a lumbering semi,
and slid back into the right lane. In minutes, a blue road sign

displayed *Exit 150, Mount Hope Road, St. Francis Pediatric Cancer Research Hospital, 1 Mile.*

A sign for the hospital directed him left off the exit ramp onto Mount Hope Road, and after passing over the interstate, another sign showed St. Francis seven miles away. The mostly flat road took him north of I-94 and into the depths of the Waterloo State Recreation Area, where trees draped their just-leafing branches over the road, creating a sun-dappled tunnel. The wild swath of south-central Michigan seemed out of place nestled amid cities such as Grand Rapids, Ann Arbor, Lansing, and Detroit. In only a few miles, James felt as though he'd slipped into another world, the highway and frenetic speed of city traffic a bad dream. He supposed the hospital's location had been chosen for that very reason.

The hospital's signs grew larger and more colorful, directing him through the recreation area and back out into open, private agricultural land. When the road skirted the northern arm of the park, James spotted two flagpoles guarding an entryway on the left; one pole proudly flapped the US flag, and the other displayed the Michigan crest a little lower. James pulled into the hospital's wide, divided-lane entrance.

Gardeners tended a maze of flower beds behind the outer curbs of the two lanes and in the median between them. Blooming tulips and daffodils wove together in a multicolored blanket, and the gardeners planted leafy clumps of perennials and tiny flowering annuals among them. A short way down the median, more gardeners waved at him while tilling the beds around a mammoth stone-and-metal entrance sign. A wrought-iron sculpture standing atop a corner of the rectangular structure portrayed the abstract outline of a robed man with a halo around his head and an arm outstretched toward a bird landing on the tip of his hand. Amazingly, it appeared that the entire sculpture consisted of a single, tubular piece of black metal that rarely doubled back on itself, widening and tapering and finally ending at the bird's beak.

The scenery couldn't stop him from breaking the posted fifteen-mile-per-hour speed limit. "Okay," he said, holding the directions at arm's length above the steering wheel, "parking deck B. Take a right at the end, then the second deck on the right." The entry road passed into a thick stand of trees, but he spotted buildings through their still-sparse branches; the road curved to the right and ended at a T intersection. On the other side, a rainbow flower bed of tulips and another stone-and-metal sign welcomed people to the St. Francis hospital complex. James turned right onto the two-lane, one-way hospital access road.

The access road circled the hospital complex. On the right spread parking lots and decks, maintenance buildings, a few small restaurants, and some nondescript buildings. On the left, curved buildings, all between five and ten stories, followed the contour of the road. In gaps between them, signs for Emergency Service Vehicles Only pointed to descending lanes for ambulances. James tried to catch peeks of what the buildings surrounded—his best guess was some sort of sprawling park. Skywalks crossed above the two-lane road, connecting the parking decks to some of the larger, interior buildings.

James discovered all this having missed the right turn into parking deck B. Back at the beginning again, he slowed to the speed limit and veered into the right-hand turn lane for his parking deck, grabbing a ticket when it popped out from the dispenser. The black- and yellow-striped gate rose, and he called Emily as he spiraled up three levels before finding the first open spot. He jogged down to the second-level skywalk and crossed over the road to the lobby of Bertoia Building East.

Suspended high above an open-air lobby, a gigantic, stationary mobile depicted the solar system, with a giant central yellow ball and smaller, colorful planets hanging at various distances from the sun. Tinted windows spanned sections of the fifty-foot walls on the far side of the vast lobby, filling the area with diffuse sunlight. A chorus of chatter and conversations rippled like a waterfall. Plush couches and chairs encircled low tables, and kids and parents lounged and talked. Some children sat in wheelchairs and read books or tapped on iPads and phones; others pointed at the planets hanging above. Giggling toddlers propelled themselves around on plastic, pedal-less tricycles, a parent following closely behind pushing each child's decorated IV pole. To James's right and left, signs directed visitors to covered walkways connecting adjacent medical buildings, and a light stream of people funneled into and out of short hallways leading to the two elevator banks on either side. Several reception and information desks sat tucked against the entry from the skywalk, and as James scanned the lobby for his wife, a receptionist asked if he needed help. But he spotted Emily standing beneath Saturn.

They hugged fiercely, and before James asked, she said, "Aaron's fine and resting. He did great this morning." Holding his hand, she guided him toward the elevators on the right. "Everyone's so nice here. I met Dr. Barna this morning. He was really excited to meet Aaron, and Aaron seems to like him. But we haven't heard any results yet."

James looked back at the lobby as they walked. "This place is huge. And in the middle of nowhere."

"I haven't had time to check it out yet."

"Well, hopefully we won't be here long enough to explore." At a service desk by the elevator, Emily showed the receptionist her patient family badge. It took only a minute for them to scan James's driver's license and get him one, which he hung around his neck. The elevator dinged, and Emily pushed the button for the seventh floor.

On seven, glass doors on either side sealed off a vestibule in front of the elevators, and Emily pointed to the right. They washed with waterless hand sanitizer before walking through the doors and into a reception area. Thin, curving strips of ceiling lights above a play table and empty chairs in the middle of the lobby morphed from one soft color of the rainbow to the next. Emily pulled James in the direction of an orange placard that read *Inpatient Rooms* and pushed a button on the wall that automatically swung open a pair of heavy doors; she introduced him at the nurses' station on the other side. The women smiled when talking about Aaron.

"He's made an impression already, huh?" James said while they walked down the hall. The eerie quiet made him feel obligated to keep his voice low.

"It's the McConnell charm. Women can't resist." Emily nudged him. He tensed. "I know." She slipped an arm around his waist. "I didn't think we'd be going through this again, either." After a few steps, she changed the subject. "I talked to Lizzie a little bit ago. She seems fine."

"Typical Lizard. I've got some drawings for you and Aaron in the car," James said, wishing he'd remembered to bring them. He glanced at the colorful wall on his left—framed photos of children and teenagers stretched nearly the entire length of the curving hall. "So where're we at?"

"Right up here, 716. Oh, there's Teri."

A short, slightly rotund African American woman in a floral print top and pink pants crept out of Aaron's room, and her white teeth shone when she saw Emily. "He's all right," she said quietly. "Just checkin' in while you were gone. He's almost asleep. And you must be Mr. McConnell." She offered her hand. "Teri Pohlman. I'll be your boy's primary nurse."

"Please, James."

"All right, but don't take offense if I happen to call you Jimmy."

"Of course not. My mom still does."

Teri laughed, bursting the stillness around them. "Ain't mommas great? We can be all grown and old, but we'll always be their babies." She noticed his empty hands. "You not bring any bags?"

"They're in the car."

"Shoot, darlin', you don't need to get 'em. Where you parked? I'll send someone out." Teri held out a hand, expecting the car keys.

"No, no, that's okay, we'll, uh, get them later," James said. As much as he appreciated the conversation, and the offer, his patience thinned. His looking over her head to try to see inside Aaron's room didn't go unnoticed.

"Bless me—" Teri held a hand to her chest—"here I am jab-berin' at you 'bout your luggage, and y'all probably want to get in there and see your boy." She stepped to the side. "Y'all buzz me if you need anything, ya hear?"

James shook her hand again and followed Emily inside.

The only area that looked like a typical hospital room lay in the staff work zone, an alcove right behind the door: a counter, bathed in fluorescent light, stocked with a variety of medical supplies; a sink; a phone with a kaleidoscope of blinking lights; and a wide, handicap-accessible bathroom at the corner.

Beyond that, if there had been a kitchenette, James would have figured he stepped into a hotel suite. Deep-burgundy walls with white trim lent a rich, homey feel to the room. A plaid couch faced two complementary recliners, all slightly angled toward a flat-screen TV in the corner, and a short coffee table sat in the middle. Behind the couch, tan floor-length vinyl drapes guarded either side of a wide window, and May sunshine streamed inside. Around the room hung artwork of spectacular cloud formations and weather patterns and land-scapes that predominantly featured the sky.

Aaron lay on a wide, thick hospital bed a few steps from the tiny living room, and monitors recessed into the dark-red wall flanked the head of the inclined bed. James sat on the edge, rubbed Aaron's hand, and kissed his cheek. Aaron stirred and squinted, smiling. "Hey, Dad," he whispered through a haze. He tried to push himself up, but James held him down.

"How'd that lightsaber feel?"

"Never felt a thing."

"We'll talk later, okay, pal? You get some more rest."

"Can you lower it for me?"

James found the bed control, and once it flattened, Aaron sank into the mattress and groaned. His head lolled toward the window, and while James held his hand, he fell asleep in min-utes. Emily tapped her husband on the shoulder and led him into an adjoining, fully carpeted bedroom.

"Why does he seem so weak?" James asked. Emily sat on the queen-size bed and patted next to her, but James wanted to pace.

"He's been through a lot the last couple days, hon."

"But—"

"And we haven't exactly started any treatment yet."

"And why is that? Where's this Dr. Barna with the results? We should've had them by now."

"We were waiting for you, like you asked us to do. Remember?"

James stopped and shook his head. "Right. Sorry. I just thought . . ."

"That he'd look like he did this morning?"

"Yeah, I guess." He sat down next to Emily and rested a hand on her knee, suddenly exhausted from all of the driving. "How're you doing?"

"I'm okay. Like I said, the people here are very nice and helpful—" she poked him in the chest like Deena had the night before—"so I don't want you causing another ruckus. Got it, mister?" He put an arm around her shoulder. "And I really need a shower and change of clothes. C'mon. I'll help you get the bags while he's sleeping."

On the walk to the parking deck and back to Aaron's room, it struck James how un-hospital-like the colorful Bertoia Building East felt. A theme of air and space gave it the flavor of a hands-on children's museum. In addition to the solar system mobile in the main lobby, murals and photographs presented stellar nebulae, stunning weather patterns, and views of Earth from space. Sculptures of lopsided planets and flat rainbows and shooting stars with tails of glittery pipe cleaners stood on pedestals like busts of philosophers or presidents.

The dark-green walls in the elevator corridors displayed other patient-created artwork, among them reproductions of famous Andrew Wyeth or Monet or Albert Bierstadt landscape paintings in an unusual medium or style, each with a picture of a smiling child next to it. Decorated ceramic tiles framed the elevator doors, and a sign near the up and down arrows explained that a tile art therapy project, purchased for the patients and their siblings through donations, surrounded every main elevator in the St. Francis hospital complex. Like everything else in Bertoia Building, the art tiles were painted with scenes of space or the solar system or the weather or the sky.

The colors of the building extended to the staff's uniforms:

brightly colored scrubs and pastel-blue, pink, green, or orange doctor's coats instead of the typical white. Most doctors, though, skipped the coat, opting instead for casual pants and a shirt with a stethoscope draped around the neck. Each carried an iPad or laptop. High ceilings abounded throughout the building and hallways, a drastic difference from the cave-like corridors of West Michigan Mercy Hospital. And the smell: instead of the concoction of orange freshener and bleach water that walloped James with a headache when he encountered it at West Mercy, aromas of bubble gum and cotton candy predominated St. Francis.

Back on the seventh floor with bags in hand, James lingered in the hallway outside Aaron's room, studying the corridor-length sunrise mural on the wall containing the framed photographs of children. The mural stretched from floor to ceiling and beyond. Near the floor, the mural's water shimmered with the colors of the rising sun. The horizon line, eye level, blazed yellows and oranges, and the colors stretched the height of the wall and into the ceiling tiles themselves, dissolving into a velvety-blue sky with pink- and orange-dusted clouds overhead.

Teri joined him as Emily continued on to the room. "Somethin' else, ain't it? Every floor has a mural like this with the ceiling tiles. And the photos."

"Who are they?"

"They're our guardian angels." She smiled. "Every patient who stayed with us longer than thirty days here on seven gets their photo on the wall. We like 'em watchin' over us while we work with the new kids. And I think the kids like seein' they ain't the only ones dealin' with this sorta thing," she explained. "We ask the parents to write up somethin' special 'bout their kids to go with it."

James skimmed some of the descriptions: *We're proud of you!... He's a fighter who won!* And too often, *We miss you so much!*

"Some of 'em left here happy and grinnin' and cured and are still cured today," Teri said, smiling. "Some of 'em never left."

James read a few more in the heavy, momentary silence.

"But your boy there . . ." She whistled and shook her head. "I've seen some fighters come through here, but that boy's got somethin' in him."

"He's a tough kid."

"Quiet about it, though, ain't he?"

James nodded.

"Well, everyone fights in their own way. Quiet strength is good. He's a bit of a baseball nut, huh?"

"You could say that. He's obsessed with statistics. Did he find out you're an Atlanta Braves fan or something?"

Teri laughed. "Well, I am from the South, but no, this place gets you on the Tigers wagon right quick."

"Then the two of you should get along great."

"He told me you're a coach? And you played in college?"

James bent his head and walked toward Aaron's room. "Yeah, I played a couple years. Seems like forever ago. And I help at one of the high schools. But now . . ." He stopped outside the room and glanced in.

"Now you gotta be a different kinda coach, huh?"

"I suppose so. And it'll be a little harder than teaching a seventeen-year-old how to bunt."

Teri patted him on the arm. "Well, you got a good team in there, Coach. And Dr. Barna'll give us a game plan in a while."

While Aaron slept over the next hour, James and Emily settled their clothes in the empty dressers, deposited the boy's toiletries in the large bathroom by the door, and arranged their bathroom supplies in the smaller, three-quarter bath off the adjoining bedroom. Emily showered and changed, and they tried to decompress some. But while she finished a light coat of makeup, Aaron called out for them.

They hurried into the other room as he pushed himself up, wiping the sleep from his eyes. He suddenly curled, grimacing at the pain in his hip and back where the samples of bone marrow and cerebrospinal fluid had been taken hours earlier. James grabbed him under the elbow and helped him sit. Aaron held up his hand to block the sunlight but asked his mom to leave the drapes open when she went to close them. They sat with him for several minutes while he woke up, blinking and squinting until his eyes adjusted to the light, and they quizzed him on how he felt from head to toe. He asked for water and his Tigers sweatshirt, and while they were in the other room, they heard a man with an Indian accent bellow a warm hello to Aaron.

Dr. Charin Barna, wearing khaki pants, a red golf shirt, and one of the few white coats James had seen, sat on the foot of Aaron's bed, smiling and chatting, cradling an iPad like a book. He stood and shook James's hand. His eyes, as coal-black as his thick hair, looked like they belonged on a giant teddy bear.

"Your son and I were going to talk about some of the things there are to do around here," Dr. Barna said.

Aaron held up a hospital magazine guide Dr. Barna had given him. "There's a planetarium and the gardens and an auditorium." Aaron tried to show James pictures.

"Sounds more like a resort," James said.

"And a resort that serves food, young man," Dr. Barna added. "I would like for you to try to eat something if you feel up to it."

Aaron nodded while reading.

"Okay then, I will have Teri come in with a menu. You will like it. Pizza, chicken fingers, cheese sticks." Emily's eyes widened at the list of greasy foods. "And all prepared to our specifications for the health of our patients, Mom," Dr. Barna said. "Does that sound okay?"

Aaron didn't answer.

"Aaron, Dr. Barna asked you a question," James said.

The boy looked up briefly and nodded again, his interest on the guide.

"Very good." He sat back down on the bed. "Tell me, when do those Detroit Tigers play tonight?"

Aaron's head snapped up from the magazine. "First pitch is at 7:05, against Cleveland."

"And who are the Cleveland again?"

"The Indians."

Dr. Barna snapped his fingers. "That is right; you told me that before. Indians." He threw his head back and laughed out loud. "How in the world could I have forgotten that?" James and Emily chuckled, but Aaron shrugged. "Well, we will make sure that you are nice and comfortable for the game then, okay? Maybe in a few days you can watch a baseball game up in the family center on the top floor, with the other patients and families." He turned to James and Emily, both of whom had recoiled at his "in a few days" remark. "Any excuse for a party for those folks," he told them through a wide smile, which he turned back on Aaron. "Okay, Mom and Dad are coming to my office for a little while. We will be back before you know it."

James and Emily each kissed Aaron on the head while he continued reading the hospital guide, but James lingered, savoring the sensation of his son's fine, short hair on his cheek, wondering how soon it would vanish. *Is this where it all changes? Is this where the fight begins, again?*

His chest thumped.

Is this the beginning of the end?

Only seconds remained of the ignorance James took comfort in the night before. The diagnosis waited down the hall in Dr. Barna's office.

He didn't want to go. He didn't want the answers he'd demanded from the other doctors.

He smoothed Aaron's hair.

Stop it. Don't waste time guessing. Let's hear it. It's time for answers. He kissed Aaron's head again.

"All right then, follow me, please," Dr. Barna said on his way to the door.

"Hey," James whispered, tapping Aaron on the shoulder. He pointed at the exiting doctor. On the back of his white coat, several colorful child handprints surrounded the words *Kick Me!* An arrow pointed down to his butt. "Maybe you can get in some free shots later."

Aaron snorted.

They walked in silence down the seventh-floor hall to a sparse room that wasn't the doctor's regular office. A meeting room or, James thought, a police interrogation room. Which was precisely what he planned on doing to Dr. Barna.

But he never got the chance.

They sat around a circular table, and Dr. Barna set his iPad down and pushed it to the side. "Okay, folks, we have a fight to deal with," he said. "Aaron's leukemia has relapsed."

Emily leaned into James, but he sat rock still.

The doctor said it with such sudden bluntness that it glanced off James's brain. An answer, just like he wanted, no more guessing. But now that it happened . . .

Emily snuffled hard and sat up. "What's our first step?"

"First, I want you to read this booklet." He pulled a brochure out of his doctor's coat and slid it across the table—*Answers to Your Relapse Questions: For Parents*, written by Dr. Barna himself. "This should cover nearly everything you will need to know. Blast cells were in Aaron's bone marrow sample, but not in the cerebrospinal fluid. We will need to treat it aggressively, at first with an induction phase chemotherapy protocol designed specifically for him."

Relapse. Aggressive. Chemotherapy. James had expected to hear these words, had anticipated the next several months and years of treatment, had played them over and over in his head, and yet . . . it seemed unbelievable.

They'd come so far. Now, everything they had accomplished up until that point, erased.

Gone.

He felt ready to throw up.

"I know that tests within your family for compatible bone marrow and previous searches on the registries have not resulted in a match, but we will submit a specific request for new searches. Many people join the registry every day. It would be very beneficial if we found a donor soon, and I will make them fully aware of Aaron's relapse and rare HLA tissue type," Dr. Barna said. "You know that an allogeneic bone marrow transplant brings its own risks of transplant diseases and treatment-related mortality, but if successful, it will give your son the best chance for long-term survival."

"Define *long-term*," Emily said.

Dr. Barna leaned back. "Oh, every patient is different. And some studies are still evaluating transplant survivors."

"Will he ever be cancer-free, if it's successful?" Emily asked.

"That is a possibility, yes."

"And chemotherapy alone won't work?"

"No, it will not." Dr. Barna leaned forward again and clasped his hands on the table. "If we rely solely on chemotherapy, we might be able to get him back into remission, but his odds for another relapse are very great."

"That's all I need to hear," Emily said. "Let's get started."

James sat motionless, dumbfounded. He normally played the professional one in these settings, rattling off the questions rapid-fire, like the night before with Dr. Adams at West Mercy, when emotions engulfed Emily. But this time, no questions came. He only saw answers. And the end result of those answers.

He just stared at Dr. Barna while the doctor continued talking. His accent—or was it James's own brain?—mangled the words until they were incomprehensible.

James clenched a fist in his lap. It shook the tighter he squeezed.

He wanted to hit something.

His face flushed, and his heart raced, temples throbbing.

He *needed* to hit something.

One of Emily's hands caressed his fist. The other lightly touched his cheek and turned his face to hers. Her eyes pleaded for him to break through whatever had seized him, that she needed him . . . but that she was there for him, too. Staring into her blue eyes, he melted.

His shoulders slumped, and he lowered his head.

And cried.

She pressed her forehead to his and joined him.

Dr. Barna retrieved a box of tissues from the windowsill and let them compose themselves. "If we are successful in finding a match, there will be another treatment regimen to go over in regard to the actual bone marrow transplant. Until then, we must focus on the chemotherapy treatment to get him back into remission, and keeping Aaron's spirits up. What do you think will do that the best?"

"Us being able to stay with him will help," Emily said. She made a final swipe across her eyes.

"So will his little sister, Elizabeth," James softly added. "The way they play . . . She helps him feel like a kid more than anyone."

"I am afraid he will not feel much like one at first," Dr. Barna said. "Are you comfortable with Elizabeth staying here and seeing what her brother will have to go through?"

They both nodded. "She stayed with my parents a lot last year whenever we had to go to Grand Rapids for treatment," James said. "Aaron missed her during the long hospital stays, so it'll be good to have her here once we've got a routine. And besides—" he wiped his nose—"like I said before, this place sounds like a resort. There should be lots for her to do here, right?"

"All of the facilities are open to any siblings the same as the patients. Our child life counselors will work with both Aaron and Elizabeth. His love of baseball will help him greatly, too. In fact, I would encourage you to decorate the room with Aaron's things, make it *his* room. I am sure you can find Detroit Tigers posters and other things to hang on the walls."

"James and Aaron can certainly go off in their own little world talking about baseball," Emily said, elbowing him and smiling.

James's lips stayed straight. He kept to himself the threat he'd made in the car earlier that day.

"Good. We have many things here that can help with that, too." He smiled at Emily. "But I will let Aaron tell you about that. Now, please, review the brochure, and let me know immediately if you have any questions."

"When does the chemo start?" James asked.

"Right away tomorrow. And then weekly treatments,

perhaps with additional oral medications," Dr. Barna said. "So let us make sure that he gets a good night's rest."

Emily and James spent a few more seconds together in an embrace before following Dr. Barna back to Aaron's room.

The boy's food hadn't arrived yet, and he still paged through the hospital magazine. His parents sat on either side of the bed, and James gently took the guide, not without a small protest from Aaron. "Dr. Barna needs to talk to you, pal," James said.

Aaron let a long moment of silence pass between him and the doctor. "More chemo, huh?"

Dr. Barna nodded.

"Like last time?"

"It will probably be stronger," Dr. Barna said. Emily and James both squeezed Aaron's shoulders.

Aaron looked to the window. Nobody spoke. James's mind raced, trying to get inside his son's head, fighting the urge to blurt out that it wasn't that bad, that everything would be fine . . . that it was okay to cry. But Aaron just stared.

Teri entered singing like a dinner bell but stopped midring when she saw the three adults huddled around the boy's bed. Her smile disappeared. She set down the tray of food on the clinician's counter and tiptoed out.

Dr. Barna patted Aaron's knee. "You are a strong young man, and we will combat this head-on."

Though still gazing at the window, Aaron nodded.

"Okay, then, I will stop by during this Tigers game for a little while if that is all right, and we can talk about tomorrow while your team scores points."

"Runs," Aaron muttered.

"Excuse me?"

"Runs. They score runs in baseball."

"Right, runs. You need to teach me more about baseball." Dr. Barna winked at Emily, smiled at James, and left.

Before either parent began to comfort him, Aaron asked his dad, in a faraway voice, if he brought his laptop. James blinked away the confusion of the request but said yes.

"Can you get it for me?"

"Sure, but don't you want to—?"

"I want to get the stats done before the Tigers start." He finally looked at his dad. His eyes were brimming. "You got the scorebook, right?"

"Uh, no, Coach said he'd e-mail you the stats from the book. They should be there now."

"But I like looking through the book!" Aaron shouted. His tears gushed. "I get to see what happened through the whole game that way!"

Emily climbed completely into bed with Aaron and cuddled him. "Shh . . . It's okay, honey. We'll get through this. This is just another step; that's all."

Through his crying, Aaron repeated that he wanted the scorebook.

James laid a hand on Emily's back when she started to reassure him again, more about the cancer fight than high school baseball stats. "Look," James said, "I'm sorry I didn't snag the book, but they need it for Monday's game."

Aaron wiped his eyes and nose.

"You know the team has to keep the book; that's something the league requires, remember?"

Aaron nodded.

"So how about I have Coach scan the pages and e-mail them next time. Then you can see the book, but they won't get in trouble for not having it. Deal?"

Aaron sniffled again, calming, and mumbled, "Okay."

"For right now, though, let's input the stats, and he can send up the scans later. I bet you'll find something he messed up anyway."

A grin trembled across Aaron's mouth, and he leaned into his mom's embrace.

A few hours later, as Aaron clicked away on his laptop, James convinced his wife that she needed a break and suggested she find a cafeteria. After she left, James stood at the window, fighting the lure of The Place. It wanted to drag him back down, deeper this time, into a pit he'd never escape.

The buildings encircled an intricate, labyrinthine nature center. A central paved path spiraled through flower gardens from one end to the other, with many mulched trails branching off; footbridges crossed man-made streams that flowed between several ponds rippling from spitting fountains; a greenhouse sat in full sun on one far side; and short ornamental trees offered scattered shady spots among numerous grassy openings. People strolled the paths; several pushed children in wheelchairs or sat on benches. Though the majority of the plants hadn't blossomed, the thousands of tulips and daffodils and other spring bloomers littered the gardens with pinpricks of color visible from the seventh-floor window. With the surrounding buildings acting as sentries to the outside world, the gardens were a sanctuary.

The call of The Place faded.

He turned and watched Aaron happily click away on his laptop. Pulling a recliner alongside Aaron's bed, he grabbed the hospital guide from the bedside stand. "So what did you find out about this place?" He opened to the center spread. "Did you see that each of the four patient buildings has a theme?"

Aaron mumbled an "uh-huh." In addition to the air and

space theme of Bertoia, another patient building was devoted to land animals, one to aquatic animals, and the last to global cultures. "I bet they'll let us visit all of them."

Aaron slapped himself on the forehead. "Oh, my gosh, I'm so stupid! I can't believe I forgot to tell you!" He saved his spreadsheet, set the laptop aside, and sat up in bed, crossing his legs. For Aaron to stop the stats, James figured it must be important. "Guess who comes and visits sometimes?"

James thought for a minute. "SpongeBob."

Aaron cocked his head at his dad.

"Frankenstein?"

"Dad . . ."

"I got it!" James snapped his fingers and pointed at his son. "Harry Potter!"

"Dad!"

"C-3PO and R2-D2."

"Curt Howard!"

James sat up, his playful grin gone. "Seriously?"

Aaron's face lit up. "Seriously!"

"The shortstop for the Tigers comes here—to this hospital—and visits?"

"I know! Can you believe it?"

"Did I hear someone say Curt Howard?" Teri said as she entered.

"He really visits?" James asked.

"Absolutely. Him and his lovely wife. They do quite a bit for us here."

"How come I've never heard that?"

"'Cause that's the way they want it."

"Miss Teri said she's going to tell him I want his autograph," Aaron said.

"Oh, *Miss Teri*'s going to ask him, huh?"

"Miss Teri—" Aaron looked at her with puppy dog eyes— "did you remember to check on when he'll be here next?"

Teri sighed and leaned down. "As if your four reminders this morning weren't enough? I ain't deaf, kiddo. But do you think I'd come in here without some news?" Aaron scooched up in bed and crossed his legs. "I heard back from the person who arranges his visits, and she called Curt's wife, told her we got this new patient who's the biggest Curt Howard fan. She said they were plannin' on bein' here when the team comes back on their next home stand—"

"That's, like, less than two weeks!" Aaron said.

"No, no, their next *long* home stand."

Aaron slumped a little. "After this series with Cleveland, they go out west for like, ten days; then they're back in Detroit for only two games and then back on the road." He fell back into his pillow in a quiet tantrum. "It's gonna take forever for them to get back here."

"But they will get back here," Teri assured him, "and when they do, on Curt's off day, he'll come see you." Teri leaned down. "And she promised that Curt will make it an extralong visit, too."

Aaron vaulted up and clapped, wriggling his whole body. And for the first time since seeing him in the ER at North Mercy, James noticed some true color blush his cheeks. Teri laughed and shook her head before leaving.

"I can't believe it!" Aaron said, clapping again.

"That's pretty awesome, buster." James leaned on the bed. "What are you going to talk to him about?"

Aaron's face froze.

"Tell you what, you've got lots of time. We'll think up a list of questions."

Aaron reopened his laptop, started a fresh document, but then stared at the blank page on the screen. Nothing.

"Don't worry; you'll think of something."

"No, it's not that, Dad." A big grin spread across Aaron's face. "You know what I just thought?"

"What's that, big guy?"

"Dad, I was *supposed* to get sick again!"

James chuckled and leaned back in the chair. "Aaron, that's—"

"No seriously! If I hadn't, I never would've, like, come down here to meet Curt Howard!" An idea struck him, and he embarked on snappy hunt-and-peck typing.

He wanted to tell Aaron not to get his hopes up. He wanted to bring Aaron back from the edge, from where he'd stood just the day before and watched his own high hope of playing catch with Aaron crumble. But he also knew that having something to look forward to was vital, crucial even. Tomorrow, the beginning of a new phase of chemotherapy, would be tough enough. A high hope for Aaron would help.

But the thought of what would happen should the ballplayer not show up wasn't what bothered him. James couldn't watch Aaron type any longer, so he paced first to the bathroom and then back to the window and the view of the gardens below.

No, Son. You weren't supposed to get sick again. Something like this is never supposed to happen to kids. Ever. And definitely not twice.

"Dad! C'mere!" Aaron waved him over like he had a secret to share with his best friend.

When James sat back down and they brainstormed questions for Curt Howard, he prayed that a tiny sliver of his son's optimism would somehow pierce his own heart.

6

CHEMOTHERAPY OVER THE NEXT FEW WEEKS made
Aaron bald again. And sick. He took longer to rebound after
each session of the new, intense induction phase of the treatment plan—which, in addition to chemo, included more
transfusions, pokes, and punctures—and he missed much
of his schooling through St. Francis's educational program.
With hair loss, vomiting, and mouth sores the only discern-
ible measurement of the chemo's effect, James failed to see how
any of it was working. He knew better, of course, but his heart
refused to wrap itself around the fact, even if his mind could.

Lizzie took the effects of the chemo on Aaron especially
hard. She'd never seen him so sick. Too young during the early
stages of Aaron's previous cancer battle, she remembered only
the end, when her brother's exams, chemo sessions, and hospital stays during his last phase of treatment kept her at her
grandparents' house. James and Emily tried insulating her by
keeping her busy with their child life counselor, Maria, but
sleeping mostly on the fold-out couch, she often woke to his

moans and crying, which led to long nights burrowing in her parents' bed.

"Dad, I think I'll let Aaron win at Uno next time," she told James over a cafeteria dinner one evening.

"Really?"

Lizzie answered with a nod as she speared her mac and cheese with a fork.

"You don't have to do that, you know. Just treat him like normal, even if that means smokin' him at Uno."

The girl shrugged, but James knew that if she was anything like her mother, she'd already made up her mind.

That evening, Lizzie held on to her Draw Fours, and Aaron milked his victory celebration. This resulted in a reminder from Emily about being a gracious winner, which devolved into a spontaneous tantrum about all of Lizzie's past victory dances.

James ended the outburst by threatening to turn off the Tigers game, overjoyed at Aaron throwing a fit about something stupid and getting in trouble. He cherished any episode resembling normal nine-year-old behavior. He longed to see more of them.

Monday, returning from a morning lumbar puncture and a round of chemotherapy in a treatment center adjacent to Bertoia Building—and the day of Curt Howard's promised visit—Aaron looked his best since the relapse. *Best* was relative, as Aaron's face, swollen from steroids, still lacked color and drooped with fatigue. But now the portacath—the round reservoir connected to a catheter through which he received his treatment—wasn't an alien attached to his collarbone, sucking the life out of him. He wore it like a badge. The steroids helped him feel a bit more like himself again, albeit with some dramatic mood swings. James knew his son didn't want to be a *cancer patient* Curt Howard visited. Aaron just wanted to be a kid, a baseball fan. Aside from fatigue and the normal nausea, Aaron felt as well as they could hope.

Emily walked alongside Aaron while James pushed him in the wheelchair. A Tigers hat covered his bald head, and nurses they passed said, "Today's the day! Are you ready?" Aaron managed as strong of a smile as he could, each a little weaker than the last.

Dr. Barna met them at the seventh-floor nurses' station. He knelt next to the wheelchair, asking Aaron how the treatment went. The boy nodded and shrugged, saying no different from before.

"You appear sleepier than usual, however," Dr. Barna said. "Do you feel sick to your stomach?"

Aaron shook his head.

"I think we can blame some of that on Curt Howard," James said. "Buckshot here didn't sleep much last night."

"Ah, yes, well, I am glad we were able to get your treatment done in the morning so that you will feel better for later this afternoon. Perhaps after a nap. I just hope I do not embarrass myself." Dr. Barna looked up at James and Emily. "I have usually stayed in my office on Mr. Howard's previous visits."

"Do you remember what position he plays?" Aaron asked. His words slurred with drowsiness.

Dr. Barna stood. "Shortstop."

"And where is that?"

"Between second base and third base."

"And what is his batting average?"

"It is the measure of how many hits one gets against—"

"No," Aaron interrupted, "I mean what is Curt Howard's batting average? Like, what number?"

Dr. Barna's eyes blanked.

"He's batting .309. Do you remember what a good batting average is?"

Dr. Barna's eyes sparkled. "I know that one. Three hits out of ten at bats, and you will go to the Hall of Fame. So is Mr. Howard in the Hall of Fame?"

The McConnells laughed. "How that works is more difficult to explain," James said.

"Well?" Dr. Barna asked Aaron.

"You'll do fine."

"As will you. But try to sleep when you get back to your room, okay?"

James began to push him down the hall again, but the doctor said he needed a minute of their time. A nurse wheeled Aaron into his room, and Dr. Barna's smile faded.

"Wow," James said, "don't hit us with all those bone marrow matches at once."

"Some early ones appeared promising, but they dropped out with further testing. We knew this would be difficult with Aaron's rare HLA tissue type, but I am very disappointed." Dr. Barna shook his head. "First, though, we must get Aaron into remission if any transplant is to have a chance at being successful. And . . ."

"And?" Emily said.

"And that is proving to be difficult as well. The latest bone marrow biopsy shows he is not responding to the treatment as quickly as we would like. He is responding, but I had hoped this stronger chemotherapy would have worked a little faster. And it may still perhaps." He looked Emily and James hard in the eyes. "But there is also a chance that he will not go into remission again. You must be prepared for that." Emily put a hand to her mouth; James rubbed his forehead. "We will forge ahead, though, and continue to hope he turns a corner and it begins to work. And then I will settle for even a close match of HLA markers if we cannot find a perfect one."

"You don't sound very optimistic," James said.

Dr. Barna gazed off down the hall as he contemplated. "I simply thought we would be a little further along in the process by now." He put a hand on each of their shoulders. "I am sorry to have to burden you with this news on today of all days, but you needed to know. Try to be strong for Aaron. He has been anticipating this more than anything. And he has taught me a lot about baseball. I might have to go see a game for myself someday."

James and Emily managed only meager smiles.

They took a second to calm themselves before entering Aaron's room. He'd already pulled the covers up to his chin and buried his eyes in his pillow.

Around the coffee table, their child life counselor, Maria, threw her Uno cards down and groaned while another girl, a year older than Lizzie and with a mop of curly red hair, gathered them up. Lizzie, sitting cross-legged in one of the recliners, swayed back and forth, her short, light-brown hair swishing in time to a bubbly tune she hummed. She waved her parents over. "I won like five games in a row!" she whispered.

"You were supposed to go easy on the new kid," Emily said. "Hey, Paige, how's your sister doing?"

"Okay," the redhead answered. "She had her first treatment today. And I start school here tomorrow."

"First grade for you, right?"

Paige nodded.

"School's pretty fun," Lizzie said. "But Mrs. Erickson gets really upset if you don't do your homework."

"Every teacher gets really upset if you don't do your homework," James said.

"C'mon, sweetie," Maria said, holding her arm out for Paige. "These folks have a busy day ahead."

Lizzie walked them to the door, waved down the hall, and scampered back to her chair. "Before Paige got here, I beat Maria like *nine* games in a row!"

Emily sat down on the couch across from the girl. "Well, I'm here now, bucko. Winning streak ends. Deal."

"You know you've never beaten me, Mom."

"Of course I do." Emily playfully pinched one of her daughter's cheeks. "You brag about it all the time."

"Are we still going to see the play tonight?"

"Absolutely. Why wouldn't we?"

Lizzie's eyes darted to Aaron, and she half shrugged.

"He's doing okay, hon. We need another girl's night out, just you and me."

Lizzie's smile dimpled her cheeks, and she started dealing.

James left them to their card game and slid a chair alongside Aaron's bed. Aaron had taken Dr. Barna's advice to heart—he snored away, his face half-hidden by the covers.

Dr. Barna's prognosis rattled around in James's head. He imagined the cancer cells as round, black, scabby-skinned gremlins, all heads and teeth, bouncing through Aaron's blood, eating everything in their path, consuming the boy from the inside out. They devoured the golden, sparkling, pixie dust–like medicine, making them swell and multiply. And they laughed, searching for more. He wanted to reach inside and squash them all like grapes, burn them alive, grind them to dust—something, anything.

He closed his eyes and prayed.

He wished that it would all stop. That Aaron would get healthy. That he could stand outside under a blue sky and play catch with his son, his healthy son.

The praying soothed him, and as he continued, he saw them playing with a baseball as bright as a ball of light, each throw sharp, each catch stinging his hand. But the serene images made his mind wander. Now, he reached into his glove and pulled out one of the black, gnarly gremlins. It laughed at him and licked its lips. The sun disappeared behind stone-gray clouds, and James couldn't stop his hand from throwing the creature at Aaron. The monster laughed louder, shriller, and Aaron ran away, crying, the gremlin bouncing after him, chomping its teeth like some murderous Pac-Man, until they both disappeared over the horizon. Laughing. Screaming. Chomping. Crying . . .

James pulled his hair into a fist, and the pain forced the images from his head. "This child needs a little victory once in a while, Lord," he whispered. "Just for today. Give him a little more strength today."

He laid a hand on Aaron's bald head.

"C'mon, Lord. Just for today."

James's prayers were answered when a nap and a hot shower later that afternoon did wonders for Aaron.

While James changed his shirt, soaking wet from helping his son soap up and rinse off, Aaron read aloud the questions for Curt Howard. He growled when something didn't sound right, and a staccato of laptop keys followed.

"How's this sound: 'What does it feel like to play in front of so many people?'" Aaron asked. He slapped the keys, frustrated. "That's stupid."

James returned to Aaron's side of the room, checking the battery on the video camera. "It's fine." He set the camera on the coffee table, unfurled another Tigers poster, and taped it on the wall by the TV. It joined two pennants and three other posters. "I think this is the last one your grandma brought."

"What about: 'Who's the toughest pitcher you've ever faced?'"

"That's a good one," James said. "But I wouldn't worry

about it too much. Talk to him like you would anyone else. Use the questions if you can't think of anything to say, okay?"

Aaron studied the laptop screen and thrummed his fingers on his leg. "'What baseball player did you want to be when you were a kid?'"

"Or not." James taped down a flopping poster corner.

"Dad, can you get my Tigers hat?"

"Sure thing, just let me . . ." He added one more piece of tape. "There. Okay, where's the hat?"

The boy shrugged, still examining his computer.

"Aaron, where did you leave it?"

"Maybe the bathroom. Or maybe I took it off before I laid down with Mom? I don't know. Maybe it's on the couch."

"So it could be anywhere in this entire room; is that what you're saying?" Aaron shrugged again, his eyes still fixed on his computer. "All right," James said to himself, "a little preoccupied, understandable." He found it in the adjoining bedroom. Aaron called for some water.

James slapped the cap on Aaron's head and set the water on a tray table pivoted to the side. "Anything else, Your Majesty?"

"How's this one? 'What's your favorite park to play in?'"

James's teeth clenched, but he smiled. "I like that one. What do you think he'll say?"

"I bet he'll say Camden Yards in Baltimore. Or maybe Yankee Stadium. Or Fenway." Aaron tapped some more on the keyboard.

"I don't know. I hear Minnesota's new ballpark is sweet."

"Yeah, but it's Minnesota. The Tigers, like, never win there. That can't be his favorite."

"Betcha a buck," James said, holding out his hand. Aaron looked at it, considered the bet, and slapped it.

Lizzie ran into the room first, followed by James's parents and Emily. "He's on his way!" Emily said.

Aaron reviewed the questions again and threw a discreet fit when James suggested he put the computer away; they compromised by leaving it powered but closed on the tray table. Aaron took some deep breaths, and James triple-checked the battery on the video camera. Laughter filtered down the hall. James stood by the TV in the corner, turned the camera on, and pointed it at the door.

Curt Howard was shorter than James expected. And skinny. With less hair. Muscles didn't ripple his untucked orange polo shirt, the legs underneath his blue jeans didn't look like tree trunks, and the hands cradling some Tigers souvenirs weren't massive webs for snagging ground balls. James could've sworn he looked like the same person who helped him at the hardware store or took his order at a restaurant or sat three pews behind him in church.

Curt's sandy-blonde-haired wife followed him in, and their faces lit up when they rounded the corner by the medical station alcove and spotted Aaron. James's eyes darted between the video camera's small screen and the live action before him.

"There's the guy I've heard so much about," Curt said, beaming. He immediately shook Aaron's hand, but he held it an extra beat until Aaron, who had glanced away, returned his eye contact. Curt waved and said hello to the rest of the McConnells and presented Lizzie with a pink Tigers cap. He introduced his wife, Kara, who, after shaking Aaron's hand, joined the others around the couch.

Curt sat in a high-backed chair next to Aaron's bed. "I've got a couple things for you." He held out a signed, home-white jersey with *Howard* curving over the number 25, then brought out a baseball covered in scribbles. "It's from the whole team," he said.

Aaron's eyes widened, and he mangled a thank-you as he studied the autographs.

Please open up; please open up, James prayed. The first few moments after meeting someone were always the hardest and most uncomfortable for Aaron, the only time he acted truly self-conscious about his sickness. Even though he wore a hat and had lived without hair pretty much half of his life, James knew that at that moment, Aaron felt naked being bald. Sometimes, Aaron's insecurity about being on display made him behave like he thought his cancer was as contagious as the flu, and he hesitated shaking someone's hand or talking directly at them. It usually took something special to open him up, and Curt's encouraging words weren't working. Aaron nodded at each reassurance and murmured some more thank-yous.

James hissed, *"Psst,"* and motioned to the laptop. Aaron glanced at it, then at James, and finally at Curt.

"You have some questions for me?" Curt asked.

Aaron shook his head.

"Yes, he does. He's been working on them ever since he heard you were coming," James said. "C'mon, pal; ask him about the park. Remember, we got a buck riding on it."

James looked back at the video screen, knowing that the camera's mic probably hadn't picked up Aaron's mumbled question.

The Tiger leaned back and gazed at the ceiling. "Hmmm . . . favorite ballpark . . . Let's see."

"I told him it was the new park in Minnesota."

"Target Field?" Curt said. "That is pretty cool, but we always seem to have a rough game there."

Aaron smiled at his dad.

"There goes my dollar."

"I'd have to say Fenway in Boston. The history and atmosphere—and the place is *always* packed. What other questions do you have?"

Aaron shrugged.

"Tell you what, I've got some questions for you. Miss Teri told me you're a bit of a stats genius, that there's no way I could stump you." He removed a folded sheet of paper from his pocket and held it up to Aaron. "But I brought some questions."

That did it. Aaron sat up in bed, his face pinkened, and his blue eyes twinkled. The tension in the room evaporated, and everyone else tried to melt into the walls to let these two—the sick boy and his baseball hero—go at it. Even Curt noticed, and he settled into the chair and winked at the camera. James flashed him a subtle thumbs-up.

"You ever hear of baseball-almanac.com?" Curt asked, unfolding the paper. Aaron nodded. "All right then: Who's thrown the most no-hitters?"

"Nolan Ryan," Aaron said. His voice cracked. "He's thrown seven."

"Good, but that was an easy one. What about . . . what's the streak for the most games played in a row?"

"Cal Ripken Jr.—2,632. All with the Baltimore Orioles."

Curt's brow wrinkled. "Can you see through this?" He flipped the paper over and checked for himself. Aaron giggled. "This is going to be tougher than I thought. Okay, I assume you know what the Triple Crown is."

"For hitting or pitching?" Aaron asked.

"Pitching."

"The person has to have the most wins, strikeouts, and the best earned run average in a season. Or be tied for the best."

"So who won the first Triple Crown?"

"American League or National League?"

"Uh . . ." Curt seemed worried. "American League."

"Cy Young with the Boston Americans in 1901."

"National?"

"Tommy Bond with the Boston Red Caps in—" Aaron looked to the ceiling for a second—"1877."

"Okay, enough with the history stuff." Curt situated himself on the chair as if he were upping the ante on the difficulty of the questions. He cupped his hand behind the paper. "Do you read baseball-reference.com, too?"

James laughed. "It's his home page."

"Oh, boy." Curt rubbed his chin. "Well, let's see how big of a Tigers fan you are. What's Tony Bozio's career batting average?"

"Including this season so far, .268."

Curt's shoulders sank. "What about Cordero Ruiz?"

"Ruiz is batting .283."

"Carl Peters?"

"He's at .311."

"How many wins does Chris Franke have in his career?"

Aaron leaned his head back in his pillow, thinking, and then shot up again. "Eighty-eight."

"Rats! Thought I had you there." Curt searched the sheet of paper for his last question. He grinned. "Okay, hotshot, how many wins does manager Ernie Mazarron have?"

"Including last night's, six hundred and—" Aaron stared at his bedcover and tapped his fingers on his chin—"sixteen. Wait! Seventeen. Six hundred and seventeen."

Curt cocked one eyebrow. "That your final answer?"

"Yes . . . no. Yes. Final answer."

Curt hung his head and crumpled the paper. "I give up." The rest of the room applauded.

Aaron smiled at the video camera. And to James, for a split second, that smile made the hospital room disappear in the camera's screen. It was just Aaron, sitting on the couch, watching a game on TV, thrilled that his beloved Tigers were winning. Everything else—the hospital, the relapse, the chemo—all of it a nightmare. James couldn't pull his eyes away from his son's grin on the video screen, terrified to lose the precious moment to reality when he looked up.

But with a difficult swallow, he did.

"Now I want you to make me a promise, okay?" Curt leaned lower. Aaron sat straighter. "You work real hard on this fight, all right? Don't give up. It's sort of like when you're facing a pitcher, and he's got you no balls, two strikes, and maybe you've never gotten a hit off the guy. With some pitchers, it'd be real easy to think you're going to strike out, and so you give up, especially if you think the guy's comin' at you with a nasty curveball."

"Dad told me that my cancer is just a curveball."

"And what are you supposed to do with a curveball?" Curt asked.

"Dad always says you go with the pitch and slap it the other way."

Curt nodded. "Your dad's a smart guy. Unless—" with his hand, he mimicked the slow-motion arc of a curveball toward Aaron—"it's hanging right there in your wheelhouse, in which case . . ."

Aaron swatted Curt's hand with an imaginary bat. "Wham! You crush it out of the park!"

"You got it! So stay strong. And make sure to always listen to your mom and dad. And don't ever forget that they and your sister and your grandparents love you very much. If you think of anything else, tell Miss Teri, and she'll get me the message, okay?"

The animation on Aaron's face vanished, and his gaze fell into his lap again.

"All right, we've got to go. You be good."

Aaron nodded, his eyes still lowered, focusing on his hands fiddling with each other.

Curt sat back and stared, visibly reluctant to ask the next question. But he leaned forward and said, "There's something you want to ask me right now, isn't there?"

Aaron glanced to James and then back to his lap. He nodded.

"What is it?"

His eyes flashed toward the camera again; then he motioned Curt forward. James's eyes flicked between watching the video camera screen and the bed in front of him: Curt lowered his ear to Aaron's mouth. Aaron whispered something James couldn't hear. Curt's grin dissolved and his brow furrowed. He looked from Aaron to the camera, then down to his hand, which the boy squeezed.

James heard only one word from Aaron: "Please."

Curt's confusion turned to concern, enough for James to ask, "What? What's wrong?" The video camera tilted to the side.

"Did you . . . ?" Curt asked, but the boy quickly shook his head. The two stared at each other before Curt's smile returned, dampened by more confusion. He patted Aaron's hand. "I'll look into it, okay?"

Aaron nodded and let go.

Kara Howard hugged everyone and waited by the door while Curt said good-bye. He shook hands with Aaron and told the boy he expected him to wear that jersey, not just hang it in a closet. Then he hugged Emily and Lizzie and shook James's parents' hands.

James pulled Curt a little closer in their handshake and whispered, "What was that all about?"

Curt shook his head. "Don't worry about it. And seriously,

if he needs anything, let Teri know." At the door he shared a last, contemplative look with Aaron, gave a small wave, and left.

Aaron's family rushed to his bedside to relive the visit. Except James. On the video camera, he replayed the last few minutes, lowering his ear to the speaker, hoping to hear what Aaron had whispered. After five attempts, he still couldn't make out anything other than Aaron's "Please."

He stopped the video. Aaron watched him over Emily's shoulder, and James shrugged at him. "What did you say?" he mouthed.

Aaron didn't answer. He just pored over the Tigers' signatures on the baseball.

7

ON SATURDAY, five days after Curt Howard's visit, Dr. Barna and Teri dropped in for an early morning, unscheduled checkup. Satisfied with Aaron's pulse and breathing, Dr. Barna draped his stethoscope back around his neck and smiled, his white teeth stark against his olive skin. "Your latest tests are beginning to show improvement," he told Aaron. "I think we might have turned a corner."

James squeezed Aaron's forearm. "Are you sure?"

"It is still early, but we may have broken through whatever kept him from responding."

Both parents took turns planting a kiss on Aaron's head, and Emily clutched his neck in a suffocating embrace.

"I haven't felt as sick this whole week."

"I am sure that Mr. Howard's visit helped," Dr. Barna said. "What is good for the mind can be good for the body."

"The only problem is he needs a little more sleep," Emily said, catching a spontaneous tear at the good news. She poked Aaron. "If you keep staying up late watching the Tigers, you're going to start feeling cruddy all over again."

"But, Mom, they're only two games out of first place! Curt had a huge game last—"

"Oh, Curt this and Curt that. Then we need to get a DVR or something. You can finish the game in the morning."

"And when I was a kid, I had a radio under my covers at night listening to Ernie Harwell call the game," James said. "He's not gonna, hon."

"I could unplug the TV, then," she said, scowling at both of them. "Or hope for some rainouts, I suppose."

"Your mother is right, young man. Rest is critically important. But perhaps—" Dr. Barna checked his watch and then nodded at Teri—"an adventure is, too."

"There's a call comin' through for Aaron in a coupla minutes," Teri said. James walked to the phone on the bedside stand, but Teri shooed him away. "I said it's for Aaron, so you just get back over there." She waggled a finger toward the couch. "He can take care of it himself."

Aaron sat up, and Teri set the cordless phone in his lap. Lizzie skipped in from the adjoining bedroom twirling a sweatshirt. Emily had promised her a walk through the hospital gardens.

"Can we go now?" she asked.

Emily helped her daughter with a stubborn sleeve. "In a minute, dear. Aaron's getting a call from someone." Lizzie flopped on the couch and picked up the TV remote. "Not right now, Liz, the call's coming any second." The girl huffed and stared at the blank black screen.

Everyone waited in an awkward silence for another few minutes before the phone trilled. Aaron answered it after one ring.

"Hello?" He smiled and looked at his dad. "I'm doing good. Dr. Barna said that things might be starting to work." James held out his hands, silently asking who it was. Aaron waved him off. "Great game last night. The double you hit was awesome."

"Is that Curt Howard?" James whispered.

Aaron, still smiling, nodded. "Uh-huh," he said into the phone. "Yeah . . ." His smile wilted, and he sank into the pillow propping him up. "Yeah, I understand." He sat silently for several minutes before his face brightened. "Really? Yeah . . . okay! Here he is. Thanks!" He handed the phone out to James. "He wants to talk to you."

"Hello?"

"Hi, James, this is Curt. He's really doing better?"

"Seems to be. His mom's a bit upset he keeps staying up late to watch you guys, though."

"Uh-oh. Then she really might not like me after this. I'd like you all to come to the game tonight against Chicago. I've already got your tickets and everything."

James's heart raced and fell at the same time. "Tonight? That's very generous of you, but I'm not sure Aaron's quite up for that yet." He glanced at his son, and now his heart shattered. Aaron's face melted, and his eyes instantly glistened, crushed. James turned away. "That'd be way too late for him, and I'm sure Dr. Barna—"

"Kara already talked to him. He said that Aaron should be good enough for this, that a little adventure might do him some good. Is he there?"

James shook his head at the grinning doctor. "Yeah, he is. And funny you should say 'adventure.' He said the same thing a few minutes ago."

"Then your wife can't argue. Tell her it's doctor's orders."

"Here, you tell her that. I'm not getting in the middle of it." James handed the phone to Emily, who tried to refuse. Her pursed lips said she already knew what Curt had in mind.

"We were just talking about you," she said in her best schoolmarm tone. She sighed and listened. "I don't know; what if—? . . . Really? Are you sure? . . . Well, I guess I'd be the worst mom in the world if I said no to that."

Aaron knelt and bounced in bed, and James slapped him a high five.

"Okay, I won't. Thank you, Mr. Howard. . . . Okay, Curt. Here's James."

"You'll have to tell me how you got her to agree," James said. "I could use the advice."

"Get all your bases covered before you even start talking. Hey, I'd like you at the park early tonight so you guys can watch batting practice. First pitch is a little after seven, like always. Think you can be there around three?"

"Wow, that's early. If Aaron's up to it, yeah, I think so."

"Okay, when you get there, use the parking lot right outside the stadium. There'll be a pass for you at the booth. Then go to the first ticket counter by the gates. There should be an older lady working there. She'll have an envelope of stuff for you and let you in. Sound all right?"

"Sounds awesome. Thanks a lot for this. This must've been what he asked you about, huh?" James said, shaking his head at Aaron. "Last time we had him at a game, he was too little to remember anything."

"Then you guys should have a blast. Gotta run. I'll see you tonight, okay?"

James said good-bye, returned the phone to its stand, and leaned over his son. "You stinker." He rubbed a hand over his smooth scalp. "You sure he's up for this?" he asked Dr. Barna.

"The steroids and other medications are working well. His white count has risen nicely in the last few days, so it will be safe for him to go to a game," Dr. Barna said. "Make sure he is washing his hands often, after every time he touches something. If it appears like it is too taxing, call it a day. But yes, he is up for this."

"But you have to catch a nap today; got it, buckshot?" Emily said.

"After breakfast," Aaron answered.

James and Emily stared, shocked. James couldn't remember the last time Aaron felt good enough to eat anything resembling breakfast.

They barely slowed Aaron down through the day. He studied and restudied updated statistics from around the major league, scribbled through a packet of English homework, and argued with his mom about whether he had promised to take a nap or just *try* to take one. Emily finally won after she swiped the TV remote and his laptop and herded everyone out of the room after lunch so that Aaron, in the midst of a grouchy, brink-of-tears tantrum, had no choice but to lie in bed. When they came back after a half hour, they found him asleep. Afterward, as he got ready for the game, he grudgingly admitted that he felt better.

They pulled into the reserved parking lot on Elizabeth Street, a half block from Comerica Park, a little after three o'clock. Aaron and Lizzie craned their heads to the sky, oohing at the massive stadium's brick facade just beginning to glow in the late-spring sunlight. Holding his mom's hand while they walked to the park, Aaron gazed in awe at the giant sculpted baseball bats and tigers that stood sentinel outside the main entrance.

An older woman waved from behind a ticket counter's Plexiglas. "Are you the McConnells?" she asked through the speaker in her window. When James nodded, she told them to meet her at the gate, picked up a phone and made a call, and disappeared through a doorway in the back of her office. She emerged on the other side of the locked gates, and an usher opened them.

"I've got your tickets here." She tapped the brim of Aaron's navy Tigers hat. "You must be Aaron. I hope you have a great time tonight, dear." The woman handed the envelope to James. "Here are some food coupons and tickets for the Ferris wheel, too, for all of you. And the badges in there will let you guys walk around without being hassled by these grumps." She elbowed the usher who had opened the gate. "Someone should be down to meet you in a minute, so wait inside here. Enjoy the game, folks!"

James hung an orange pass around each of their necks, and Lizzie dragged Emily toward the carousel of tigers in the Big Cat Food Court inside the front entrance. James and Aaron walked past the white bronze statue of Ernie Harwell, the famous Tigers radio broadcaster, and toward a kiosk displaying historical placards of former players and past teams. Maintenance crew smiled when they saw their badges, tipped a cap or waved, and kept sweeping or securing fresh bags in the trash barrels, prepping for the onslaught of people at the opening of the gates still hours away.

The crack of a wooden bat hitting a ball splintered the relative quiet, and the historical exhibit suddenly lost its appeal to Aaron. James called for Emily and Lizzie, and they jogged across the concourse circling the stadium and toward the field. They stopped alongside another kiosk selling souvenirs, behind the top row of seats of the park's lower bowl.

Starstruck, Aaron murmured, "Whoa." James whistled, and Lizzie said, "Wow, that's really cool."

Emily knelt next to her son and put her arm around him. "Pretty special of you to ask for this."

The field was amazing, yet, from how far away the

McConnells stood, it looked like a postcard. Only two people were on the field: a batting practice pitcher on the mound and a hitter inside a dome surrounding home plate. It took a second for the sound of each hit to reach them, the balls barely specks off the bat. But they watched, mesmerized.

The sound of thick heels clunking on concrete distracted James and Emily from the bat cracks. A young, dark-haired woman wearing gray slacks and a lightweight Tigers jacket approached from down the concourse.

"Mr. and Mrs. McConnell?" she asked. "I hope you didn't have any trouble getting here." She shook their hands. "My name's Michele. I work in the front office. Mr. Howard asked me to come get you."

"No trouble at all," James said. "Guys, this is Michele," he said to Aaron and Lizzie. "She works for the Tigers."

"You kids ready to have a good time?"

Aaron, still speechless, jittered. Lizzie leaned against her mom's leg.

"All right then, right this way." Another bat crack.

"Is that . . . ?" Aaron started to say.

"Excuse me?" Michele said.

Aaron nodded down to the field. "Is that . . . Shawn Janneson down there?"

Michele peered at the field. "He must be getting in some early swings."

"Where does he play?" Emily asked.

Aaron gazed at the field in a trance. "Right field."

Crack! This one sounded thicker, denser, and the ball ended up clattering in the right field seats.

"Full batting practice doesn't start until later," Michele explained. "I'll take you out beyond the fence in left field so you can have a chance at some home run balls. But first I want to show you the suite where you'll be watching the game." She led them down the concourse and toward a set of glass doors, beyond which lay the secure lobby for the administrative offices.

"Suite?" James asked.

"Oh, did I forget to mention that?" Emily said, smirking.

"Mr. Howard is letting you use his personal suite for the game tonight. He knew you'd be worried about Aaron during the game, and a suite will have much better access to medical attention if he needs it," Michele said. "It's on the upper level of suites. When you get up there, you can order food off the menu, and everything will be brought right in."

She held open the glass door and directed them through a metal scanner archway, where a security guard inspected Emily's backpack. Once clear, a plump, balding gentleman behind the welcome desk called two elevators that filled one side of the room. While they waited, Aaron pointed out the black-and-white photos of Tigers elected to the Hall of Fame; he spouted several statistics about each one.

Both elevators opened at the same time, and Curt exited the one on the right. "You made it!" he called. Dressed in his home-white pants and a navy batting practice jersey—with the Tigers' *D* emblem over the left breast, white patches on his shoulders, and white stripes from his armpits to his waist—he pointed at Aaron's jersey, the one he made the boy promise not to hang in a closet. "You're lucky you wore that. We'll match later tonight." He turned to Michele. "Can you take the girls up to see their seats?"

"That was the plan."

"Plan?" James said.

"Yeah, can I borrow you boys for a few minutes?" Curt asked.

"Hey, don't look at me," Emily said to her husband's confusion. "He told me about the suite but not about any plan."

Curt took a step toward the elevator he had come from. "C'mon, guys." James followed, but Aaron froze like Ernie Harwell's statue.

"Aaron, let's go," James said. The boy shook his head and edged closer to his mom. Out of reflex, she placed a hand on his shoulder. James walked back to him. "Buddy, come on. Curt wants to show us something." He gently pulled Aaron's hand toward the elevator. Aaron resisted, slipped from James's grasp, and hugged Emily's side.

"You don't want to come?" Curt asked. Aaron vigorously shook his head, and the two shared a long stare. Curt nodded. "I gotcha. All right, c'mon, James; it'll just be a few minutes."

But James squatted. "Hey, what's wrong? You feeling sick?"

Aaron shook his head again, still silent.

"Why don't you want to go?"

Aaron shrugged and studied his shoes. James leaned in close and whispered, "This is what you wished for, right? So let's go. We might never get another chance like this."

Still, Aaron didn't move. James straightened up. "Well, if you're not going, I'm not going."

"But . . ." Aaron looked at Curt for help.

The ballplayer smiled and held out his hands at Aaron. "It's your choice."

Aaron took a deep breath, and a grin fluttered across his lips. He joined Curt in the elevator.

James mumbled to Emily, "That was weird," and followed.

"So the suite," James said when the elevator door closed. "That's what you meant by having your bases covered."

Curt laughed and pushed the button for the lowest level. "Always smart to have the questions answered before they're asked."

"What do you need to borrow us for?"

"I've got some more stuff for the kids I wanted to give you before the game. The guys signed a few more things."

James nudged Aaron with his elbow. "Thanks a lot for all of this," he said to Curt. "You've done more than enough already." Although a few years older and with a nearly identical height and build, James felt like a little kid next to the professional athlete. "You have no idea how much it means to this guy. Actually, we all needed this right now."

The door opened into an alcove in an underground, brightly lit tunnel that encircled the park. Several guards manned barriers like airline security checkpoints, and signs directed personnel to where they could and could not go. James immediately spotted one of the bullpen pitchers—Riley Josephs, Detroit's red-goateed, eighth-inning setup man—chatting with a woman about the same age. In his street clothes and no ball cap, he didn't appear quite as imposing as he did on television when he took the mound. James whispered something to Aaron; Riley nodded a long-distance hello.

"Where do you want us to wait?" James asked.

"Wait? You didn't think I'd bring you guys down here to wait in the tunnel, did you?" Curt led them toward a set of double doors with the Tigers' emblem on it, his metal cleats crunching on the concrete.

"Is that . . . ?"

"The clubhouse? Yeah. Some of the guys want to say hi." He tapped the bill of Aaron's hat. "Aren't you glad you came down with us?"

James's imagination of the behind the scenes of a major league baseball complex—the areas only players, coaches, and reporters saw—always vacillated between extremes. On the one end, based on his two years of college baseball, he pictured a dank, dark, cold underground; one with low ceilings and yellow flickering lights. In this vision, the superstar athletes skittered through the shadows like an army of rats, toiling away in a locker room infested with nine kinds of fungus and a haze stinking of mildew, body odor, and ripe socks. And before every game, each player sacrificed a dollop of sweat and fingernail clippings into some hag's cauldron for a potion that spit them onto the field in sparkling-white uniforms.

On the other end of the spectrum, golf carts whisked the players from their limos in some top secret parking garage, down a red carpet, past a bank of flash-popping paparazzi, and into a clubhouse that shamed the Waldorf Astoria. Thick carpet . . . luxurious leather chairs . . . players in white bathrobes with their names and numbers on the back and fluffy orange- and black-striped slippers . . . a staff of butlers ready to bring a player whatever he might need before and after a game—steak, champagne, the keys to a new Cadillac.

Reality was far more benign and clean and, frankly, boring. The service tunnel, by no means red-carpet worthy, wasn't seedy or nefarious, either. And the clubhouse beyond the double doors Curt opened felt more like an office than a dungeon or a resort. The breeze and echoes from the tunnel ceased when the doors shut, leaving them in a short, quiet, carpeted hallway. For all James knew, they could've been heading to an afternoon college class.

With Aaron by his side and James a step behind, Curt played tour guide, pointing out the glassed-in office of the clubhouse manager directly to their right and portraits of prominent Tigers of the past on the wall. In a dozen steps, the hall ended at another set of closed, steel double doors, also with the Old English *D* emblem. To the left of those doors, next to a closed office, a blue plaque read *Video Room Manager*.

"You know what we do in there?" Curt asked.

"Watch videos of the other pitchers and hitters?"

"You got it. The video manager puts all of that together before each game. It's one of our best scouting tools. But we also watch video of ourselves hitting and throwing, to see what we're doing wrong."

The warm hallway stretched a considerable length to the left of the video room. Yellow cinder block walls held a modest number of pictures and plaques, and more doorways opened every ten to twelve feet on either side. "Those are just offices, meeting rooms, the manager's office—"

"Ernie Mazarron?" Aaron said.

"The one and only. The other coaches share a spot." Curt turned and led them back past the video room. "This way to the dugout." He rapped his knuckles on the steel doors at the T junction. "And down here . . ." In a handful of steps, they stood before another set of doors at the end of the corridor. James and Aaron didn't need to be told what lay beyond.

Curt opened the doors. "Well? What do you think?" he asked Aaron.

The boy plastered himself against his father's leg, unable to answer. James wasn't much help.

James had only ever seen fragments of the Tigers' clubhouse on TV. Postgame interviews with sweaty players captured bits of the caramel-colored wooden lockers behind their heads, a swarm of postgame microphones, recorders, cameras, and lights hovering in front of them. Now, the rest of the picture filled in. Though it wasn't opulent, it surpassed every other athletic locker room he'd ever been in.

The same stiff navy-and-orange woven carpet from the hallway spilled into the spacious, windowless clubhouse. The square room bulged at each side, lending the impression of being circular. Once inside, a door opened on James's immediate left—he caught a glimpse of a huge fitness room packed with bikes, treadmills, elliptical machines, and a host of other equipment—and on the far side, players entered and exited the bathroom and showers. Curt let James and Aaron wander to the center of the room, where the ceiling recessed up into the lights, creating a ledge with a wide face that ringed the room. One side of the ledge's facing read *DETROIT TIGERS*; more black-and-white photos from memorable games in the Tigers' past—a theme Comerica Park celebrated throughout the stadium—continued all the way around.

Several players were present, some of whom, in fact, walked around in white bathrobes with their names and numbers on the back, albeit without the tiger slippers James had pictured. A few sat on leather couches, watching one of two mammoth TVs standing back-to-back in the center of the room. One looped the current ESPN news broadcast; the other flashed from one picture to the next in hyper channel surfing. Someone fussed about playing *Halo*, but the others shot him down.

"Boz always wants to blow something up before batting practice," Curt said. James glanced down at Aaron—their open mouths matched. One of the faces of the franchise stomped away from them, laughing and pouting at the same time— Tony Bozio, the hulking, superstar left fielder. When Boz sat down in front of his locker, he flung a roll of athletic tape at those on the couch. Aaron giggled.

"Over here, guys," Curt said. His locker stood by a short, windowed hallway that looked into the fitness room and led to an airy trainer's room. He swiveled around his navy-blue leather office chair with a white *D* on the headrest. A box, *McConnells* scrawled on the side, filled the seat.

"Hey, Howie, is this them?" A lanky African American walked over, twisting a navy wristband onto his forearm.

"Carl Peters, James and Aaron McConnell," Curt introduced. They all shook hands.

"I hear you know a few stats," Carl said to Aaron, who grinned and leaned against James. "Well, who won the 1982 World Series?"

Aaron didn't answer. He just stared, deer in the headlights.

Curt leaned down. "C'mon; you're making me look bad," he whispered.

Aaron snickered. "The St. Louis Cardinals."

"In how many games?"

"Seven. Against the Brewers."

Carl humphed and adjusted his wristband again. "What about 1981?"

"The Dodgers. In six games over the Yankees."

"How about 1971?"

Aaron thought for only a second. "Pittsburgh Pirates over the Orioles in seven games."

"Dang!" Carl said. He pointed at Aaron. "You best study up 'cause I'm gonna stump you one of these days, all right? Even if I got to go old-school."

"I think he likes the old stuff best," James said.

"Then *old* old-school." Carl held out a fist for Aaron to bump, and he returned to his locker.

Curt rifled through the box—pulling out another jersey, some more signed baseballs, wristbands, hats—and handed each item to Aaron with an explanation.

James's candy-store eyes gaped around the room. Here he stood, smack in the middle of a fan's dream with his son, rubbing elbows with a clubhouse of professional, larger-than-life ballplayers. Up close and witnessing the behind the scenes of Major League Baseball, The Show. He'd heard that men were from Mars and women from Venus, but to him, professional

athletes came from an entirely different galaxy. One very
far away.

But here, now . . . suddenly, what was happening and what
he saw caught up to him, and everything he thought he knew
about major league baseball, from a fan's perspective, disintegrated. The press had it wrong. The fans had it wrong. *He* had
it wrong.

A few of the Latino players—Alejandro Santana, Cordero
Ruiz, and Carlos Espinoza—chatted up one another in a blur
of Spanish. James caught another player, starting catcher Tyler
Cavanaugh, talking about his son's Little League game. First baseman Dawson Frye tapped a text into a cell phone. Carl Peters sat
in his chair and flipped through a scouting report. . . . These men
before him—regardless of endorsement deals or multimillion-
dollar contracts or the national spotlight—were just that: men.
Men with names. And first names, not just what displayed on
the back of a jersey. Regular guys with a most decidedly irregular
profession. James couldn't comprehend how they played for their
jobs every single night under such a public, unforgiving spotlight.
Yet they came and went through the clubhouse, mostly in silence
in their pregame routines, with a remarkably ordinary air about
them as they "got ready for work." Sure, exceptions existed, but
most players were grown men with families.

They were fathers. Like him. But they worked in an office
where their job, unlike almost any other job in the country, was
relentlessly scrutinized—and sometimes ridiculed—by a truly
clueless audience.

Curt's kindness, the refreshingly regular clubhouse, the
men—James had all the proof he needed: major league baseball
players were normal, regardless of the few prima donna super-
stars or what the countless talking heads would have the world
believe.

When he turned back, Aaron and Curt were closing the box of souvenirs. "Okay, follow me, you two," Curt said.

A few more players interrupted their walk out of the clubhouse, wishing good-lucks and hang-in-theres to Aaron. James thanked them for their autographs on the baseballs, Aaron bumped some more fists, shyness sealing his lips, and they reentered the warm, school-like hallway. Curt pushed open the steel doors leading to the Tigers' third-base dugout.

"Holy smokes, buddy," James whispered to Aaron. "We're going to the dugout."

A major league dugout.

A place James once wished to be a part of.

Curt tapped Aaron on the shoulder. "I'll race ya." He jogged forward; Aaron surged ahead as fast as he could, and Curt slowed down so that the boy took the lead.

Curt's cleats thudded on the hard rubber floor. Fluorescent lights lined the tunnel, which dropped down two short flights of stairs. At the end of the corridor, he held out his hand for the wall but let Aaron touch it first. "Aw, man!" They slapped hands. "Good hustle."

He pointed to a door on their left. "You guys ever hear during a broadcast that someone's getting in some swings during the game? Underground batting cages."

James and Aaron ducked their heads inside. "Awesome . . . ," Aaron muttered.

They veered to the right through an open doorway and into an anteroom, and a warm breeze washed away some of the tunnel's stuffiness. Before them, through an archway, rose a set of stairs.

There, at the top of those few steps, the dugout. And then, at eye level, twenty yards away, sunlight, and a thin line of green. James drank in the smell of freshly cut grass.

Curt and Aaron bounced up the half-dozen steps to the dugout. James took each one deliberately, as if he were creeping out of the tunnel to avoid security. Aaron explored the gigantic space, its floor made of the same rubber material as the tunnel; aromas of pine tar and wood and leather hung like smoke. Curt popped open a bucket of bubble gum on the ledge behind the wooden bench and helped Aaron stuff his pockets, extracting a promise that he had to check with his mom before having a piece. Bat racks and helmet cubbies were empty. James didn't have a very good view of the stands from inside, but their enormous, hulking presence loomed all around him.

The wide-open field called. His eyes drifted to the diamond, so bright and green and open. Shawn Janneson had completed his early batting practice, leaving only a groundskeeper or two working near the stands, the pitching screen in front of the mound, and the batting dome around the plate.

"Listen, I've got to run and get something real quick," Curt said. "Why don't you guys take a walk out there."

James's gaping mouth said, *Are you crazy?*

"Seriously, we've got some time before BP. Go on. Take a look around."

James surveyed the field. "I feel like we should take our shoes off first. You sure it's okay?"

"You won't get tossed off, if that's what you mean." Curt hopped up the steps and waved to one of the groundskeepers, hollering that some friends were coming onto the field and pointing down at James and Aaron. "Don't Taser them or nothin'; they're with me!" He clapped James on the back, gave Aaron a nod, and shuffled down the stairs to the clubhouse tunnel.

Father and son stood alone in silence, awash in the warm sunshine and breeze and smell of the grass. James couldn't take his eyes off the field before him, but he also couldn't move his legs. The memory of letting go of an old dream—his younger dream—refused to let him move, to walk up onto the field and experience what he'd turned his back on more than thirteen years ago.

But the person who was alive because he did turn his back on that dream squeezed his hand.

"C'mon, Dad," Aaron said. "Let's go see it."

8

AARON GAVE JAMES'S HAND A TUG, and they stepped onto the field and crossed the section of grass in front of the dugout, stopping at the baseline path between home plate and third base. The white stripe had not yet been chalked for the game. Out of habit, James hopped over the smooth, supple red dirt, not wanting to leave a footprint, and Aaron squealed when James yanked his hand and swung him over as if the dirt were a mud puddle. They walked and turned in circles on their way to the center of the infield, captivated at the panorama of the stadium.

They stopped on the grass between second base and the pitcher's mound, and Aaron craned his head back. "Wow," he whispered.

James had always wondered what it must feel like to stand in the middle of a professional baseball field, a *major league* field. The towering stands, the scoreboards, the light stanchions . . . He'd heard a variety of descriptions—that it felt like playing in a canyon or being on stage or, really, like nothing much at all. But one description he had heard before fit perfectly.

A cathedral.

Electronic messages scrolled across the video displays encircling the stadium were glittering, living frescoes. The upper deck reached skyward like the lofty reaches of the nave. The towering scoreboard in left field shimmered—a giant, digital Michelangelo, animated with players' faces and fiery cartoon baseballs and advertisements. But they stood in the middle of the infield, the sanctuary. James spun slowly, unable to breathe. He felt so small, so insignificant, and everything around him seemed so . . . *holy*. A manifestation of that fleeting, golden, glowing moment that happened during the evening games back home. That moment had always feigned a transformation of the high school field into something bigger than itself, into the only thing that existed. But here, now—this *was* the only thing that existed.

He could never have fully appreciated Comerica Park's master architecture while viewing it only from the stands. The perfect proportions of the rising stands and excess grass and dirt in foul territory made the infield seem bigger than it actually was, even though the dimensions were the same as the high school field back in the swamp: ninety feet between bases; sixty feet, six inches from the mound to the plate. The scene in the basketball movie *Hoosiers*, in which Gene Hackman's character measured out the height of the rim and the distance to the free throw line in the massive Hinkle Fieldhouse court, came to mind. It showed the bug-eyed farm kids from Hickory that no matter what else happened around them, the court, and therefore the game, were exactly the same as back home.

But now, the surroundings overwhelmed James. Standing at the nucleus of the regular-size baseball diamond in the midst of a major league stadium was too much. Way too much. He suddenly felt he knew nothing about how to play this game.

He stood and stared for several minutes. The Pepsi Porch sign beyond the right field seats stood lifeless and dark; the behemoth scoreboard in left field blipped only test messages and player videos beneath a pair of giant, prowling tiger statues. The bright-blue sky above and gentle breeze confounded him with the sensation of being simultaneously inside and outside.

Breathtaking. Something he had dreamed about, and something still out of a dream even as he gazed around, fully awake.

Bigger than life. A place where giants played. Sure, they might have looked normal in the clubhouse, like regular dads, but out here . . . out here the players became superheroes.

Stadium and stands and lights and scoreboards aside, he prized one part of a baseball field more than anything else, for it was a part of every field he had ever played on.

The grass.

He squatted and flattened his palm on the grass. Soft, almost springy to the touch, yet the individual, freshly cut blades were stiff, too. Uniform. *No wonder there aren't any bad hops in the big leagues.*

Aaron's face glowed, wide in wonder at the structures around him. He appeared so tiny set against such a massive backdrop. "C'mere," James whispered. Aaron knelt. James told him to spread his fingers, and he slowly pressed his son's hand down into the grass. "Pretty soft, huh? Here, go like this." James brushed his own hand back and forth over the tops of the blades. Aaron did the same. "Now . . . slowly. Really *feel* it. And smell it."

Aaron closed his eyes and drank in a heavy breath through his nose. A look came over his face, one James hadn't seen in a long time.

Absolute calm.

"For me, baseball is all about the grass. For you, it's stats and numbers. But those stats are made here, on the grass. When you've played as much as I have . . ." James trailed off, trans-fixed as he swept his hand back and forth. The grass connected him to Little League with his dad, and the high school state championship he won as a freshman, and every college field he played on as he built himself a pro scout–worthy career. A horde of baseball memories, of summer days in the grass.

Aaron was in none of them.

He possessed no memory of playing catch with his son in the grass. No pretend games in the backyard as James caught balls and strikes, ghost runners loading the bases in the bottom of the ninth in the World Series. No ground balls or pop-ups or double plays or bunts. No cheering at T-ball games, no coach-pitch game interruptions when an entire team would stop playing to watch a plane fly overhead, no running the bases and those first tumbling slides, no coach-and-son pic-tures, no picnics after the last game of the season.

Only the glove he bought him last Christmas. The one that still sat atop the bookshelf back home, alongside all the other ones Aaron had never used.

Then James realized that Aaron had no baseball memories for himself, either.

Until now.

The boy still brushed his hand across the grass, his eyes closed and his face gripped by unusual calm, when James took his hand again. Aaron opened his eyes.

"I'm sorry," James said.

"Why?"

"I didn't mean to say that what you like about baseball, the stats and numbers . . . I'm sorry. I wish . . ." James shook his head. The knot in his throat wouldn't budge.

"It's okay, Dad." The calm vanished, replaced by his usual humble grin.

"But we're here now. I'm on the best grass I've ever seen. With my best buddy. And you know what? It's my new best baseball memory."

"You think I'll ever, you know, be strong enough to play someday? Like, on a team?"

James pulled Aaron into a firm embrace. "Absolutely." He cleared his throat. "You heard what Dr. Barna said. We turned a corner." He let Aaron go and held him at arm's length. "You'll get on your own baseball field someday, and you can kneel down right in the middle of the infield and feel the grass. And then I'll have a new best memory."

They walked on the pitcher's mound, around the L-screen that stood in front to protect the batting practice pitcher, and down the dirt strip from the mound to home plate. Their voices echoed through the cavernous stadium while they wandered back to the mound, pointing out the press box high above home plate, the bullpens beyond the left field fence, and the giant Belle Tire sign in right field.

"Well?" Curt called as he strolled from the dugout. He held a dark-tan ball glove closed against his chest. He also hopped across the dirt baseline.

"I feel like those ghost ballplayers coming out of the cornfield in Iowa," James said. "How can you guys stay focused on the game with all this around you and when all those seats are filled?"

"Here is fine, when they're cheering *for* you. Yankee Stadium?" Curt shook his head and hissed. "Yeah, that can get a little distracting."

"Home field advantage, eh?"

"It's bigger than you think."

"But—" James waved his arms around—"*all* of this. Does it take something away from the game?"

"If you let it, yeah, it can. But everything's moving so fast that if you let it take something away and affect how you play, you won't be here long. What do you think?" he asked Aaron.

"This is really awesome."

"Listen, guys, I gotta get loosened up a bit." Curt winked at Aaron and then grinned at James. He opened his glove at James. A matching mitt lay nestled inside the pocket. "Wanna play catch?"

James looked at the offered glove as if it were about to attack him.

Curt and Aaron laughed. "Glove? Catch? Ball?" Curt said slowly, waggling the mitt. "You do remember how to throw, right?"

"I know we can't play catch, Dad, so I thought . . ." Aaron glanced up at Curt.

James stared at his son. Such a little guy. And so much a grown man.

He fought hard against the welling in his eyes and nodded. He handed Aaron his light fleece coat and slid on the glove. Aaron pumped his fist, and after he and James shimmied through a sequence of high fives, low fives, forearm bumps, and wiggling fingers, the three made their way to the outfield grass, with its perfectly mowed diagonal paths alternately light and dark green.

Curt bent down to Aaron. "You gotta be my scout, okay? Watch close."

"Can I sit on second base?"

"Best seat in the house."

Aaron shuffled to the dazzling-white base and planted his bottom on top. He clapped three times. "Let's go, Dad!"

Curt rubbed a brand-new baseball into his glove, and once they were a few paces behind the infield's dirt skin, he jogged toward the left field foul line. On the grass behind shortstop, James swung his arms around in giant windmills, grabbed his right throwing arm and pulled it behind his back, then over his head, then across his chest. His shoulder, tight from not throwing for nearly a month, resisted each stretch, but he didn't care how sore he'd be.

"Now, I heard you were a coach," Curt said from across the span of about sixty feet. "You wouldn't let your players get away with that little bit of stretching, would you?" James laughed and spent a few more minutes loosening up.

Curt threw him the ball. It sparkled in the sunlight like a shooting star and slapped into the borrowed infielder's glove. James took it in his hands, gazed around at the stadium again, flashed his son a grin and a wink, and fired it back.

As they tossed it back and forth, James took some satisfaction in how his throwing and form matched almost exactly with Curt's. It made him smile inwardly. *Maybe I've been teaching it the right way after all,* he thought. The throws from both men got harder and crisper the more their arms loosened.

"So I heard you played college ball and looked you up," Curt said. "Shortstop, right?"

Smack into James's mitt.

"Yep."

"What happened?" Curt asked.

James stopped in midthrow and held the ball. "Excuse me?"

"Your second year. You batted, what, .390?"

"You really did look me up." James threw the ball again. ".396."

"So what happened? Injury?" The ball streaked back to James.

James packed the ball in his glove a couple of times. "I met a girl."

"She make you quit?"

James laughed and threw. "No. Baseball just, I don't know, lost a little off its fastball, if you know what I mean."

"And would this happen to be the same girl you came to the park with today?"

"That's the one." Curt threw one low, but James short-hopped it cleanly.

"Sounds like there's a story there, to make a guy give up the game."

James paused, the ball in his glove. "No, not much. Boy meets girl. Boy goes bonkers for her and forgets how to hit a curveball. Girl takes pity on him and marries him. Same old story."

"C'mon; there's gotta be more to it than that."

James caught the ball and inspected it. "We started dating toward the end of my sophomore season, my .396 season. Em's a year older. That fall of my junior year, I was—" he snapped a throw to Curt—"preoccupied with her, I guess. Did horrible in fall ball and lost my job to a freshman. Coach wanted me to keep pushing." He caught the ball again. "I tried for a little while. But he had to break the news to me. I'd always been a starter, so I hung 'em up. He let me stay on as sort of a junior coach, help the younger guys with the ropes and classes and college life, all that." James's next throw sailed high, but Curt jumped and snagged it.

"So you just walked away after one bad season of fall ball? From all those dreams you had as a kid?"

"Hey, don't go making me think twice! Em did fall in love with me as a ballplayer, after all." Now James jumped a few inches to catch a high throw. "But she was in a good program, biomedical engineering of all things. We got married and moved to North Carolina while she finished up a master's degree."

Curt whistled.

"Oh yeah, she's got the looks *and* the brains of the family. Doesn't she, bud?" he called to Aaron. The boy didn't answer, his face screwed down tight, serious, studying them.

"I tried to find it again on a team at a small college down there. I had a couple years of eligibility left. But it . . ." James paused, staring off into the grass between them. "It wasn't happening. I lost it." He tossed the ball back. "Anyway, Em's parents both passed right after we got married, and we didn't want to start a family in North Carolina, that far away from my parents, the only grandparents. So we moved back to my hometown up north, I got to be head coach right away at my old high school, and things seemed—I don't know—to work out how I guess they were supposed to. That's it. That's the long version."

"And you're still coaching?"

"Yep. Part-time assistant. At least I was. Guess we'll see what happens next year." James bent down to catch a low throw, and he quickly flicked back a sidearm without straightening. The ball arced perfectly to the right, and Curt caught it at his chest. "The hours needed to be a head coach didn't sit well with a young family. And then, with . . ." He nodded at Aaron but didn't say anything; Curt showed his understanding with a raised hand. "I couldn't keep up. They hired a new guy, great guy, and he let me stay on for whatever I wanted to give them. It gave me lots of time to be with Aaron for appointments and tests." James absently patted a fist into his glove.

"You know, losing the touch like that and then walking away from playing the game must've been hard. You ever regret it?"

James caught the ball and held his arms out to Comerica Park. "Looking around here now, I sure do! This is torturing me. I could've gotten used to playing in a place like this."

Curt's laugh bellowed through the stadium.

"Seriously, though . . . yeah. There were regrets. What-ifs. I always wondered if I gave up too easily. Sometimes those regrets really stung." James surveyed the exquisite infield, wondering again if he did give up too easily. Then he saw the boy on second base and smiled at him.

"But all those major league dreams I had as a kid, like you said? All those changed the day that guy came along and I bought him his first glove. That's when I got a new dream." He studied his mitt and rubbed the ball into the pocket. "Still waiting for that one to come true. We thought this was finally going to be the summer, that we'd finally get our chance to . . ." His eyes flashed to Aaron, and he fought the lump, holding a finger up to Curt that he needed a second. "Losing that chance? Now *that* stings."

"Yet," Curt said. "You just haven't gotten a chance *yet*."

James stared at the ground.

"You stay in shape?"

James resumed throwing with his hardest fastball yet, welcoming the change in subject and the twinge of pain in his shoulder. "I try to throw most days, even during the winter. We have gym workouts for some of the players, and I usually run those."

"What about hitting?"

James let out a belly laugh. "I've been in the cage a few times. That ball's smaller and faster the older I get."

"That's practice is all. You obviously had it at one time. Best I ever hit was .372 my junior year."

"So I've got a question for you," James said. "Why all the questions?"

Curt used his glove to wave it away. "Just curious."

When Curt next caught the ball, he flicked his mitt toward the grass. "All right, Mr. Scout, pay attention!" he called to

Aaron. He tossed James a soft grounder. Instinct kicked in, and James fielded it and fired it back. For the next ten minutes, Curt threw him ground balls, varying the speed, and many to the left and right. Thanks to his less-than-new sneakers with slick soles, James slipped repeatedly, fielding everything off to the side, unable to get in front of the ball. But he gobbled up every one using the expert form he taught his high school players. Backhanders, to his glove side, short hops—they all cushioned gently in his glove and ended up right back at Curt's chest.

James had a pretty good sweat going when Curt finally brought it to a close by flinging a high fly ball. Using his glove to shield the sun, James caught it with two hands, right above his head, like the final out of a game. Clapping skittered from the dugout. Emily and Lizzie walked onto the field and joined them by third base.

"Well?" Curt asked his scout. "Give it to me straight."

Aaron thought for a moment, looking his father up and down. "He's still throwing pretty strong. Accuracy was good. For the most part. He did sky one."

"Huh?" James said.

"Looks like he might've lost some range left and right," Aaron continued. "He wasn't getting in front of the ball."

"It was the shoes!" James said, showing them his spike-less soles.

"But his hands looked really solid. Good on the short hops, good throws. All in all, not bad. I think he's still got it."

"Well, I'm glad you approve, Mr. Scout," James said. He flopped the borrowed mitt on Aaron's head and playfully pushed him away.

"So what do *you* think?" Aaron asked Curt.

"It might be tough. But it could work."

"What could work?" James said.

Curt motioned to Aaron, who, suddenly shy, leaned against his mom. They all stood in silence.

"Go on," Emily said. "Tell him."

"Tell me what?"

Aaron looked away. But a deep breath appeared to give him some confidence, and he stepped forward. "You asked me what I said to Mr. Howard in the hospital."

"Yeah. But I know now. This whole day, right? Pretty cool." James flicked Aaron's hat.

"That wasn't it." Aaron straightened his hat. "This isn't what I asked for. It wasn't my wish."

"Um . . . okay." James glanced at Emily and shrugged. "What was it then?"

"My wish was for you, Dad."

"Right. To watch me play catch in the outfield. Aaron, I—"

"No. To *play* here."

"Yeah. Catch. You said—"

"No, to play a *game* here. A major league game."

"One game," Curt said. "One night. What do you think?"

The air sucked completely out of James. Mouth agape, he looked from one person to another.

One game?

An incoherent sort of half stammer, half grumble tumbled out of his mouth that everyone took as a yes.

His family laughed and cheered, and Curt flashed a thumbs-up sign toward the row of suites high above the third base dugout. Emily hugged him, and Aaron hollered a *Woo-hoo!* that raced around the stadium. Curt patted James on the shoulder, and still, James hadn't said a word. When Emily released him, he couldn't look at Aaron.

James finally cleared his throat yet found only a dry and

crackly voice. "There's no . . . I mean, how could I . . . ? I'd only . . . I can't . . ."

"Just hear us out, okay?" Curt said.

"Us?"

"I want you to talk to a few other people first. It's not all up to me. Those ground balls were to see if you could still catch and throw. I think we can take it to the next level."

"Next—"

Curt put a hand on James's back and steered him toward an open gate directly behind home plate, where Michele stood waiting. The stands rose up on either side of the ramp that descended back into Comerica Park's service tunnel. "Michele will take you up to the real bosses, and then we'll talk later." Curt shook James's hand again and thanked him for the catch, then improvised a quick handshake with both Aaron and Lizzie, who giggled, and jogged back to the dugout and clubhouse tunnel.

Michele led them to a suite where three men sat on a leather couch and two high-backed bar chairs, waiting for them. Two rose and greeted James at the door. "Lou Schelling," the tallest of the three said. "I'm general manager for the Tigers. This—" he held a hand out to a much shorter man—"is my assistant GM, Wes Marco. And this—"

"Mr. Mazarron," Aaron said, his eyes widening. The gray-haired, uniformed manager rose from the couch on bowlegged knees and shook the kids' hands first. He looked like even more of a drill sergeant in person. His wrinkly face and silver-stubbled chin rose with a wide but chiseled smile, and his handshake was solid.

"Please, please, have a seat," Lou said, returning to his stool. James stayed standing, but Aaron and Emily sat on the couch. Lizzie climbed into her mom's lap. "Are you folks enjoying yourselves?"

"Uh . . . ," James stammered.

"It's been a lot of fun already," Emily said.

"And the game hasn't even started yet," Aaron said.

"Well, I hope the boys make it a fun game tonight," Lou said. "The White Sox have a good ball club this year."

James opened his mouth to say something but stopped.

Lou and Wes laughed at James's bewilderment. "I suppose I'll get to the point," Lou continued. "Curt's filled us in on everything, and judging by the thumbs-up he gave us, we'd like to make this work." He turned to Aaron. "We want to help make your wish come true, young man."

Aaron beamed.

James's smile twitched and crumbled. "That's very kind of you, but . . . I . . . Everything you guys are doing today for Aaron, for us . .. . that's more than enough, really. I don't . . . I just don't think . . . I mean what if . . . ?"

"We researched your college stats," Wes Marco said. "I even called your old college coach yesterday. You had the talent at one time, Mr. McConnell. Pro scouts were high on you, too, from what your coach said. And we've got ballplayers older than you getting ready for batting practice right now. You just need some work."

James shook his head, about to speak, when the skipper's raspy voice stopped him. "You're rough, that's all. A little time in the minors'll round you into shape."

"But—"

"There's some contract stuff to work out," Lou said. "You can't simply suit up. There's all sorts of hoops to jump through to get the proper paperwork filed with the league, even if it's only for one day. But Wes is a guru at that sort of thing."

"But I can't—"

"You'll go through the ranks like everyone else—single-A up

to triple-A—but we'll move you up the ladder a little quicker," Wes explained. "Our minor league coaches and roving instructors will focus on you, and you'll get a few games down there. Lou thought that to make it easier on your family, we'd keep you around the area: West Michigan, Erie, and Toledo. We won't send you down to Florida."

James held up a hand and finally found his voice. "Gentlemen, please. That's all . . . Look, this is all just really fast right now. I appreciate the time you've taken with this, but I'm not comfortable leaving my family. Not to mention I'm not exactly major league material, even if it's for one game. I've been away from it too long."

"That's what the training's for," Lou said. "All you have to do is—"

"That's beside the point, Mr. Schelling," James interrupted. "I'm sorry, but that's not what's important." He rested a hand on Aaron's shoulder, but his son fixed a stare on his lap. "I'm sorry, buddy, but I just can't."

Lou leaned forward and rested his elbows on his knees, clasping his hands. The back of his gray suit coat stretched tight around his narrow shoulders. "This is a once-in-a-lifetime opportunity, Mr. McConnell. I know Curt has mentioned it to some of the other players, and they all think it's a great idea."

"But what about—?"

"I'm just asking you to consider it."

"But Aaron's treatment is in full swing right now."

"Just consider it."

James focused on his son, whose eyes remained in his lap. "What if the coaches and instructors say I can't hack it?"

"It's only a cup of coffee," Mazarron said. "But—"

"Cup of coffee?"

"A quick stay in the bigs. That's what we call it. But if they say you can't hack it, your cup will be more of a sip. And it'll be in the minors."

"Well . . . ," Lou said. "C'mon, Ernie; he'll be fine. He'll make it up here."

"Don't get me wrong; I think this is a wonderful idea, but you're not gonna get any slack from me. If we gotta kibosh this whole thing and wash you out at Erie or Toledo, so be it. I won't put a team out there I don't think'll get us a win, and I don't want you to embarrass yourself. Or us."

James respected the manager's honesty. "I appreciate that," he said. "I wouldn't even think about doing this if I can't help the Tigers."

"All right, then," Mazarron said.

"I'm not saying I'll do it."

"But you'll consider it?" Lou asked.

James looked at his family. Emily gritted a smile; Lizzie hadn't been paying attention, her eyes fixed on the suite's glass front.

But Aaron. He watched his father hard, his blue eyes pleading. They appeared in pain, and in a flash, he looked much older than nine. Or maybe he just looked sicker. His mouth formed one word, the same one he had whispered to Curt Howard back at the hospital: "Please."

The silence and pressure washed over James. "I'll consider it. But Aaron's doctor has the final say, and Em, too. If they don't think I should be gone, then I'm not." He bent toward Aaron. "Even one day in the big leagues isn't worth not being there if you need me, pal." Aaron's lips trembled, and he leaned his head against his dad. James wrapped him up in his arms.

The three Tigers rose. "Wes will be in charge of this," Lou said, and the assistant GM handed James a business card. "Let us know as soon as possible, though. I thought that Father's Day would be perfect."

"That only gives you a few weeks to get your—" Mazarron glanced at the two kids and Emily—"uh, stuff together. Get your eye right again. You'll have to bust your hump if you want your cup of coffee in my dugout."

James shook his hand.

"Okay then, I got a lineup to put together." He softened when he took Emily's hand. "Was a pleasure to meet you, ma'am." He pinched Lizzie's nose, tapped the brim of Aaron's cap and shot a finger pistol at him, and left.

The White Sox roughed up the Tigers' number four starting pitcher for six runs in the first two innings—he never escaped the second inning—and the Tigers couldn't recover. The 8–5 loss, however, didn't dampen the excitement of the game, nor the afterglow. Whereas Aaron would've moped after watching the Tigers lose on TV, he made it through the game at Comerica Park all smiles, only mumbling, "Rats," at the fly ball to center field for the final out. He even watched the White Sox players congratulate one another on the field afterward. But only for a minute.

Ten minutes into the late-night ride back to St. Francis, Lizzie and Aaron passed out, their mouths open. While James navigated the maze of interstate exit ramps and merged onto westbound I-94, Emily reached back and propped up the kids' heads as they rolled forward or to the side. She finally turned around with a satisfied sigh.

She tried to ask James about Aaron's wish of his playing in one major league game and how the Tigers wanted to help, but he squinted at the oncoming headlights and murmured an occasional "Uh-huh" or "Yeah, I know." She gave up and closed her eyes.

The images blurred in his mind as he drove in silence until

he didn't know what to think. From meeting a whole team of pro baseball players to walking out on the infield and playing catch in a major league stadium, every moment seemed surreal. And the offer—to fulfill a childhood dream if only for one night. Every time he tried to contemplate it, headlights singed his eyes and scrambled his thoughts. Finally he forced them out, closed his mind, and drove, concentrating only on what existed in the dome of his headlights.

They carried still-sleeping children into a tranquil, dim Bertoia Building lobby. A staff member near the elevator found a pair of wheelchairs, and with a groan and some huffs, James and Emily deposited the kids into them. With the couch in their room already folded out and made up for Lizzie, they roused the kids enough to go to the bathroom one more time, helped them change into pajamas, and slipped them under the covers. Emily flicked on the bathroom night-light and closed the adjoining bedroom's door behind them.

She flopped on the bed. "What a night. I wish they would've played better."

"White Sox are pretty good this year," James said from the bathroom. "Should be a three-team race between them, the Tigs, and the Twins."

"I can't stand the Sox," Emily said.

"That's why I love you." James collapsed on his back next to her. They stared at the ceiling together in silence.

"You know I have to ask you," she said. "I gave you plenty of time to think about it on the drive back here."

"I can't believe he wished for that." James tried, unsuccessfully, to rub the fatigue out of his eyes.

"What do you mean?"

"I mean, why would he do that? He could've asked Curt for anything."

"He loves you," Emily said. "And if he can't play right now, he wants you to. He knows . . . you know."

"Knows what?"

"How hard it is on you, not being able to play catch with him, to teach him how to hit, to throw. He wants to do those things as much as you want to teach him."

"I know. That's what he sort of told me out on the field." James propped himself up on one elbow and faced his wife. "He doesn't think I blame him for us not having played catch, does he?"

"Of course not. He just . . . feels bad. He knows how much you want to do that with him. And with the way you guys talk about baseball and you relive your games for him—he knows all your stats from college. He knows how much you miss playing."

James stretched out again and pushed a long breath out of his nose, his eyes still on the ceiling. "Hon, I can't do it."

"Sure you can. I watched you in college, remember? It'll all come back; you'll get your timing. All you need is—"

"No," James interrupted. "I mean . . . I *can't do it*." The simple admission hung in the air like a blanket of smoke, suffocating the room. Even their breathing seemed to be sucked away as the walls closed in.

Emily sat up and turned, her legs dangling over the edge of the bed, her back to her husband. "You don't really have a choice."

Now James sat up. "What do you mean I don't have a choice? Of course I do. They're not forcing me to do it, and I'm not going to leave Aaron for the next three weeks so I can go goof around at some sort of fantasy camp."

Emily stood and faced him. Her neck flushed as her temper bubbled to the surface. "This is not a fantasy camp, James; this is the real thing," she said quietly so as not to wake the kids in the other room. "And it's for your son."

"And being with my son is the most important thing right now." James didn't bother to keep his voice down.

Emily sat next to him. Her neck drained of color. "I know it is," she said. "But *you can do this*. Aaron's not going anywhere right now. We can check with Dr. Barna, and if chemo's going to work like he thinks and it'll start picking up . . . honey, you won't be missing anything here."

"Won't be missing anything?" James shouted, standing. Emily held out her hands for him to be quiet. "I'd be missing *everything*! We've danced around it, so I guess I'll be blunt: What if he's only got a few months left to live? You're asking me to miss that to go play in some stupid game?"

"You playing in that 'stupid game' is your son's *dying wish*! And you're only going to think about how this affects *you*?"

"You don't get it."

"I get it perfectly! You want blunt? Fine. You can't bear the thought of . . . of *all this*, so you're going to suffer in silence and sit at his bedside and wait for that day to come while he wastes away."

"Don't talk like that," James said quietly.

"And all the time, Aaron will be looking at you, wondering why you're there, *ignoring him*—"

"I'm not ignoring him by wanting to be with him!"

"—*ignoring him* by ignoring the one thing he wished for, the *one thing* he wants to see more than anything else before he . . ." Tears interrupted, and she buried her face in her palms. James pulled her close, and their bodies shuddered.

"How can I be gone?" James whispered. "How will I be able to look at him when I get back, when I wouldn't have been here for three weeks?"

Emily wiped her nose and eyes. "How will you be able to look at him if you stay?"

James sat on the bed, leaned forward, and pressed his fingers into his eyes.

Emily rested a hand on his back. "If this treatment won't work, if this really is . . ." She took a breath to calm herself but didn't finish the sentence. "Would you rather spend that time sitting next to him watching ball games with him on TV? Or would you rather make his dying wish come true and be *on* that TV, playing *for* him?"

"Why didn't he just wish for a signed bat or something?"

Emily chuckled and sniffed at the same time. "I know. Or if he asked some wish foundation for a fishing trip to Canada. Or a Disney vacation." She pulled his face up to hers and cupped his cheeks. "But he didn't, James. He asked *you* to make his wish come true."

"And you're fine with all this."

"This is the path before us right now," she said. "We can't sit on the sidelines and let the situation tell us how to act. We have to choose to move forward with happiness. And *life* and living. For whatever time we have left with him."

"Just like that."

"Yeah, just like that."

"That's not as easy for some people as it is for you, Em."

"But that doesn't mean it's not what we're supposed to do."

James walked to the window. He slipped his hands in his back pockets and gazed upon the dark gardens far below. Solar-powered lights illuminating the main spiral path shone like stars that some cosmic force had shaken free from the heavens. "What about something during spring training next year? Like in a game that wouldn't count?"

"Before we came and got you, I met Lou Schelling, and he

told me everything and brought that up," Emily said. "But I guess Curt talked to Dr. Barna, and they think that Aaron . . . They think it'd be best to get this done now."

All the more reason not to do it. James's shoulders sagged. That line of argument would get him nowhere.

"You saw how he's been ever since he met Curt," Emily continued, "and tonight, at the game. Do you remember seeing him that . . . energetic? That—I don't know—full of life? I even had to get after him when he wouldn't share popcorn with Lizzie. They were *arguing*, James. *Arguing*. When was the last time Aaron's had the energy to argue with that girl?"

James snickered.

"And remember what Dr. Barna said: 'What's good for the mind can be good for the body.' Honestly, seeing you do this, following your progress, keeping stats, *your* stats, watching you in that game, that could be exactly what he needs. Even if it's only a short-term bounce back." Emily walked up behind James, slipped her arms around his waist, and laid her head on his back. "I really believe this will make him stronger. He'll have a goal, just like you. You think he's not going to fight with everything he's got to make it to that day? When he can watch you—*you*—play on his favorite team?"

James hadn't considered that. He turned and settled into Emily's embrace. They held each other, motionless, for several minutes.

"And you think I can still hit a fastball?" he asked.

"Of course. Curveball, on the other hand." She hissed and shook her head. "I know what my scouting report would say."

He playfully slapped her on the bottom.

"Absolutely." She rose on her tiptoes to peck a kiss on his lips. "And I still haven't seen a better fielder than you."

"This happens right away, you know."

"I know. And for right now, Aaron's just got chemo, and they'll be finishing up school. And we can call you if something changes, and you'll be able to get back here within three or four hours, no matter where you're at. Remember what Wes said. They won't send you to Florida; they'll keep you with the minor league teams close to Detroit."

James kissed Emily once more and turned back to the window. Everything tumbled together in his head like roiling storm clouds.

Aaron's smile gleamed through it all.

He knew he'd never see a smile bigger than the one Aaron would wear the day his dad ran onto the field in a Detroit Tigers uniform.

"Okay," he said. "I'll do it."

Before he changed his mind, he pulled out Wes Marco's business card, and Emily found his phone. After two rings, the assistant general manager answered.

"I'm in," James said. "I can't promise it'll work, but I'll give it a shot."

"Fantastic. We'll work out some kind of contract that meets league requirements tomorrow," Wes said. "Be down here tomorrow afternoon to take a physical and sign the contract, and you'll ship off to Grand Rapids on Monday."

"I don't even have my glove," James said.

Wes laughed on the other end. "I think we can dig one up around here for you to borrow."

9

JAMES STAYED AT ST. FRANCIS for Aaron's Monday morning chemotherapy session and an early lunch with Lizzie. Afterward, Aaron, on the verge of another nap, offered a weak good-bye hug while in bed.

"Knock it out of the park, Dad," Aaron whispered, snuggling under thin covers.

"To the moon, buddy. We'll talk every day, okay?" Aaron didn't stir. James's lunch flopped in his stomach when he kissed his son a final time. "Keep him safe, Lord," he whispered, pressing a hand on Aaron's shoulder.

In the hall, he swung Lizzie around his waist until she giggled, squeezed and kissed her again, and turned her over to their counselor before her welling eyes made him cry, too. "You watch over Mom, okay, Lizard?" The girl nodded and leaned against Maria, who steered her back into the room.

Emily walked him down to his truck. They didn't say a word and simply stood, embracing, in the parking lot. James couldn't let go.

With a final kiss and whispered "I love you," Emily gently pushed away.

"Love you, too." He hugged her once more and, through blurry eyes, hurried into the truck and pulled away.

He arrived at Fifth Third Ballpark on the northern outskirts of Grand Rapids, Michigan, in the early afternoon. In a section of the parking lot designated for employees, several cars shimmered under a cobalt-blue sky. James pulled alongside—an employee, at least for a little while. He tried Emily's phone again. They had talked only a few minutes during the drive, and he wanted to see if the nap had done Aaron any good. The call went right to voice mail. "I'm here. Try you in a bit," he said. He followed it with a text of the same message.

In front of the stadium, concrete stairs rose up to the ticket gate and main concourse, and at the bottom of the steps, a video crew that had been dispatched by the Tigers—over James's objection—stood filming him in the truck. One cameraman and one producer/sound tech. Wes Marco believed that a video of James's journey could generate some PR, from both a baseball standpoint and a cancer awareness perspective. Plus, Wes wanted Aaron to see his dad's journey through professional baseball from beginning to end. James lost the argument after hearing that, accusing Wes of going right for the throat.

And now there they stood, rolling.

James left his suitcase in the truck and grabbed a duffel containing workout clothes and the borrowed glove from Curt Howard, the one he used to play catch at Comerica Park. With a check of his phone to see if he'd missed Emily's return text, he opened the door.

Immediately, James knew the video crew—whom he met back in Detroit the day before during his physical and minor league contract signing—wouldn't cause problems. They melted into the background, remained silent, and used the zoom lens as much as possible. James nodded a hello as he walked by them and headed up the stairs outside the ballpark.

At the top, a young man in a royal-blue West Michigan Whitecaps polo shirt leaned against a wall texting on a cell phone. After a flimsy handshake, he introduced himself as Cole, an intern for the public relations department. "They told me to take you to the clubhouse."

Less than two hours from home in northern Michigan, Fifth Third Ballpark—the home of the West Michigan Whitecaps, one of two Class A minor league affiliates of the Tigers—was a much cheaper alternative for quality baseball than an excursion to Comerica Park. James had been to several games, but he never knew that the player clubhouse sat on the concourse level surrounding the park.

Cole held open what looked like a plain service door tucked near a concession. "Good luck, man."

An older man in a similar blue Whitecaps polo shirt, and whose spilling gut completely engulfed his belt, waited inside. "There he is! Sal Bradon, clubhouse manager and general all-around babysitter. Good trip?"

James shook his hand. "Yeah, thanks, no problems getting here."

"Well, right this way, young man." Sal walked only a handful of paces before extending his arms upon his kingdom. "The luxurious accommodations of the West Michigan Whitecaps at your service, Mr. McConnell. Not a dive like some of the older minor league clubs in the Midwest, but we don't coddle 'em like some of the newer places, either."

A familiar, game-day tingle quivered in James's belly, something he hadn't felt since college. Royal-blue lockers fronted by one long, continuous wooden bench lined three of the four white cinder block walls, and thin, hard carpeting showed the cleat wear of hundreds of ballplayers through the years. An old plaid couch and matching love seat sat perpendicular to each other in the center of the room, facing a tube TV mounted on the wall near the ceiling; an oven, refrigerator, and a long counter containing a sink squared out the room. In all, it was about twice the size of the kitchen–dining–living room area in James's tri-level house. And for a couple dozen grown men.

Sal pointed to the far side—closest to the bathrooms and showers stood the only locker not heaped with clothing and equipment. A new shoe box sat on the bench in front, and four jerseys and two pairs of pants hung inside. "They said you was an average-size feller, so I think your uni will fit fine. Hat size?"

"Uh, seven and a half, I think."

"I'll dig up a couple. Different days, different uniforms," Sal said as they walked to James's locker. "Home whites, road grays, Sunday afternoons are white pants and blue jerseys. Practice jerseys, too. We didn't have enough time to get your name stitched into 'em. The old lady in town who does it was off visitin' her grandkids yesterday, and 39 was the only number in your size." Sal flicked a toothpick into the corner of his mouth and nodded in the direction of the pants. "Let me know if the pants don't fit, but don't go try tearin' out the hem to make 'em longer. We'll need those for the next Joe comin' through here. You can pull 'em up to your knees if you want 'em shorter."

"No problem. Nice, normal length for me."

The toothpick rolled to the other corner of his mouth. "Lemme run and get Skip." Sal waddled more than ran.

James dropped his duffel on the bench, unpacked his glove into the locker, hung up a sweatshirt, and removed the white jersey. His fingers ran over the embroidered *West Michigan*, and he turned it over: *39*. His jersey. And not one to wear while coaching. Those old butterflies roused from their thirteen-year-old cocoon, and they were hungry.

He took out his phone. Still no text. *They must be with the counselors right now.* He snapped a photo of the jersey, took another of the clubhouse, and sent them to Emily.

After a few seconds, the phone vibrated. Nice! We're hanging in there. Heading to gardens. Talk later.

The short text did nothing to lift the weight of worry. *Hanging in there? What does that mean? If he's not feeling good, don't take him to the gardens.*

While he tapped a return text, Gary Trombole, the manager, said behind him with a voice that spoke of too many years of cigarettes or barking at young ballplayers, or both, "Those'll be a little stiff." Trombole's hands rested in the back pockets of his white uniform pants, and the sleeves of a royal-blue Windbreaker were pushed up to his elbows.

"Excuse me?"

"The cleats. Be a good idea if you broke them in the next couple days."

James opened the box, and brand-new size ten black cleats shone back at him.

He shook hands with the manager. "Who's breaking me in?"

"He's waiting in the dugout." Trombole stood for a moment, hands sliding back into his pockets. His gut gave Sal's a run for its money. "Wes Marco said to put you at second base. You good with that?"

"Played shortstop in college, so yeah, that'd be great."

"You still got some arm strength?"

"So says my scout." James smiled. Trombole's lips didn't move. "My son, Aaron. But I'm guessing your instructors will be the judge of that."

"Can you hit a fastball?"

"That'll need some work, I won't lie to you."

"'Preciate the honesty. Most kids come in here think they're the next Tony Bozio and can't get their heads through the door. My job at this level is to knock 'em down a peg."

"You won't have that problem from me."

"Good. Learn to hit that fastball quick before we ship you off to Erie. Right now, strength and conditioning coach is in the dugout. Get changed. White pants, BP jersey, meet him down there. And leave your glove in your locker."

They shook hands again, and Trombole left. No mention of Aaron or the uniqueness of the situation, no "getting to know you" or how this had all come to be. Just baseball.

The two-man camera crew, pressed in a far corner of the clubhouse, smiled and held a thumbs-up to the newest member of the West Michigan Whitecaps. James took their picture and sent it to his wife.

Two hours later, when James returned to a clubhouse thumping with raucous music, he wondered if he'd ever lift his arms again, let alone put on his glove for infield practice. The strength and conditioning coach had pushed him through a torturous boot camp; any thought James had of already being in good shape lay sprawled, gasping, somewhere out in right field. The idea of sitting on the clubhouse couch for a few minutes seemed like manna.

The couch and adjoining love seat were full: five ballplayers—three in street clothes and the other two in socks, sliding pants, and holey T-shirts—scrunched together, watching some sporting event on TV.

James's only option, the hard bench in front of his locker, felt glorious. He begged his legs to stop screaming. They laughed at him.

The rest of the players were in full warm-up uniforms, and over the music and TV, James heard the murmurs: "Is that the guy? . . . We got Gramps for Bobby? . . . Only for a few days, though, right? . . . Dude's kid's sick, man; give him a break. . . . A PR stunt. . . . Just a cup of coffee, no harm. . . . Tags was going on the DL anyway."

James didn't care. The only thing that mattered was ibuprofen.

Although a few players introduced themselves, most remained at their lockers getting ready for early infield and batting practices. James caught their wary glances. After gulping down a few pills, he grabbed his phone. Before he checked it, though, a kid not much older than the boys he'd been coaching just a few weeks ago sat down.

"Hey, man," the kid said, "how you doing?"

"I'll let you know as soon as I can feel my legs. And arms." They shook hands. "James McConnell."

"Ben. So we heard about everything. Pretty weird, huh?"

"What did you hear?"

"Just that you're here to play for your son. He's . . . How's he doing?"

James checked his phone. No calls. No texts. He waved it at Ben. "Wish I knew."

Ben's eyes narrowed.

"Sorry. He was fine this morning. Treatments are going good; thanks for asking." But without a message from Emily, a swarm of images flashed, all revolving around the black, gnarly cancer gremlins surrounding Aaron, ready to pounce.

"So are you gonna be here long?"

"I think a week. But I suppose that's up to Skipper."

"Are they really gonna bring you all the way up to The Show?"

"I suppose that's up to Skip, too. The 'Big Skip,' anyway. I just hope I can throw the ball today."

"Yeah, Coach Varger'll have some fun with you. So what position do you play?"

"Second base, I think."

Ben straightened up. "Oh. Really? Well . . . um . . . look, I gotta, uh, get something from Sal. See you out there."

"Yeah, see you out there."

James hit Emily's speed-dial number but hung up when the door to the coach's dressing room near his locker burst open. A short, squatty coach—Mickey Rooney in a baseball uniform—emerged, whirling a fungo bat like a wrapped-tight umbrella, and strode into the center of the clubhouse.

The coach wiggled into a comical batting stance, wound up, and whacked the couch. The players didn't flinch. "How you ladies doing today?" His red blotchy face, painted with glee, took in everyone present, and the man's eyes sparkled when they landed on James. "New meat today, gals!" He burst into a gurgling cackle. "Be nice seeing the old-timer run around the outfield tonight, but first he needs some work on ground balls." Some jeers murmured from the corner, but Mickey rounded on them with a wide smile and sharp tongue. "You're one to talk, Sanchez! Two errors last night—"

"On the same play!" another player said.

"On the same play!" the infield coach added. "You get extras today, buddy. You *comprende* that *inglés, amigo*?" Sanchez offered something disparaging in Spanish, sending the coach into another cackle. "All right, Marys, get down there. Extras for everybody, especially with our new meat here. It'd be nice if you didn't embarrass me tonight."

James stood—painfully—and exchanged his phone for his glove. A handful of other players filed to the clubhouse stairway that led down beneath the stands and into a tunnel to the dugout. But the coach stopped by James's locker. "Mike

Varger," he said, shaking his hand. "Don't take any offense to what I might say to you over the next week. Hope this all works out for you and your boy. But you gotta get in shape with me now." The liquid laugh returned. James brought up the rear of the group of infielders.

After playing catch with a teammate whose name he never got, James trotted to second base, but Varger, at home plate next to two catchers in shin guards, stopped him. "Head on over to third for some, Jimmy. Stretch that arm out. Then take some at short and then scoot to second. Let's see what you got at each place. Who knows, maybe Sanchez there—" he jabbed his bat at the shortstop—"could use a breather for a week."

James jogged on the outfield grass to join two other fielders at third base. Right as he arrived, his turn came up, and he shuffled forward onto the infield dirt, sinking into his ready position—butt down, knees bent, arms flexed and ready, hand and glove open and rigid several inches off the ground. The stretching that came from throwing and the adrenaline of anticipation reduced his pain into a dull ache.

All right, Aaron. It all starts here.

Varger stopped before he tossed the ball out to hit. "Here he is, ladies; pay attention! New meat here's gonna show us how it's done! Make sure you all watch him real careful. You feel that, Jimmy? You feel 'em watchin'? We're ready to be dazzled. You ready?" He made to flip the ball in the air but held it. "You sure you're ready? I'm gonna toss this ball and hit you a grounder, Jimmy, all right? All you gotta do is pick it up and fire it over to first. Here it comes, okay? Comin' at ya! Right now!"

James's heart no longer thudded in his chest—it simply stopped.

Varger flipped the ball out front and topped it. It dribbled as harmlessly as a bunt, not even halfway down the third base line. James straightened up, relaxing, but Varger attacked. "Getitgetitgetitcomeoncomeoncomeon; he's gettin' down the line!"

James immediately sprang into action, eyeing the slow roller, instantly deciding to barehand it instead of using his glove. He shuffled his steps, planning to plant his left foot next to the ball as he stooped to scoop it with his throwing hand. From there, pure training would take over as he'd throw off-balance while still running forward, arcing the ball right into the first baseman's chest.

But as he bent down to pick the rolling ball out of the grass, his left foot, just before planting, kicked his glove. His feet tangled, and as the ball glanced off the heel of his right hand and underneath him, James's right foot rolled when it came down. All of his momentum carried him forward, and he couldn't brace himself in time. He sprawled flat on his face and slid, his chin plowing through the grass.

"Geez, Jimmy," Varger said while James remained spread-eagle on the ground, trying to find his breath. "I don't know how you played ball at that fancy college you went to, but us professionals pick it up and throw it. Now, what you do with a baseball in your spare time's your own business." The players exploded with laughter, and Varger turned on them. "And all you Nancys shut up! You all've done somethin' worse with a ball, and don't pretend ya haven't!" The laughing subsided but didn't stop.

James gathered himself to his knees. Varger squatted near the plate, only several feet away, and tipped his cap back. "You need a minute, Jimmy? I mean, yer pretty brave, tryin' that right in the middle of the field in front of us, but ya know, most people like a little privacy." He winked.

"Hit me another one of those, you geezer."

The coach's smile widened, and he stood; a catcher flipped him a ball.

James trotted back to his position, the other third basemen hiding their faces in their mitts. In the stands a row above the first base dugout, the Tigers' video crew filmed.

Great, he thought. *Aaron oughta get a kick out of that.*

A pit hollowed his stomach. Another baseball memory that didn't include his son.

He pounded a fist in his glove. On the next slow roller, he didn't end up flat on his face, but his throw pulled the first baseman off the bag.

For the next half hour, James wavered somewhere between *meh* and not bad. Ground balls occasionally handcuffed him, and a few scooted between his legs, but then he'd stretch out in a backhand, snag a one-hop line drive, and fire a strike to first base. Any instructions from Varger were shouts about what he did wrong: his glove wasn't down, his throws were low, his throws were high, he wasn't getting the ball out of his glove fast enough. He played his best at second base, thanks to the shorter throw. And he earned a glove slap from Ben, another second baseman, on a shallow pop-up near the foul line in right field that James caught going away over his shoulder. The next grounder, though, skipped off his glove, then his forearm, and rolled into center field.

The other shortstops and second basemen inundated him with defensive schemes, cutoffs, double plays, relays, and how they communicated to one another on the infield. The first couple of double play attempts were rusty around second base. On the next one, he completed the turn but buried the throw to first in the dirt. Mercifully, Varger hit him a final, soft, straight ground ball, and he fielded it as routinely as he had at Comerica Park with Curt Howard.

His next stop, the batting cage. After picking out a thirty-four-inch, thirty-one-ounce pale ash bat from Sal's extra equipment, James met the roving instructors, who traveled among the Tigers' minor league teams, in the cages behind the center field wall. He demonstrated his form and mechanics by hitting off a batting tee into a net, but after a dozen swings, the two instructors asked him to start over.

James backed out, wrung the bat handle, and stepped up to the tee. He pretended the pitcher, sixty feet, six inches away, had gotten the sign from the catcher and come set. In his mind, the fastball streaked for the plate, James loaded his weight on his back foot, his eyes zeroed in on the stationary ball on the tee, and—

"Hold on," Steve, one of the instructors, said. "Open up your front foot, drop your hands three inches, and on your follow-through, extend your arms more."

"And bend some more on your back leg; you're too upright," the other instructor added.

"Like this?" James asked. He lowered a little. His right leg strained.

"A little more."

His thigh quivered.

"There. Now bring your hands in fast. We shouldn't even see the barrel of the bat through the zone."

James swung and topped the ball off the tee. He grabbed another and set it on top.

"Again," Steve said. "And crouch more this time. Try lowering your hands another couple inches, too. Now swing in slow motion, and let's take a look."

James felt like an idiot, but the two instructors liked what they saw. It didn't work. The hits weren't nearly as sharp, and the more James held the new batting stance while pretending to wait for the pitch, the more his muscles ached. His body naturally reverted to its old form right as he began to swing.

Steve interrupted him when his hands slid into the swing plane. James straightened, thudded the barrel on his shoulder, and glared.

"You're doing it again," Steve said. "Your hands—"

"It's not his hands; it's his hips," the other said. "What you need to do—"

"I can't even get comfortable," James finally snapped. "Look, this is how I've always swung, and I hit .396 in college."

"This isn't college, rookie."

James's hands twisted around the bat handle again, but he tried to smile. "I realize that. I just need a steady supply of fastballs. It's all timing."

The instructors looked at each other. Steve shrugged, and the other said, "Let's do some soft toss then."

James paused a few extra seconds between each toss from an instructor, who squatted off to the side and flipped balls in front of James. He incorporated some of what they tried to teach him but still ended up back in his old form with mixed results—some hits popped up; others squared off the bat. After a quick refresher on bunting, he pushed on a batting helmet and stood in against a pitching machine.

Two years ago, Aaron sat in a dugout and cheered him on during another Old West–style showdown with a pitching machine, and the sudden memory sucker punched him in the gut. It forced him to back off the plate inside the batting cage. He stalled, adjusting his helmet and batting gloves.

He held the bat up straight and stared at the Louisville Slugger logo on the barrel.

Okay, buddy, this is for you.

James never saw the first dozen fastballs. As some players

gathered around to watch, he pressed, gripping the bat tighter, his swings feeling slower and heavier even as it seemed the balls gained speed. A few players chattered encouragement to "Drive it" and "Relax" and "Hang in there." The instructors remained silent.

"Hang in there." What in the world did Emily mean that they were hanging in there?

More misses, terrible misses, close misses, and nowhere-in-the-same-zip-code misses. The wooden bat swung like a tree branch.

James finally held up a hand to the coach feeding the machine and grabbed a ball from the growing pile in the back of the net. In a snarl, he flipped it in the air and ripped through it.

There! That's what it feels like!

He closed his eyes, trying to recapture that day on the field with the pitching machine, when he began lousy but ended up driving balls deep into the outfield, his son cheering him from the dugout each time.

James stepped back in, missed again, but fouled the next one off. Then he topped one off to his right. Some *attaboy*s murmured through the player spectators.

Finally he cracked a line drive right back at the machine.

"Good!" Steve shouted among scattered whistles and slow, sarcastic claps. The coach switched off the machine. "Remember that one right there. Time to get ready for the game anyway."

James flicked the bat into the net, disgusted, knowing that sorry hitting display had the instructors wondering if his .396 college batting average had instead been from beer league softball.

Back in the clubhouse, the manager told James to suit up that evening even though he wouldn't be playing except in a dire emergency. "Don't mean you ain't got somethin' to do, though," Trombole mumbled. As he left, James's confusion turned ominous when some of the players, who had left him alone most of the day, gathered around and escorted him down to the tunnel and the first base dugout.

They maintained the suspense as the stadium filled in the clear, warm evening, a perfect night for baseball. James threw a little more, stretched, and ran some tentative sprints in the right field grass, hoping he looked like he knew what he was doing. Knowing that he'd spend the game on the bench tempered any apprehension, so after loosening up, he simply sat in the grass behind first base and stretched some more as other players threw. Fifth Third Ballpark seemed so huge, yet it felt like three of them could have fit inside Comerica Park.

"Hey, rookie," one of his teammates called, waving him into the dugout. They presented him a long, rolled-up flag with the reverence of a sacred artifact in a thousand-year-old ritual.

"What's this for?" James asked. Then it dawned on him. He'd seen this flag before. "You're not serious."

"All the new rooks gotta run it out their first night here," one of the players said. "You can thank Bobby Taggert for making sure we didn't forget."

Bobby Taggert. The kid whose nagging back pain sent him to the disabled list, conveniently opening a roster spot for James. He knew he couldn't escape the mild rookie hazing now, and he hung his head. "When do I head out?"

His teammates pounced on him, smacking his back and bouncing up and down as one mob.

After the announcer introduced the visiting Dayton Dragons, music rumbled through the loudspeakers, and the fans rose to their feet. The announcer's bland, mono-tone voice morphed into that of a radio disc jockey and game show host rolled into one. "And now . . . let's meet the starting lineup of your . . . West . . . Michigan . . . Whiiiiiiiiiiiitecaaaaaaaaaaaaaps!" The crowd roared, James got his signal, and he sprinted from the dugout. The royal-blue flag displaying a white *CAPS* unfurled, and James ran around the outfield like a college cheerleader, like a fool, like a rookie . . . like a teammate. He waved it back and forth over his head, jabbed it high at the calling of each name and roar of the small crowd, and slapped the starters' hands on his way back to the dugout.

The game moved fast as the Whitecaps won, 7 to 4, in a very businesslike manner. James remained on the bench the whole time, his attention trading between the game on the field and the phone in his locker, wondering if it chirped with a message from Emily. In the clubhouse afterward, the music blaring once again, he found only one text, a smiley face icon in response to the photo of the Tigers' video crew. He tossed it back on the shelf in his locker. Trombole let the players enjoy the postgame while Varger harangued Sanchez, even though the shortstop played a flawless game. Before James knew it, the players had showered and headed out. He still sat in his uniform, staring up at his phone.

Near midnight, James drove the quarter mile to a Comfort Suites, his home for the next week. He tossed his duffel on the bed and called Emily. At each ring, his temper boiled. And it didn't settle when she finally picked up. By the sound of her voice, she'd been asleep.

"So how'd your first day in professional baseball go?" she asked through a yawn.

"Probably would've been better if I'd heard from you at least once during the day. At least a voice mail or something." He didn't mean it to come out so harsh, but he didn't apologize, either.

"We had a busy day, too, you know." She sounded a little more awake. And annoyed.

"Well, sorry, but I was worried. You said he was 'hanging in there,' and then I get nothing."

"All right, I'm sorry."

"Didn't he have a good day?"

"He just couldn't keep lunch down. I didn't send him to class again, so we spent some time outside. The fresh air seemed to help." Drowsiness replaced some of Emily's annoyance. "How did it go?"

James sighed and sat on the bed. He rested his elbows on his knees and stared at the floor. "I don't think I'll be able to move tomorrow. Did Lizzie head back with my folks today?" He kicked his shoes off and rubbed his eyes.

"Tomorrow. She's ready. They're getting on each other's nerves."

"That's the steroids."

"I know. So tell me about it. How did you do?"

"*Rusty* isn't quite the right word. You'll laugh when you see this film. But it felt pretty neat being back out on the field again. I had to wave that stupid flag around the outfield tonight while they announced the lineup."

Even her laugh sounded exhausted. After a long pause, her deep, comfortable breath filled the phone. "Hon, I've got to get some sleep."

"Okay. But promise me you'll keep me in the loop more, okay? Just some texts—that's all I'm asking for."

"I'll try. Night."

The click of the phone sounded so final and left James so very alone.

The next day, Varger worked with only James and a first baseman on the infield while the roving instructors watched from the dugout. James remained at second base and fielded grounders until his cottonmouth forced him to take a breather. Sanchez jogged out to shortstop, and the two practiced double plays, cutoffs, and relays. Then, standing around second base, he listened carefully to the shortstop's broken English about the Whitecaps' situational defenses and other schemes.

While James felt his fielding improved, his hitting didn't, and Trombole wouldn't let him take swings under the batting dome on the field with the other players prior to the game. He stayed in the cages beyond center field, trying to imagine the pitching machine back home, envisioning each ball as one of the cancer gremlins in Aaron's body. This was his chance to smash them to dust. But they kept winning.

His chance to get into a game came as a late-inning replacement on Wednesday—his third day there—a day that saw some line drives in the batting cage earlier. In the bottom of the seventh inning of a blowout—the Whitecaps on the short end—Trombole sat down next to him in the dugout. The Whitecaps power hitter Rodney Dunning walked to the plate amid a screech of incomprehensible hip-hop music, quickly followed by a chorus of boos when the Dayton Dragons pitcher fired his first pitch wide for ball one.

"They're pitchin' around him," Trombole said. "They don't want him to get somethin' started." After three more quick pitches, Rodney trotted to first while more boos rained down on the Dragons pitcher. The crowd turned again when

Alberto Santos flicked the bat weight aside and strode from the on-deck circle.

"Make 'im pay, Al!" Trombole hollered. He leaned over to James. "Al's had this a few times already this season, teams walkin' Dunns to get to him. Really ticks him off that they think he's an easier out."

"Is he?"

"Yeah, but it still ticks him off. Swings outta his shoes at it."

Alberto stayed true to form, trying to pummel the ball into orbit. He succeeded only in lifting a routine fly ball to right field to end the inning.

"You ready?" Trombole asked when James leaned back and slid his hands into the pocket of his blue Whitecaps pullover.

James's breathing clutched, but he kept his cool—not too scared, not too eager. He hoped his reaction said, "Whatever's needed to help the ball club."

Trombole saw through it and laughed out loud. "Second base, Jimmy."

At the changeover to the top of the eighth inning, the other position players were all out of the dugout by the time James grabbed his glove. With a gulp, he jogged up the dugout's three steps, praying he wouldn't trip his way onto the field.

The field.

He was on the field again.

The years of being on the field as a coach couldn't compare to those first few seconds running out there as a player. Those people filling the stands . . . none of them came to see the coaches coach. They paid their money to see the players play. And that's just who he was. A player again. All of those old dreams of nights under the lights and his picture up on the scoreboard and his name blasted through the loudspeakers flooded back.

"Now playing second base, James McConnell," the announcer said. Monotone, no fanfare, random applause from some of the few remaining fans, the others not bothering to recognize another name paraded through the farm system.

But for James, it came with fireworks.

It was that same golden moment from the high school field all over again. Only instead of a sinking sun, stadium lights cast a white glow. And instead of sitting in the audience, he stood center stage. The long-ago doubts that whispered at him silenced. The years peeled back. He hadn't walked away from baseball. He was an all-American, drafted, and took the field to begin his professional career. He'd made it.

His teammates nodded at him, pointed, or tipped a cap. Sanchez met him at second base and gave him a fist bump, trying to calm down the rookie. James fielded the practice grounders from his first baseman cleanly and snapped them back to his glove. Adrenaline added a little extra pop to the throws.

And in those few brief seconds after the practice balls bounced back to the dugout and the batter swung through his routine, before the pitcher came set and stared in for the sign, everything seemed to pause and take a deep breath. James's heart caught, poised on the cutting edge of that breath, ready for action, ready for *anything*.

He was back.

It felt good. Really good.

He ended up being more of a spectator in that inning and the ninth as well. Four fly balls, a strikeout, and a grounder to third accounted for the Dayton Dragons' six remaining outs—and the Whitecaps' two most efficient innings of the entire game. And when the final—and thirteenth—Whitecap struck out in the bottom of the ninth, James stood in the on-deck circle, his chest pounding as if the game were on the line. At the last out, he simply shrugged "Oh, well" at the manager.

"Don't worry, Jimmy," Trombole said. "We're off tomorrow. But you're startin' on Friday. You'll get your cuts. More BP and infield tomorrow, though. Be here at three. I'll give Wes at the Tigers a call and let him know what's happening."

When James reached the hotel and dialed Emily, he had every intention of asking her to wake Aaron so he could tell him about getting in his first game. He didn't need to. Emily sounded very awake—and unhappy. James heard moaning in the background. Baseball vanished.

"What's wrong? What's going on?" he asked.

"He's having a hard night. He fell asleep three different times, but he keeps waking up." Equal parts frustration, concern, and fatigue tugged at her words. "Dr. Barna thinks he might be fighting a little infection, too."

"An infection? What's—?"

"A *little* infection. It's not a big deal right now. They're taking care of it and watching his white blood cell count. He just needs to keep taking it easy, and frankly, I think he overdid it the last couple days with you gone."

"Why? What's he doing?"

"I'll let him tell you."

Something rustled on the other end, and then Aaron snuffled into the phone. "Hey, Dad." So weak and just . . . sick.

"Hey, buster." James's voice trembled. "Mom said you're feeling kinda lousy, huh?"

"Yeah."

"Well, maybe this'll make you smile: I got to play in a game tonight."

"Really?" Aaron's voice perked slightly.

"Yeah, second base. Played the eighth and ninth innings," James said. "We got creamed, though, 8 to 1."

"You get any hit to you?"

"Nope, nothing close. And I was on deck in the ninth when we made the last out. But guess what? I'm starting on Friday."

"Seriously?" He felt Aaron's soft smile through the phone. "They don't put those games on TV, do they?"

"'Fraid not, kiddo."

"How've you been doing?"

"Oh, you know, a little rusty. But that grass is pretty nice. Gobbling up the ground balls, just like with Curt. Looking forward to swinging the bat on Friday. Have to knock it right back up the middle. Maybe I'll try for a double."

Aaron giggled, but it faded quickly.

"So Mom said you're working on something." James heard the covers shuffle again, and he imagined that Aaron sat up in bed.

"I started a website. Well, Maria's helping me."

"A website? For what?"

"For you. For the baseball you. For your stats and stuff."

James chuckled. "Well, there aren't gonna be a lot of numbers on there, playing only one game and all."

"I know. But it'll still be cool. Maria said we'll put some photos on it, in your different uniforms and stuff and—" he took a deep breath—"you know." The fatigue seeped through the phone.

"Sure thing, kiddo. Why don't you get some sleep, okay?"

"Okay. Bye, Dad. Good luck Friday."

Emily came back on the phone. "He looks a lot more relaxed now. I'm going to sit with him until he's really asleep. I'll talk to you tomorrow."

James whispered, "Okay," and hung up.

James spent most of Thursday waiting for Emily to call back—he reminded her with several voice mails and twice as many texts—but they didn't talk until the evening. James's parents had brought Lizzie back down, and she and Emily spent the day shopping at a nearby mall while Aaron spent some time with his grandparents. James and Emily's conversation at night simply recapped their days: Aaron's infection seemed under control; lots of new clothes for Lizzie; manicures for the girls; James still behind on the fastball.

The game jitters that attacked James during the two innings on Wednesday devoured him on Friday. The uniform and cleats were beginning to feel comfortable and familiar, but in warm-ups before the game, his glove and bat still clunked in his hands.

He settled when familiar faces appeared in the stands waving homemade signs—his parents; Greg, the high school athletic director; Tom, the head coach; and a handful of varsity players from back home. There wasn't much to watch, though. He handled three of the four ground balls that came his way easily enough, airmailed the first baseman on the other, and fed Sanchez perfectly on a double play. At the plate, his only contact dribbled back to the mound; none of his other swings came close. Even with the submediocre play, Trombole stopped by James's locker and told him to hit the road to Erie, Pennsylvania, in the morning to join the next team.

"I don't know if he'll have anything to put on that website," James told Emily that evening as he packed.

"What do you mean?"

"All the zeroes are going to look a little funny. I'm not exactly lighting things up." He folded a pair of pants and put them in the duffel. "Is his infection getting better?"

"Yes, it is." James heard a door closed. He could tell she had moved into the bedroom. "But why aren't you?"

"Huh?"

"James, Aaron's obsessed with this website. Keeps telling everyone how well you're doing, 'gobbling everything up,' and that his dad is going to have his own line in the *Baseball Encyclopedia*. But you need to get to the majors first."

"Em, don't worry about it; it's just kinks I have to work out. I sugarcoated it for Aaron, that's all."

A thick silence filled the phone.

"What?" James squeezed a rolled-up pair of socks. He hated it when his wife went silent. "I can't do that to cheer him up?"

"How are you going to sugarcoat not making it to the Tigers?"

"What—?"

"You do remember what Ernie Mazarron said, right? He said that if they had to wash you out at Erie or Toledo, they would. And you're going to Erie tomorrow. But that's not Aaron's wish, James. You with the Tigers is his wish. Not Erie. Not Toledo."

Now James threw the socks onto the bed. "I'm trying! But it's kind of tough when I'm worried about you guys and nobody's telling me what's happening."

Emily's heavy sigh rattled his ear. "He has all of his doctors and all of his nurses. We're fine. But you're not. You've got to focus."

James rubbed his eyes. "It's just . . . hard. Really hard."

"I know. But this is your son. This is his wish. It doesn't matter if it's hard. You've *got to do this*."

He picked up the ball of socks and chucked it at the window. Then he held his breath until his chest hurt.

"Look, it's almost a six-hour drive tomorrow. I gotta get to sleep. I'll call you from the road." He caught himself. "Or you know, if that's too much, you can call me if you want."

"James—"

"Love you. Kiss the kids for me."

"Yeah. Okay. Good night."

He tossed the phone on the bed.

10

JAMES AND EMILY'S ONE AND ONLY CONVERSATION during his five-and-a-half-hour drive from Grand Rapids to Erie didn't extend much beyond mutual apologies for their argument the night before. Somewhere in the middle of the Ohio Turnpike's monotony, James coasted on cruise control in the relative silence of small talk. Update on the weather: not bad, kind of sunny, supposed to be warm; update on the roads: clear. They even covered the important things in only a few words: infection gone, transfusion later, Lizzie on her way back home for her last week of school, James certain he figured out a glitch in his hitting.

They both broke the tension by stating their promises at the same time, then shared a laugh. Emily started over first. "I'll leave you a text about the transfusion because you'll be practicing," she said. "You won't have to ask."

"And I'll write back telling you I drove one into the gap in left-center field."

But that afternoon, at Jerry Uht Park—home of the

Double-A Erie SeaWolves—he fouled off the first five pitches.
Steve, the roving instructor, called him to the edge of the net.
"Are you ready to try my way yet?"

"I'll crouch a little more, but I can't lower my hands any
farther. The ball gets on top of me too fast."

"Okay, but flatten the bat, then. Concentrate on slashing
through. Quick hands."

The same foul balls resulted: a scarce clip of the ball, which
lifted straight up only an inch and ended up in the back of
the net.

"Here, try this." Steve lifted up the net and handed James
a black bat. "An inch shorter, an ounce lighter."

No luck.

James stepped out of the batter's box and tore three full-
speed swings in his old college form.

"Maybe it's the long drive. Why don't you take some infield."

James didn't argue. He tossed the bat into the net, ripped
off his batting gloves, and stuffed them in his helmet.

The long drive, apparently, was also to blame for his
fielding. After the third throw in the dirt, the first baseman,
Lincoln Church, a brick house of a man as dark as his black
mitt, took two long steps off the bag and glared at James,
holding his hands out. "What's your problem, man?"

James held up his mitt. "Blame Curt Howard."

Lincoln replied with another glare before firing the ball
back to the catcher at home plate.

In the break between practice and the game, James sat at
his clubhouse locker and checked his phone. One text from his
wife, keeping her end of the deal: Transfusion went well. He's eating and says hi. How'd the line drive feel?

He couldn't text back the truth, not even a stretched truth,
so he tossed the phone aside and rubbed his eyes.

James felt the floor quiver. Lincoln sat down while wrapping his left wrist in athletic tape.

"So did all that look as bad as I think?" James asked.

"Quit tryin' to recapture your glory days, man. Those're long gone. It's all 'bout right now. And right now, you gotta get your throws up." He slid a black wristband down from his elbow to cover the tape. "Look at me. I ain't no small target."

"I know. I'll get 'em there."

"You better. How'd you do at West Michigan, anyway? Coach Varger still hollerin'? Who's his whippin' boy now?"

"That'd be Felipe Sanchez."

"Yeah, shortstop. Varger's got a thing 'bout middle infielders. So how'd you do down there?"

"Okay."

"Not what I heard."

"You are blunt."

"You hit the ball in the game you played?"

"Sure did."

Lincoln cocked his head to the side.

"Once. Back to the pitcher."

Lincoln rested his elbows on his knees and leaned toward James, searching him for a tense minute with his dark eyes. *Here it comes,* James thought.

"You'll straighten out." He held James's gaze another few seconds, nodded once, and left.

James lay low in the dugout during his first game with the SeaWolves on Saturday. Sunday morning, the bat still felt unruly in his hands, and the batting cage's net continued to billow behind him instead of beyond the pitching machine; some weak ground balls sprayed to the right as he swung late on the pitches. A short break let him decompress in the clubhouse, and he dashed out a text to Emily and his mom while sitting at his locker, asking for a photo of the two kids at that moment, whatever they were doing. Neither replied. The Tigers' film crew, tucked in a corner of the clubhouse, kept the camera steady on him. All they captured was the number 61 on the back of his jersey.

That early evening, after the midday game, a SeaWolves win, they weren't the only camera in the clubhouse.

James's call-up from single-A to double-A had gone unnoticed on Saturday, but it didn't escape the scrutiny of the league transaction wire on Sunday. When the clubhouse door opened after Sunday's game, a horde of cameras and reporters scorched a path to his locker, where he sat in his stark-white uniform. And there were more than the usual few local beat writers and news stations.

The questions came fast.

"How is your son?"

"What hospital is he at?"

"Did you ask him to make this wish?"

"Why do you think you moved up so fast, when you struck out three times in your only game at West Michigan?"

"Some are saying this is just a PR stunt for the Tigers. What do you say to that?"

The lights, the microphones, the huge cameras, the onslaught of questions—James blanked in front of all of them. He tried to answer but only stammered out gems such as "Uh . . . "; "Um . . . "; "Well, that's not . . . "; "What was the question?" Every time he paused, trying to think of what to say to these people, five more questions piled in. Camera clicks popped like popcorn, the flashes like fireworks. The throng bore down on him, inching closer, until he had to stand, backed up against his locker. And still, the questions came. And still, he stammered attempts at answers.

"Hey!" Lincoln shouted. He elbowed his way through the crowd. "One at a time. Give the man a chance to answer." He scowled at each person holding a phone, recorder, camera, microphone, or light. They cowered. "All yours, man," he said to James.

"Did you ask your son to make this wish?"

"Uh, no, I didn't ask for this. He just, you know . . ."

"How hard is it? You've had a long layoff since you last played; how would you grade your progress?"

"Um . . . just, you know, trying my hardest. Gotta . . . just gotta keep working."

"Is your son really dying?"

What kind of a question is that? he wanted to scream. *What kind of absurd question is that?* But no scream came out. Only astonishment. Disbelief.

Lincoln stepped in front of the cameras and said they were done, that lots of other guys in the room had actually played in the game tonight, that James had no further comment. He stood guard, turned away any last questions, and remained several minutes after the last camera left.

"Thanks, Linc."

"Jackals." He rounded on James. "But you gotta show 'em you belong here." He stepped closer and burned James with his glare. "You gotta show *us* you belong here, that you're a ballplayer. And right now, you ain't shown squat. You show us you're a SeaWolf, and we got your back. Got it, rookie?" He swatted James once on the shoulder.

James snatched his phone and texted Emily: Don't watch the news tonight.

Before pregame batting practice on Monday, manager Kevin Burkes summoned James to his office. When James had first arrived, Burkes—only a few years older, and balder—had wanted to hear the whole story of Aaron's wish and playing catch at Comerica Park. But when James stepped inside his office this time, Burkes's face stiffened, dour. And James didn't notice Tigers assistant general manager Wes Marco sitting down until the door closed behind him.

With the click of the door, it hit him.

It's over. One week. I lasted one week. I didn't make it.

He sat, but his mind flew back to the hospital. He saw Aaron sitting up in bed, working on homework or watching *SportsCenter* or continuing his plans for the James McConnell Major League Stats website. He saw himself walking into the room, his duffel in hand. He saw Aaron's face melting to tears. "I'm sorry, buddy. Those guys are just too good," he heard himself say. "I tried my best."

"Did you, Dad? Did you really try your best?"

James shut his eyes. Emily was right. There was no sugar-coating this. Aaron had made a wish. Perhaps his dying wish. And James had failed to make it come true.

"We got a problem," Wes said.

"Yeah." James leaned forward and looked at the floor. "Yeah, I know."

"You did terrible in that interview yesterday."

James sat up. "What?"

"The interview. I'd play it back for you, but I don't think you want to see it."

"You're here because of the interview?"

"Yeah, why else? I was in Toledo over the weekend, getting them ready for you, when I caught your performance on the late news."

"I thought you were here to tell me to pack up."

"'Course not." Wes glanced at the Erie manager.

"Not yet," Burkes said.

That dangling threat put James on edge again. But with the reprieve, he sat at attention.

Wes leaned against the edge of Burkes's desk. "I knew we could sneak you into West Michigan, but I thought we'd have a worse time moving you up than we did. But the story's out now. Someone in our front office got called last night, wanting info on you. I think one of our people made an innocent comment; then it went up the food chain."

"So what do I do?"

"The cameras will be a part of your life now, besides the one we sent to follow you. I'll run interference as much as I can and keep them away from you. But at some point you'll have to deal with them. And that group last night? Those were just local guys. The story's national now, so don't turn on the radio or read the Internet. Like, at all. Marketing and media relations back in Detroit put together a few things, including some pointers to make sure you sound like a ballplayer and not a PR gimmick."

"But right now you're playing like a PR gimmick," Burkes said. "That's gotta stop."

James didn't acknowledge the manager, for his stomach turned at a sudden thought. "They won't send cameras to the hospital, will they?"

"They'll try, but they won't get in," Wes said. "Still, give your wife a heads-up. I already talked to the hospital administrator today, and he'll let the staff know. Don't worry; Aaron will be protected."

"Thanks. And sorry for yesterday," James said. "I guess I expected it at some point, but I didn't really expect . . . *that*."

"I'll hold a press conference today, without you. Ask for some privacy for you and—" he looked at Burkes—"for the team. That sort of thing."

"I don't know," Burkes said, grinning. "PR gimmicks aside, it's been a while since we had that many cameras in here. It was kinda entertaining."

Wes chuckled. "Right now, though, you need to have a little private press conference." The manager opened a laptop on the desk, and in a few taps on the mouse pad, a Skype Internet call rang through the speakers. He turned the computer toward James.

After a few rings, Emily and Aaron appeared in a box on the left; Lizzie popped up, along with his parents, in the one on the right.

"I thought this might help with your slump," Wes whispered. He and Burkes left James alone in the manager's office.

James spent the first several seconds staring at everyone, unable to speak. Emily and Lizzie appeared normal, and James's parents waved in the background. Aaron was pale. Ghostly.

"How'd chemo go today?" he finally asked.

Aaron shrugged, his eyes darting back and forth between his computer's monitor and the webcam.

"He did great, like always," Emily said.

"And what about you, Lizard? Good to be back in your own school today?"

"Yeah," she said loudly and slowly. James and Emily recoiled. "Nice. To. See. Every. One."

"Honey, talk normal. We can hear you fine."

"Oh." Her head disappeared beneath the screen. "Grandma, where's the microphone?"

"It's on . . . ," James tried to say, but he just laughed.

"How's it going for you?" Emily asked.

"Nice interview yesterday," his dad said.

"You caught that, huh?"

"Don't worry about it," Emily said.

"Wes told me I'm going to get some media training along with lessons on how to—"

Emily's eyes widened, and she shook her head quickly, glancing to Aaron.

"Uh, how to handle whoever's pitching on Father's Day."

"I checked," Aaron said, his voice weak, "and if the Twins don't have any rainouts, it'll be Ramon Mendez. He's really good, Dad."

"Your old man can take 'im," James's father said.

James forced a grin. "That's right, buddy. Let me at him."

Aaron whispered something to Emily.

"Hey, he wants to lie down, so we're gonna go."

James put a hand to his mouth. He didn't want them to leave so soon, didn't want the call to click off and their screen to go black. But he nodded. "Okay. Hey, Aaron?"

"Yeah, Dad?"

James bit his tongue. "How are . . . how are the Tigers doing? I haven't been paying attention."

Aaron fidgeted a bit, jostling the laptop and camera. "They're three games out of first. Boz is in a slump, and Chris Franke lost the other day." As Aaron spoke, his eyes fell closed.

"All right. You lay down and take a nap. But . . . I'll talk to you tomorrow, okay?"

"Okay, Dad."

"Hey, pal?"

Aaron's eyes flitted open.

"I sure could use one of our handshakes."

With a fading smile, Aaron held his hand out to the camera, and James did the same. Each pretend slap and each fake bump brought James's tears closer to the surface.

"Good luck tonight, Dad. Bye, Grandma and Grandpa. Later, Lizard."

"Daddy, let's do a computer kiss," Lizzie said. Her pursed lips lowered to the monitor so that her forehead filled the tiny camera. "Are you kissing? I can't see you."

"You bet, sweetie," James whispered. He kissed his fingers and touched them to her forehead.

"Mommy, now you computer kiss me." Lizzie's forehead filled her screen again; Emily's lips blacked out their monitor.

"And here's one for you, Mr. Ballplayer," Emily said.

James pressed his fingers to his computer's webcam and closed his eyes.

Both calls flicked off, their screens black, and James stared at the monitor. Burkes finally came and got him for batting practice.

Although roughly the same size as West Michigan's Fifth Third Ballpark, Jerry Uht Park seemed immense, even with the close fence in left field begging hitters to try to bash home runs. Just like everything else. Baseball. His place in it. Family. Aaron's wish. *Maybe I should swing for the fences,* James thought while waiting in his batting practice group for his turn at the plate. Although he'd never been a power hitter, maybe, he thought, trying to crush the ball would straighten his eye. Maybe it would straighten everything. *Maybe it's time to get angry.*

The Skype call helped with that. At first, he wallowed when the call ended, and he carried that despair onto the field. But the sight of the outfield and the cracks of the bat and the home run balls and the press throng above the third base dugout just made him mad. Mad at the cancer—he wrung the bat handle, heating up his gloved hands. Mad at the bone marrow registry for having no matches—he tapped the bat against his forehead. Mad at himself for stinking up, so far, two baseball stadiums—he smacked the bat's barrel against the inside of his cleats as if knocking off dirt.

His teammates laughed and joked with one another. They were so confident in their abilities. So smooth. James knew he played like that once upon a time. Once upon a *long* time.

He lifted the bat to his shoulder. It thudded like an anvil. The anger disappeared.

He already knows who Minnesota's starting pitcher will be. James shook his head. *And I can't even touch a single-A prospect.*

He glanced up at the stands. The crowd of cameras had tripled in size from what had stood in front of his locker the night before. And they were all zoomed in on him, their national story.

News at eleven, he thought. *Kid's dying wish swings and misses.*

James's turn at the plate came up. He didn't want to go. He didn't want to continue the charade any longer. He knew it: he should never have tried this. *How can I make it up to Aaron? Where could we go? What could we do instead? Because I sure can't do this.*

I can't do this.

When the words formed in his brain, he heard only the monstrous, black cancer cells applauding. And it made him mad.

He couldn't say the words "I give up." He wouldn't. *Better to be told to go home than to give up.*

A few teammates chattered encouragement when he stepped up. Steve stood behind the dome and leaned on the fencing, reminding him to keep his hands on a short, straight path close to his body, turn his hips, and extend the bat through the zone.

He popped up the first two bunts before dropping the next only a few inches in front of the plate. But he pushed two perfect bunts down the first base line and angled another two closer to the third base line.

"Thataway!" Lincoln called from the on-deck circle, where he worked pine tar onto his bat.

When it came time to swing away, though, the foul balls resumed. Straight up into the dome, topped off to the side, lifted straight up and to the back of the cage. He pulled two pitches foul down the third base line, but only because the batting practice pitcher had lobbed them in. He stepped out of the batter's box and held his bat out front, staring at it. *Why won't you work?*

"Someone here to see you," Lincoln said.

From the dugout, in white baseball pants and a Tigers batting practice jersey, looking the same as he did when they played catch at Comerica Park, walked Curt Howard.

James was both relieved and embarrassed.

"Did you call him?" James asked the big first baseman. Lincoln held up his hands, innocent.

"I wanted to check up on my second baseman," Curt said. He walked around the dome and stood in the left-handed batter's box. They shook hands across home plate. "You can thank the lady in your life for suggesting how I spend my off day. She said you needed your compass corrected."

"You didn't have to come all this way to tell me to buckle down. I've gotten a few earfuls about that already." James scuffed the dirt with his bat.

"Well, I would've asked Linc to talk to you, but he's still too much of a ladies' man."

"What has that got to do with me playing like crap?"

"Hey, guys, can you give us a minute?" Curt asked the few people loitering around the dome. When they left, he held his hand out for the bat.

Although he batted right-handed, Curt took a few slow, perfect swings left-handed. He extended his follow-through, gazing skyward at an imaginary ball sailing over the right field fence. "It's your hips. You're not driving them through."

"That's what they keep saying. And that's what I keep trying. I just feel nowhere close, like my coordination is shot."

"Your coordination isn't shot."

"I can't square up the ball."

Curt handed back the bat. "Let's do a little Whac-A-Mole training."

"Whac-A-Mole?"

"Yeah, I just made it up. Hold the bat by the barrel and tap my hand with the handle. Don't think about it; just hit my hand." Curt held out a flat, steady palm as if it were a pitched ball frozen over the plate. James tapped it. Curt moved his hand higher. James tapped it again, right in the center. "Now . . . faster. Don't think. See it. And hit it."

Curt's hand blurred over the plate—high, low, inside, outside. James smacked the center each time. All instinct and reflex.

"See?" Curt said, taking the bat again. "Your coordination is fine. But you're swinging with all arms. Your hands are coming through nice, but your hips are lagging behind. You open those faster, concentrate on driving your right hip forward, and your bat will follow. And you just showed that it'll be in the right spot." He rested the bat on his shoulder. "But you know all that. Don't you?"

James looked at home plate. He nodded. "When did Emily ask you to come down?"

"On Friday. After you talked to her that night. And I heard you had a video call with them today, too."

"Wes set it up."

"That's nice and all, but I wouldn't have done it."

"Excuse me?"

Curt dragged the end of the bat through the dirt. "Look,

this is going to sound cold, but for a little while, you need to forget you have a family."

James laughed.

"I'm serious. You got tossed into this. You didn't have time to come up real young when all you had to worry about was baseball so that when you got married and started a family, you already had your routine and your focus. The simple fact is you're trying to do too much. You can't worry about them and play baseball at the same time. Not at this level."

"He's got cancer, Curt. How can I not worry about that?"

"Aaron's in a hospital, he's in his treatment, and he's being watched 24-7. You need to let him and Emily and the doctors do their thing. *You—*" he pointed the bat at James's chest—"need to do yours. You don't think they'd find a way to get ahold of you if there was an emergency? And even if you had your phone in your hand and they needed you, it's still five hours back to St. Francis. James, *you're not there*. The problem is—" he tapped home plate—"you're not *here* either."

Curt took another couple of slow, left-handed practice swings, glancing back and forth to James as if instructing him, all for the sake of the cameras in the stands. "Now look. Emily wasn't the only one who wanted me to come talk to you. You used your get-out-of-jail-free card from Lou and Wes already, when they moved you up from West Michigan when you didn't deserve it." He started to swing again but this time drew attention to his hips, showing how they opened up, and dropped the barrel of the bat into the hitting zone. "Mazarron's put his foot down. He said that this ends here if you can't turn it around. Like, now. And the only way that's going to happen is to forget you have a family. You're not a husband. You're not a dad. You're a baseball player. Stop calling. Stop texting. What's happening, how you're playing right now, it's not for lack of talent. It's lack of focus. You need to focus on nothing but baseball." He rested the bat on his shoulder again.

When James nodded, he held it out. James took it.

"Now show me."

Slowly James mimicked Curt's form. Curt adjusted his hands a touch, pushed his right hip forward, then stood back and watched two full, fast swings.

But like Curt said, James knew all of that.

"I feel like I'm back in fall ball all those years ago. When I lost it."

"You need to find it. And you can't do that with a cell phone in your back pocket."

"I walked away from baseball for them, you know."

"But now you have to *play* baseball for them. To get to that game, so you can play for Aaron, you've got to push him away. For a little while."

The two men stared at each other. James lowered his gaze first.

"Okay. Let's work on that swing off a tee. Away from those guys." Curt motioned to the cameras.

That night before bed, James sent only one text to Emily:
Thanks.

Curt's talk, however, wasn't enough. If anything, James played worse during the next day's infield practice. Every hop seemed in-between, every pop-up in the sun. Between his legs, off the heel of his glove, up into his cup . . . every possible way to miss a grounder, and even a couple he was sure he invented.

It's not talent. It's focus. So focus.

Another ball jumped up onto the heel of his glove and deflected off his right hand, dribbling away. James picked it up and, snarling, hurled it over the right field fence.

Burkes strolled out to second base, his arms crossed, and pulled within a nose of James. "Get that outta your system?"

"Not really. Sorry about that," James muttered.

"Don't be sorry. Be better."

"Right."

"Curt told me what you guys talked about. I don't want to be the one to send you packing and crush your boy's dream. So *be better*. You got this. Pretend you're showing the kids back at your high school. Watch the ball and eat it up; don't let it eat you."

"I know." James scuffed the dirt with a cleat. "It's just . . . *them*." He waved his glove to the stands alongside the third base dugout and propped his hands on his hips.

Burkes didn't need to look over his shoulder to see who James waved at—the camera clicks *tick-tick*ed throughout the stadium like raindrops pattering on the metal awning. "You're their story now. Wes ran cover for you yesterday, but like he said, you'll have to face them some time. Probably tonight after the game."

"Can I do it now? Get it over with?"

"What, like *now* now?"

James didn't blink.

Burkes waved to the dugout, and Wes trotted out in dress pants and shoes and an open navy blazer.

"What's going on?" Wes asked.

"Rookie here wants to get his presser over right now. Do you have his statements ready?"

"I don't need a statement," James said.

Wes hissed. "We all saw how it went last time you winged it."

"I learned my lesson. I'm not going to take any questions or anything right now. I just want to let them know where I'm at. Where my mind's at." He looked at Burkes. "What Curt talked to me about yesterday? I think I just need to say it out loud to someone. Might as well be to them."

Wes finally agreed but said he'd end it at the first sign of a repeat of his previous performance in front of the cameras. The manager told the players to keep taking grounders, and the three of them walked across the diamond.

"Right behind you, buddy," Lincoln muttered, marching after them.

The camera clicks intensified when James stopped on the field a few feet in front of the rolled-up tarp nestled against the wall, and questions poured down upon him. With Wes on his right and Burkes on his left, James held up his hands. The chatter intensified when he appeared about to pick questions. No one heard his pleas for quiet.

"Pipe down!" Lincoln shouted, stepping next to James. "Why do I gotta keep yelling at y'all to shut up?" When the only sounds were more camera clicks, the big man crossed his arms, warning the crowd with a glower.

James turned to the media. "How's everybody doing?" he asked. No response. "So last time . . . you guys kinda caught me off guard. I should have used the clichés from the movie *Bull Durham*." He smiled. Still nothing. "You know: 'We gotta play 'em one day at a time.' Uh, 'I'm just happy to be here. Hope I can help the ball club.' 'I just wanna give it my best shot, and the good Lord willing, things will work out.'" More cameras. "C'mon, guys, *Bull Durham*? Really?

"Okay, well, I know Mr. Marco gave you guys a statement yesterday and took some questions. I'm not going to take any today. I just wanted a few minutes to talk to you a bit. This— right now—is the only time I'm going to do this. I'll do stuff with you after this all finishes in Detroit. But I learned a pretty valuable lesson yesterday, and I think I needed to tell you guys, to say it out loud, so I could believe it myself.

"I have to focus on baseball. I've got to focus on getting to that day. I've been trying to do too much, trying to keep in contact with my family too much while my boy goes through his treatment. But I've got to put that aside for now. And you know what? It stinks. But I've got to do it. For Aaron. I've got to trust the doctors and nurses and my wife to be there for him while I—" his throat clenched for a second—"while I can't.

"Part of his treatment is the hope of seeing me play for the Tigers. You guys all saw Curt Howard here yesterday. He told me I won't get there with a cell phone in my back pocket. But seeing you guys today, I'm pretty sure I won't get there with your cameras in my face, either."

"What Mr. McConnell means," Wes interrupted, "is that—"

But James held out a hand to cut him off. "I got this," he said. He turned back to the crowd. "Look, I'm not saying I won't talk to you. Just . . . for right now, you get the short version. This all started when my son made a wish to Curt Howard of the Tigers. And Curt and the Tigers took it upon themselves to make Aaron's wish come true. They aren't doing this for publicity; they don't need help filling the seats. And their minor league teams got on board, too."

Some of the cameras lifted up and pointed over his shoulder, and James glanced back at the field and found that a handful of players had gathered behind him, the others on their way. He nodded a thank-you, and several tipped their caps in return.

"I'm trying to show these guys I belong here, but I haven't earned anything from them yet. But they're supporting me, supporting my family, sacrificing some time until I get my act together. Some guys even sacrificed their roster spots. Bobby Taggert at West Michigan and Cesar Vasquez here at Erie. The same thing'll happen at Toledo and Detroit, guys giving up a couple days in the sun so that I can have one night under the lights.

"So now I'm asking all of you. The teams and front offices, the coaches, the players—they're all doing their part to make this happen. I've had to make, well, sort of a brutal decision to separate myself, emotionally as well as physically, from my family for a little while. I think now I'm really ready to do *my* part." He looked at each camera. "I'd really appreciate it if you all would do *your* part. Let me focus on baseball. It's no guarantee I'll get in that game for the Tigers. I've got to relearn how to hit a fastball, for one thing. I'm not asking you not to film—I mean, the Tigers sent their own film crew." James jabbed a thumb to the two-man crew on the left field foul line. "But if you could, I don't know, be in the background, I guess. And whatever you do, don't go to the hospital to try to interview my wife or son, please." He straightened up. "For the sake of a little boy undergoing treatment for cancer, please, don't."

James pounded a fist into his glove. "Now, we've got a big game tonight against Altoona, and it'd be nice to find out if I can still pick up a grounder or hit that fastball. So thanks a bunch, everybody."

Reporters' questions and camera snaps skittered down to the field when James turned his back on the media horde; his teammates surrounded him, and James bumped fists with each one. As one unit, they jogged back onto the field and dispersed to their positions.

The ground balls resumed. James waited his turn, his glove to his mouth and his eyes closed, pushing each image of his family out of his brain.

I'm a ballplayer, he told himself. *These guys took a chance. They just showed me. Now I've got to show them I belong here. I belong here.*

He stepped up, squatted into his ready position, and focused on home plate. On the next ground ball to him, the hop bounced true into his glove. Perhaps they had always been true, only now his eyes were clear. He cushioned it to his chest and snapped a perfect throw to first. His teammates razzed him with mocking applause—Lincoln even gave him a we're-not-worthy bow—and James held up his hands, allowing the other second baseman to push him around. The weight of the cameras lifted from his shoulders, and the banter of the players consumed the sound of their clicks.

Not only did James's fielding begin to climb out of the cellar after the press conference on the field, so did his hitting. He noticed it on the very first batting practice pitch: the ball floated toward the plate. He jumped on it and lined a hard ground ball out to shortstop. It sent a charge through his hands. He fouled off the next few pitches, settled down with a breath, and then drove another grounder, this one to second base.

The other SeaWolves noticed the change, too, in both his performance and in his mind-set. James had become a true teammate. A ballplayer deserving of a chance.

"C'mon, rookie, is that the best you got?" Lincoln said behind the batting dome.

"Hey, at least it's going in the right direction," James said. Another pitch, and the ball not only looked slower, but bigger, glowing white. His eyes widened—another cut, another screaming ground ball.

The next morning, James showed up at the clubhouse and received the highest honor for a new ballplayer: a nickname. Nothing too outlandish or contrived, just a mash-up of names that happens to nearly everyone, but a nickname nonetheless. Walking into the strangely quiet clubhouse on Wednesday morning—the only camera the Tigers' video crew—James found his locker plastered with newspapers, all containing articles and photos of him, from national opinionators to beat writers.

It wasn't only the chair in front of his locker and the inside walls and shelves, either—his bottles of shampoo, deodorant, glove, cleats, jerseys, pants, even the hangers were all wrapped like Christmas presents. The players pounced on him, beating his back amid shoves and shouts of "J-Mac's our boy!" and "Here's J-Mac the star!" Newspapers and baseballs begging for autographs waggled in front of his face.

Later that morning, the team boarded a bus for a two-game series in Harrisburg, leaving James with Jerry Uht Park all to himself, along with Steve and a smattering of cameras in addition to the Tigers' film crew.

The day began with classroom work on the Tigers themselves—a three-ring binder full of signs and defensive plays, and a scouting video of the Minnesota Twins, the team he'd face on Father's Day at Comerica Park. It all muddled together in his brain during lunch.

"Take the afternoon off," Steve said while James finished his club sandwich. "Be back here at eight tonight. We'll switch up practice a bit."

"Under the lights?" James took a drink of his Gatorade.

"Yeah, Wes called. You're not playing a day game on Father's Day. It got bumped to ESPN's *Sunday Night Baseball*."

The Gatorade nearly sprayed out of his mouth. "Wait—what?"

"National television. So some more nighttime practice oughta help."

The sandwich grumbled, threatening to come back up.

James didn't eat anything the rest of the day, nor did he relax. Instead of lounging at the hotel, where it would have been too tempting to fill the downtime with phone calls and texts to Emily, he spent it at the clubhouse, watching the scouting video three more times and studying the Tigers' instructional sheets.

Steve found him hunched over a small conference table, his hands on his forehead. "Let's go, J-Mac. Lights are fired up."

James warmed up with one of the teenage batboys who hadn't made the road trip. His panic about the game being nationally televised had dissipated over the long day, and when he trotted onto the field, lit up like noon, his stomach fluttered with a tinge of excitement. As he played catch, he paid closer attention to how the ball glowed under the lights. His throws seemed faster, more crisp. He tried to imagine a packed Comerica Park watching him, but the empty Erie stands—which, when full, only seated 4,200 fans—couldn't mimic a sold-out major league ballpark.

Something felt different on the first grounder hit to him. Under the lights, the ball streaked like a star across the grass, but he corralled it without even thinking about it. Effortless. He tossed a laser beam to the batboy, now playing first base. The next grounder seemed to track right into his glove on its own, and in a flash, his hand picked the ball out of his mitt and zipped it to first. Steve laced a two-hopper far up the middle, but in three light strides, James backhanded it, planted, and put all his strength behind the throw. It felt a hundred miles an hour.

He lost track of the number of ground balls he fielded, all without an error.

He couldn't stand still. Sensing "the zone," that magical place every athlete dreams of reaching, where everything clicks, he jogged to the dugout and grabbed a bat. Steve hustled the L-screen out to the mound. James didn't bother bunting. In his eagerness, he swung for the fence and topped the first few.

Stepping out of the batter's box, he took a breath, then calmly placed his right foot first and dug it into the dirt. Then he set his left foot down in position and raised his heel off the ground.

"No step. Straight hands. Drive hips," he muttered. "Hands and hips. Hands and hips."

The *crack* shocked the still stadium.

A line drive to left field.

A no-doubt base hit that rolled to a stop in the middle of left field.

The instructor's grin gleamed as bright as the lights. He reached into the ball bag and took out two more.

"Don't stop now," James said.

By the time they were done, baseballs littered the outfield.

After showering in the clubhouse, he picked up his phone and hit Emily's speed dial. It rang once. Then he hung up. He squeezed the phone and brought it to his forehead, closing his eyes. He said good night to his family in his mind.

Friday afternoon, while James waited in the empty clubhouse for the rest of the team's arrival, he didn't even look at his phone; he simply slipped it out of his pocket and tossed it on the shelf in his locker. Changing into running shoes and shorts, he hit the field to jog laps.

The sun beat down and the sweat felt good, but breaking out of his slump the previous night during the solitary practice did little to clear his head. While jogging from foul pole to foul pole along the outfield's warning track, his shoes crunching dirt, he heard Aaron's voice, over and over: *"I know we can't play catch, Dad."* . . . *"I know we can't play catch . . ."* And then he saw the boy kneel down and brush his hand along the grass.

James fought the images. They needed to stay away. For

him to be a ballplayer, a successful ballplayer, they needed to stay away.

He slowed and stopped somewhere around left-center field.

He took a few steps off the dirt warning track, squatted, and held his hand inches above the grass. But he wouldn't touch it.

"I can't think about this right now," he said aloud. His hand trembled and then clenched into a fist. "Sorry, pal. But not right now."

An hour later, Lincoln found him sitting at his locker clutching his cell phone like a quitting smoker on the verge of giving in.

"Hey, what happened?" Lincoln asked. "Is Aaron—?"

"No, no, he's fine," James said. "At least I don't think anything's wrong, or I would've heard. Just really tough today, not calling them." It took a few deep breaths for him to set the phone down.

Lincoln slapped him on the back. Hard. "Don't be like that, J-Mac. You had me freaked out!"

"Sorry, big fella. I know how sensitive you are."

"Yeah, well, don't go blabbin'. Got a rep to maintain. You ready for tonight? Skip says you're startin'. And I heard you might've finally got some glasses that work."

"Zoned in, Linc."

"You hear that, gang?" Lincoln bellowed. "J-Mac promised gettin' his first hit tonight!" A few whistles and hoots raced through the clubhouse, and Lincoln smacked him on the back once more.

After warm-ups, while the team changed from batting practice jerseys into their pin-striped home whites, Ralph, the clubhouse manager, shook a clipboard at James.

"What's this?" James took it and sat down.

"Form for the equipment companies. Glove preference, size,

color, four-pane or solid basket, ash or maple for your bat and length and weight, that sort of thing."

"For what?"

"You serious?" To James's empty look, Ralph chuckled. "You're a star. Between your little speech on the field and someone filming your batting practice the last two days, people are lovin' it. Everyone wants to send you their stuff for you to use, hoping it makes it to Detroit."

"What, you mean for free?" James scanned the sheet.

"Of course for free." Ralph eyed him. "This kinda stuff happens all the time, J-Mac."

James studied the list and handed back the clipboard. "I'm fine."

"You're saying no?"

"Yes, I'm saying no. I bought my own batting gloves, I've got a glove on loan from Curt Howard, and I finally got my cleats broken in, the ones the Whitecaps gave me. And I'm not going anywhere without those two bats I've been using lately." James flicked his head at the clipboard and retied his cleats. "If those companies really want to give stuff away, tell them to give it to some of the teams' foundations. They all sponsor youth baseball."

"Really?"

"Really." He finished. "I'm going to throw. Thanks, Ralph."

"All right." Ralph shook his head. "Good luck tonight, J-Mac."

Luck didn't find James against the Richmond Flying Squirrels that night, a 4–2 loss. At the plate, the pitches weren't as big or slow as during his breakout batting practice session.

"You'll get 'em next time," Lincoln said, swatting him on the butt back in the dugout after his first strikeout. And second strikeout.

After his third strikeout, James jammed the bat into the rack and pressed his helmet between his hands, hoping it would shatter. But he just slammed that into its cubby, too.

"Next one, J-Mac," Lincoln said, meeting him at the Gatorade jug. "Next one. I feel it."

"Did you actually see my last swing?" James slugged the drink and tossed the empty cup in the general vicinity of the trash barrel.

"Brilliant, if you ask me, you wavin' up there like you're swattin' at a fly. They think they got you all figured out now, but you're settin' 'em up. You ain't foolin' me."

Lincoln's tiny confidence boost almost worked: James's fourth time up to bat nearly resulted in his first hit, if not for a stellar play by the second baseman, who leaped to snare his line drive. The Flying Squirrels zinged the ball around the infield before James even dropped the bat.

But James's heart soared. Inches away from his first hit. Lincoln stood on the dugout's top step and clapped at him all the way back to the dugout.

He carried that spark of confidence, along with an errorless game in the field, to the next night.

In the bottom of the sixth inning, while James swung a weighted bat in the on-deck circle, Lincoln whistled him over. "You might not get up again, so make this count." They bumped fists. "Don't do this for nobody else but you. *You* need this, J-Mac. Now, come on!"

As James walked to the plate, the half-full stadium appeared empty. The pitcher stood alone. The ball looked like batting practice.

And on a one-ball, two-strike pitch, James looped a soft line drive to left field.

One hit among many in a lopsided SeaWolves victory,

and one hit that incited a Gatorade shower in the clubhouse afterward.

In the midst of the spray, Lincoln stood on a chair above his teammates. "It's about time this old man put up something other than a goose egg in the box score and officially got a batting average!" The players cheered. "Where's Skip? Skip!" Burkes stood at the door to his office. "Can I tell him? Lemme tell him. C'mon, man."

Burkes waved a hand in a flourish. "The floor's all yours."

"All right, listen up. J-Mac, get up here!" James stumbled forward, shoved and jostled and hauled up onto a chair next to Lincoln. "Now, J-Mac, Skip got the call . . . and you've been released, man. Been nice knowin' ya!"

The players booed and sprayed more Gatorade at Lincoln.

"All right, all right . . . you're leavin' for Toledo in the mornin'!" Another round of cheers. "And we all got you a going-away present, too. Somethin' for The Show!"

A small box passed among the crowd until someone flung it at Lincoln, knocking his drink out of his hand. After cursing amid the howls of laughter, he picked up the box and held it high; the players whistled.

Depend adult diapers.

Linc draped his arm around James. "Where you're goin' . . . you're gonna need these."

11

WHEN JAMES SPOTTED FIFTH THIRD FIELD in downtown Toledo—with its left field scoreboard and yellow foul poles rising above a neighborhood street and light stanchions rimming two city blocks—he stared at his toughest test yet: his last stint through the minors with the Triple-A Toledo Mud Hens. Father's Day, and his major league debut, loomed one week away.

Focus on baseball for one more week, he thought, turning in to the stadium parking lot. *Don't screw it up now.*

After an early morning text from Emily, that focus came easier and clearer. But when he turned the car off, he allowed himself a few more minutes to be a husband and father, reading the text again: Aaron doing great, close 2 remission. Lizzie back here. Go Mud Hens!

He reread the text, several times.

Remission.

A fountain of magnificent news in one spectacular word.

He smiled and closed the text, squeezing the phone in a short prayer of thanks, and took off his husband and father cap.

Time to be a Mud Hen.

Manager Martin Malcolm met him in the tunnel outside the Mud Hens clubhouse. "Mr. McConnell, I presume?" He held out a thick paw of a hand, as big as the catcher's mitt he used in the majors for eleven years; it swallowed James's hand. "First, baseball: I thought I'd sit you today and tomorrow, let you settle in and practice hard, and then you'll start on Tuesday against the Knights."

"Sounds great, thanks."

"Now, how's your boy?"

Not quite ready for the question, James stammered, falling back on an old platitude. "He's a tough kid. Hanging in there."

"Good, good. Come on, you can meet the gang."

James froze in the clubhouse doorway. The uniformed gang, all twenty-four of them, waited for him, silently seated in their chairs in the center of the room; three sat on the far side in high-top chairs, their legs and arms crossed. Every face stared at him. No one smiled.

"Crap," Malcolm muttered, standing next to James. He pushed his cap to the back of his head.

"What—?"

"Kangaroo Court," the manager said. "Honest, I didn't know they had this planned as your welcome party."

"Kangaroo Court?"

"If you do something stupid, somebody files a charge, it goes to court, and if you lose, you pay a fine." He nodded at the three players sitting on the high seats. "And with Larry, Moe, and Curly there for judges, just about everyone loses."

"But—"

"Sorry, can't help you."

"Are you the rookie James 'J-Mac' McConnell?" the judge on the left stool, "Larry," asked in a deep voice.

"Uh, yeah."

He held aloft a piece of paper. "There's a charge against you."

"I—"

Moe, the center judge, silenced him by rapping a baseball bat on the arm of his chair. He held out his hand for the slip of paper. "Mr. McConnell, it says here that, as witnessed by clubhouse manager Ralph MacAllan and reported to first baseman Lincoln Church, you stand accused of—" Moe squinted at the paper—"'denying the benefits befitting a professional baseball player while in the employ of . . .' Pablowski, you wrote this, didn't you?"

A skinny player in an impeccably white uniform stood. "Why do you say that?"

"Because it's got Ivy League written all over it," Moe said. "Anyone else would've wrote, 'He turned down free stuff.'"

"Well, I can't help it if all you curs have no—"

"What's a cur?" someone asked.

"How about *moron*? Do you know what a moron is?" A flying sock chased Pablowski back to his chair.

"I'll spare you hearing Ivy League's version of the charge, J-Mac," Moe said. He folded the piece of paper and examined James. "You turned down free stuff. How do you plead?"

"Uh—"

"Your Honor, I object," another player said, rising to his feet. "And I'd like to represent Mr. McConnell."

"Interesting development," Curly, the judge on the right, said, rubbing his chin.

"Does anybody have a problem with that?" Moe asked. Pablowski started to rise. "Anybody *other* than Pabs?" He turned to James's lawyer. "What's your defense?"

"Your Honor, the charge itself is my defense." Murmurs bubbled through the crowd until order returned after a thirty-four-inch, thirty-two-ounce maple gavel whacked the side of a chair. Pablowski stood, ready to defend his accusation. "It says it was witnessed by Ralph MacAllan and Lincoln Church."

"So?" Pablowski said.

"And where are they, genius?"

"At Erie."

"Precisely. So J-Mac would have to stand trial for this charge at the court in Erie." James's lawyer sat down.

Pablowski held out his hands, his mouth open that the tribunal would even consider dropping the charge, but that's just what they did, huddling.

"Case dismissed on a technicality." Moe banged the gavel again.

"But we're not done with you, J-Mac," Larry continued. "A charge has also been filed on behalf of the entire Toledo Mud Hens—"

"Here we go," Malcolm said.

"—that while you're here, Skip expects us—"

"It was a suggestion," Malcolm interrupted. "One I know you bunch of—"

"Careful, Skipper, you know there's no cursing in Kangaroo Court. Automatic fine."

Malcolm's jaw bulged. "That I know you bunch of 'curs' will ignore all to—"

"Ahem . . ."

Malcolm patted James on the shoulder. "Good luck, pal." He retreated to his office.

"So Skipper said that while you're here, we are to act like professionals. Mr. McConnell, how do you plead?"

"Uh, I—"

"We'll take that as guilty as charged," Curly ruled. "You're fined twenty-five dollars for bringing such an impossible burden to this team, and because you'll only be here a week, we require the money immediately." He held high a cardboard box decorated with the Mud Hens logo, stickers, and the calligraphed words *Kangaroo Court Fines*.

Just as when he entered, the room fell silent, every eye on him.

James sighed. He dug through his wallet and held up two bills. When he deposited them into the Kangaroo Court Fines box, the players surrounded James for a genuine welcome to the Mud Hens, which involved being directed to a locker filled with Bengay, Rogaine, the latest copy of *AARP The Magazine*, and a gigantic pair of Harry Caray glasses.

"Glad to see you took Skip's suggestion," James said.

The mild rookie hazing of Kangaroo Court immediately folded James into the team, and it carried onto the field, where he shagged fly balls from one end of the outfield to the other. But it also relieved some of the pressure of the clock in his head ticking down from one week, and sharpened his baseball focus.

His first batting practice pitch looked like an overstuffed marshmallow, and he smashed it to left field.

"Quit lobbin' 'em in there!" a player called from behind the batting dome.

Another line drive, this one directly over the pitching screen.

"Save some of those for Detroit, man."

He laced three more, all up the middle, and stepped out to a ripple of applause. "Rookie's got a stick!" someone yelled.

As at West Michigan and Erie, James spent his first game with the Mud Hens on Sunday afternoon sitting in the dugout and watching. Monday's practice centered on him, but he took the field with many of the butterflies banished.

The first ground ball of infield practice streaked in the hole between first and second base. James dove, his glove a magnet, and he gathered to his feet and flicked the ball to first.

"Maybe we should quit right there!" the infield coach yelled.

But the coach didn't quit. And neither did James.

He was one of the boys again.

During a break, he gazed around the field. At Erie, the confidence of the players had been palpable, particularly because he had none at the time—an outsider looking in, a pretender. Now, he surged with that same confidence, fielding ground balls and ripping drives as well as any of them.

He stepped into his ready position for another grounder and turned an effortless double play with the shortstop.

Regret pricked him like a pin. That hadn't happened in years.

I really could've made it. I could've been a ballplayer.

He pounded a fist in his glove.

I am a ballplayer. This day, right now. For a little while longer.

More grounders, more batting practice, and another game watching from the dugout.

That night, back at the hotel, he slipped off the ballplayer hat, picked up the phone, and found a text from two hours ago: Did u win? -Aaron

Yep. 9-4. Didn't play. How u feeling?

James waited only a few seconds before the phone jingled with a return message. His heart sank. It's me. Kiddo's in bed. Doing great.

Awesome. Practice went well. Sorry I missed Aaron.

It's ok. I'll show him in morning. When will u get in a game?

I start tomorrow nite. Off day Wed.

Great! Good luck. Get lots of sleep. Only a few days left! Love u!

Love u 2.

Tuesday night, James jogged out to second base to start against the Charlotte Knights. The Mud Hens' Fifth Third Field, one of the nicest complexes in minor league baseball, was pristine even if the weather wasn't—cloudy, windy, and spitting sprinkles. Not enough to delay the game, but enough to soak the field. After fielding the obligatory warm-up grounders from the first baseman and flipping the game ball around the infield, he judged where he should play the left-handed leadoff hitter and settled into his ready position.

"Hey, J-Mac," the first baseman called after the first pitch, nodding toward the stands by the Mud Hens' third base dugout.

James's mouth went dry.

He'd been here before, a month ago, his attention on a game, distracted by a player who motioned for him to look outside the field. And last time, he saw an SUV careening toward the field with the message that his son's cancer had relapsed.

He heard Curt's voice again: *They'd find a way to get ahold of you if there was an emergency.*

Emergency.

But when he searched the stands for the emergency, he didn't spot anyone frantically waving, as Greg had. Just one person, three rows up behind the on-deck circle and in the aisle, bouncing a hot-pink umbrella up and down to get his attention.

Emily.

The smack of the catcher's mitt startled him back to the present, but her pink umbrella, waving side to side as she found her seat, kept drawing his gaze, making him late for a cutoff on a single to right with two outs. And he didn't even remember the first two outs. When the last batter struck out, Emily skipped down to the railing.

"What are you doing here?"

"I heard Toledo called up their new prospect," she said. "Hoping I could get his autograph."

"He's sitting tonight. They put me in instead."

"Well, I guess you'll have to do."

"You know, this probably isn't the best thing. Not supposed to be a husband or father right now, remember?"

"Then pretend I'm that college girl in the stands you used to knock yourself out to impress."

James grinned. "Hey, Dougie," he said to the batboy, "get me a ball and pen, will ya?" He scrawled something across the ball—not his autograph—and tossed it to her. She blushed.

The hard rain held off, and after his first at bat in the third inning, a hard single to right, he stood ten feet tall on first base, a college sophomore again. Emily's hollers carried above the crowd, and her umbrella waved up and down again. On the next pitch, the batter drove a deep fly to left-center field, and the crowd swelled as he blazed the wet, slow base paths, scoring on the double.

"Way to go, babe!" Emily cheered as he jogged back to the dugout, his uniform dirty from sliding into home plate, even though he didn't have to.

In the field, he tugged at his glove and pulled his hat down. "Come on, number 58!" Emily shrieked. James strutted around second base, flicking the ball around the infield and sinking deeper into his ready position. A routine ground ball bounced out to him, and he casually sidearmed it to first for the last out of the inning.

Emily cheered during his entire last at bat in the eighth inning, and James caught an outside fastball on the bat's sweet spot. The drive over the first baseman's head rolled to the wall, and he legged out his first extra-base hit, sliding in headfirst a second before the throw. Emily's "Wooo!" drowned everything else.

James stood with one foot on the base, his hands on his hips, refusing to brush any dirt off his chest. He pointed in Emily's direction.

Oh, man, did I just point at her? he thought. He started laughing.

Emily continued hooting through the Mud Hens' postgame on-field congratulations; then she and her pink umbrella scampered up the aisle and to the covered concourse.

The clubhouse manager found James at his locker, changing without showering. "Hey, J-Mac, some chick's waitin' for you outside. She's pretty smokin' if you ask me." He announced it loud enough for everyone to hear, drawing whistles. "You want me to go get her so you can introduce her around?"

"Not on your life," James said, tugging on a shirt.

"Aw, come on," one of the players yelled. "You gotta let her meet a *real* man!" Bare-chested, he flexed, bouncing his pecs.

James didn't bother responding. He just snatched his wallet and keys and raced out. As the door closed behind him, he left the ballplayer inside.

Even with the umbrella, Emily's damp brown hair had lost all its body and lay flat to her head. Her pink cheeks puffed in a radiant smile, and in a navy Tigers hooded sweatshirt and jeans, she was the most beautiful woman James had ever seen. He swept her up in his arms, kissing her deeply when he set her back down.

"Aaron's fine," she said. "When your parents brought Lizzie back down, they said they'd keep an eye on everybody while I snuck out. Surprised?"

James answered by kissing her again. "You don't know how I needed this."

"And the best part? I don't have to be back until noon tomorrow. Aaron's got a later appointment, so they told me to get a good night's sleep." She stepped back and batted her brown eyes. "Do you know where I could spend the night, Mr. Baseball Player?"

"You're terrible at that, you know," James said, laughing.

"But it worked, didn't it?"

Arm in arm, they jogged to the parking lot.

Nearing one in the morning, they both still lay awake, Emily's head on James's bare chest. He gently rubbed her back, staring off into the dark hotel room. "It was pretty neat watching you play again," she said softly, drowsiness slowing her words. "Just like college."

"Nice to be watched."

"I'm sorry I had to push you away. And then have Curt come do it, too."

"It's okay. I needed to hear it. I know it's only been a week with this sort of separation, but I think I'm getting the hang of it—letting go to play, but then coming back to you guys in the morning or at night. The last couple days have been easier, anyway. Tonight sure helped with that." He kissed her head.

"For a long time I didn't understand why you gave it up," she said. "I never asked you to. And the way you played tonight, after so much time off . . ."

His eyes glazed over as he watched the ceiling, his hand still absently stroking her back.

Could I have done it? Could I have had the baseball life and the girl, too? All these years . . . the coaching, the desk jobs . . . Maybe I was wrong.

The regret wasn't a pinprick anymore.

It stabbed him like a dagger.

To rekindle this youthful dream, to have this taste, to see for himself that he could compete, to wonder what his skills would have been like had he not quit thirteen years ago, to glimpse a life . . .

He forced the images of that life out of his mind. He couldn't return to that fork in the road.

"I know you never asked me to," he whispered. "It was my choice."

She rose up on one elbow. "Then why did you?"

"I've told you before, Em. When you came along, baseball just wasn't . . . I don't know; it wasn't fun anymore. Not like it used to be, anyway." He thought back to that moment his college coach told him he'd been demoted and how easy it had been to say okay and walk away. "I followed my heart and picked a different path. One with you. And one that led to Aaron and Liz."

"But now you've found your way back." Something in her voice sounded thrilled. And afraid.

"I didn't find my way back. Aaron gave it to me. It still amazes me that he wished for this. Pretty selfless thing to do."

Emily nestled back against his chest. "I guess we did something right."

"I hope this game on Sunday gives him something back, something to help him."

"It will." Though her head remained on his chest, she reached up and caressed his face. "A wish come true. You should see him. And his website to you. He still has ups and downs, but he's so excited."

"Has he been okay with me out of touch? Did you tell him why?"

"I did, yeah. It turns out you didn't need to sugarcoat it for him. He knew things were going rough."

"Mr. Scout knows all, eh?" They lay a minute in silence, both of them melting into the mattress. "I can't believe Dr. Barna thinks he's getting closer to remission."

"It's not *complete* remission," Emily said. "Just the end of the induction phase."

"I know. But it's a step closer."

"Then maybe we can go home for the next phase." She rubbed his chest. "This whole thing you're doing has a lot to do with that. And you know what? You got a wish come true, too."

"It's not the one I have right now."

"I know," she said. "But all we can do is hope and pray and keep—"

"—livin' life," James finished.

"And then you can get that new glove off his bookshelf."

They kissed again, and Emily snuggled back down. In a few minutes, James felt her body rising and falling rhythmically, and with her tight to his side, he drifted off into the first peaceful night's sleep that he'd had in a long time.

Heavy rain moved into the area before dawn, and they slept in on the Wednesday off day, sharing a continental breakfast in bed. James pulled the car under the hotel check-in port, and they remained in a tight embrace.

"A couple more days," James whispered, his face buried in her hair. "Good news or bad news, I'll be back with you guys in a couple days."

"It'll be good news. I know it." She pressed another light kiss to his lips, and James watched as she pulled out of the parking lot and down the road until traffic swallowed her.

The rain canceled his off-day practice and forced James into the fitness room. He ran hard in warm-ups before Thursday's game, didn't play especially well that evening—let a potential double play ground ball eat him up for an ugly error—and took the infield early on Friday for a solitary workout. Although the occasional thought of Aaron or Lizzie no longer made him flub a ground ball, he wouldn't let himself get complacent. The official word from the Tigers hadn't come yet. Being washed out and sent packing still lurked as an option.

Before Friday's batting practice, James sat at his locker, changing into his pin-striped, sleeveless jersey, when Malcolm yelled, "J-Mac!" The clubhouse froze. "Need a word." Every head turned.

James left his jersey unbuttoned. His two hits and solid defense on Tuesday fizzled in his mind. All he saw were Thursday's botched double play and two strikeouts.

Three weeks of minor league training boiled down to this moment.

Malcolm told him to close the door and motioned to a seat.

"Well, Jimmy, Mazarron's called me every day for updates. I just got off the phone with him again, in fact. And I honestly didn't know what to tell him."

James went numb. Malcolm's voice drifted away, replaced by the beeps from medical monitors. By a Tigers game, quiet, on the TV in the corner of a hospital room. By the soft crying of his son.

He couldn't sit there and listen to it, but he also couldn't move his legs. He closed his eyes. This entire last week, thinking maybe he'd made the wrong choice about baseball, that he'd picked the wrong path . . . and now, the if-onlys and second-guessing of that long-ago decision withered, the furthest thing from his mind.

There was no wish come true for Aaron.

He opened his eyes and stared at the manager.

"Maz wanted you to stick around for one more game tomorrow," Malcolm said. "I thought you could use a day off with your family."

Day off?

A deep, baritone roll of laughter puffed Malcolm's cheeks. "This is my favorite part of being a manager." He leaned his elbows on the table. "Jimmy, the big club's noticed, and I got the call. Pack your bags. You're goin' to The Show, kid." He stuck his hand out, and James stared at it, unable to speak. They shook. "I'm going to trot you out there for a couple innings tonight against Pawtucket and then pull you. Then I want you to hit the road."

James first nodded but changed his mind. He swallowed, painful across his dry throat. "I appreciate that, Skip, but I think I'll stay. These guys have been great. You, too. I don't want to ditch you halfway through a game."

"You sure?"

"It's a short drive. I'll be all right." They stood. "Thanks, Martin."

"Hey, it was my pleasure. You knock 'em around on Sunday, okay? And you tell that boy of yours . . ." Malcolm's lips pressed together. "You tell that boy of yours he's got a clubhouse full of fans back here in Toledo." They shook hands again.

James walked to the door, turned around, and looked at the floor. "Goin' to The Show," he muttered. "So that's what it feels like."

"Everything you thought?"

James shook his head. "Honestly? I'm just going home."

After midnight, with a cardboard box of Kangaroo Court money tucked under his arm as a call-up gift, James McConnell jogged through the lobby of Bertoia Building East at St. Francis Pediatric Cancer Research Hospital. He felt stronger than ever, solid, his chest deeper and his arms and legs thick and firm. And his mind, no longer muddled like when he left for the West Michigan Whitecaps three weeks earlier, raced in anticipation of the coming days. He paused at the door to room 716 and collected his breath.

Crepe paper streamers hung from the ceiling on the other side of the medical area like the entrance to a tattoo parlor. Soft lights glowed on the other side, but silence pervaded the room, broken only by the waterfall white noise from Aaron's sleep machine. He didn't expect a rowdy welcome, but he thought someone would be awake, particularly since he had called from the road.

He swept aside the streamers and set the box down. The room's burgundy walls were plastered with handmade Welcome Home signs, the kids' versions of the Whitecaps, SeaWolves, Mud Hens, and Tigers logos, and huge cutouts of the various numbers James had worn so far—39, 61, and 58. Colorful J-Mac signs filled the gaps.

Emily dozed on the couch, a magazine having slid off her thigh and onto the cushion. She smiled and reached up to embrace his neck, asking in a whisper about the game and his trip. He shrugged them both off.

"Lizzie's in the other room," Emily said. "They're both out. Aaron wanted to stay up, but he crashed right after you called."

As James walked to his son's bedside, his heart raced faster than when he stepped to the plate for his first at bat with West Michigan. And it leaped higher than when he collected his first hit with Erie. And it ached deeper than when he committed his first error with Toledo.

In the warm, low light cast by the bedside lamp, Aaron looked perfect. Bald as a cue ball and sick, but perfect, lying on his back, mouth open in a deep sleep, a foot sticking outside the covers, both arms askew—one over his head, the other stretched out to the side. His chest rose gently with full, comfortable breaths. James put a hand to his mouth, and he heaved in a swallowed, silent cry.

The last three weeks felt like a lifetime.

He reached out to touch Aaron but pulled his hand back, afraid the boy would vanish into memory.

Emily rested her hand on his back and her head on his arm. "He's getting close. Dr. Barna likes the blood results better every day."

James nodded. He couldn't talk.

"What is it, hon?"

He wiped his nose and eyes. "The last week and a half, ever since Curt talked to me . . . it was like a different life. One without him. A few times—" he looked away—"I didn't think of him for so long that it felt like he wasn't even here."

"In the hospital?"

"No. *Here*. Like he had *never* been here. And now, seeing him . . . All these guys, these professional ballplayers I've played with, played catch with . . ." His voice trembled. "I've just wanted him to be the one to catch it." He broke down again.

Emily took his hand and rested it on Aaron's forehead, just as James had pressed Aaron's hand into Comerica Park's infield grass. "He's *here*, James. He's right here."

The touch freed him. He kissed Aaron's forehead, no longer afraid he'd disappear, squinting his eyes to try to hold the tears from falling onto his bald head. It didn't work, and James wiped them away with his thumb. He laughed through his crying. "I'm gonna be a wreck on Sunday. I wouldn't be surprised if I get yanked right after being announced."

Emily patted his back. "You'll do fine. Like you told me in Toledo, you've learned how to handle it. And having Aaron there, watching? I bet you'll be even more focused."

"He's going to do more than watch." To Emily's wrinkled brow, he only said, "It's a surprise."

They stood a minute more and watched Aaron sleep before

switching off the light. In the adjoining room, Lizzie sprawled across their bed. James wriggled in alongside and laid an arm across her. She thrashed, sinking a foot into his stomach, like she did whenever she snuck into their bed back home, then curled up and snuggled against him.

In minutes, the lights of Comerica Park glimmered in his dream, and he trotted around the bases after smacking a game-winning home run. And his son waited for him at home plate.

12

THE TENSION MOUNTED. They eyeballed James, waiting for him to make his move, and it unnerved him, leaving him sweating. He reached out his hand, then curled it back into a fist. He knew what he had to do; he just couldn't make himself do it. Leaving it up to fate churned his stomach, but fate waited, tapping her fingers, each *thrum* thudding deeper in his chest.

He'd stalled long enough. It all came down to right now. He closed his eyes and begged fate to turn her wrath on someone else.

He pushed the button, and the Uno Attack! machine beeped but remained still.

James deflated, awash in relief, and pushed back his new *America's #1 Dad!* hat. Tugging at a necktie splashed with baseball players and gloves and pennants and bats, he turned the machine to Emily.

She didn't hesitate, deciding to rip the Band-Aid right off and go for it. Fate found her victim. With a beep, a flurry of cards spit out at her, raining down upon the few homemade Father's Day cards on the coffee table. James and the kids whooped, and Emily tickled Aaron in the ribs when he shimmied a victory dance in his chair. The next card he played left him at Uno.

"I hope you bring those cheers to the game tonight," Curt Howard called from the doorway. "Your dad's gonna need them."

"Hopefully he won't play second base like he plays Uno," Emily said.

"That hurts." James tapped his chest. "Right here. In my heart. Ow."

"So you feeling strong, big guy?" Curt asked Aaron. "Ready for all the excitement?"

Aaron flashed him two enthusiastic thumbs-up.

"Speaking of all the excitement . . ."

"You ready to go?" James asked.

"Thought you'd want to get there a little early today and settle in."

"You know what that means," James said, and he divvied up his cards three ways.

Lizzie grinned with new life. Emily grumbled, "That's lovely," under the weight of more cards. Aaron, so close to winning, groaned.

"Okay, buster, I need a special one for this game day." And as on the days he coached, James and Aaron slapped their short handshake routine. He slipped off the baseball tie and draped it around Aaron's neck, then hoisted Lizzie over his shoulder, playfully whopping her on the bottom as he spun in a circle. She shrieked, clutching her cards, and pecked a kiss on his cheek when he plopped her back in the chair.

Emily followed them to the door. "Don't let this guy freak out," she said to Curt, who stole a hug from her.

"Me? Freak out?" James said.

Curt told her that Kara would pick them up for the game. Emily tried to protest, but Curt didn't budge. "Consider it a final present."

Emily rose to her tiptoes for a long embrace with her husband, whispering, "Good luck."

"I'll see you there. Make sure he gets a little rest."

"Yeah. Right."

Subdued conversation about anything other than baseball filled the ride to the ballpark in Curt's black Escalade—so much focus over the last two weeks, and now Curt tried to keep James's mind off of it. But when the buildings of downtown Detroit sprouted on the horizon and the first green highway sign displaying directions to Comerica Park appeared, James fell silent.

"Nervous?"

"Glad I had a light lunch. Did they have to make this a nationally televised game?"

"I promised your wife I wouldn't let you freak out, so don't freak out."

"I'm just ready for this to be done." James stared out the passenger window.

"Well, try to enjoy it, too. Because once the stadium starts filling up, this game will fly by faster than any of the ones in the minors."

They pulled into the players' parking garage across the street from the stadium and, on their way through the underground tunnel, reviewed the things they'd practiced the day before. The few guards standing outside the clubhouse nodded a hello and wished him luck.

Last time, James walked through the security line as one of Curt's guests.

Now he was a player. A Tiger.

When the heavy metal door closed, the silence of the office-like clubhouse enveloped them. "Let's go to work," Curt said.

In the empty clubhouse, Curt changed into exercise clothes and shut himself in the adjoining fitness room, leaving James alone. He dressed quickly but partially—white pants, navy socks, and a navy-and-gray short-sleeved undershirt—and sat in his leather chair with the Old English *D* on the headrest. Leaning back, he stared at his locker, his mouth pressed into his clasped hands, and tried to focus on breathing.

The sparkling white jersey hanging in his locker hypnotized him: *McCONNELL* arching over *51*. Not a souvenir from the gift shop or some sporting goods store. His jersey. A game jersey. Perched on the edge of disaster for three weeks of minor league baseball, he now sat hours away from a major league game. *His* major league game.

He reviewed the scouting report in his head. He visualized a perfect swing. He—

He pictured Aaron on the mound.

Baseball. Right now, baseball.

He imagined turning a flawless double play, Comerica Park's lights glittering off the grass.

Adrenaline seeped throughout his body, numbing any lingering soreness.

A clatter of doors startled him. "Hey, Howie, we got a zombie out here," Carl Peters called into the fitness room.

Curt joined him at the door. "I don't think he's moved."

"Do you think he's breathing?"

"I remember my first game," Curt said. "Scared out of my mind. I made two errors that day."

"I lost one in the sun," the center fielder said.

"And I bet it wasn't a big-time nationally televised game, either."

"No, sir, it wasn't."

"You guys are hilarious," James said, still staring.

Carl patted James on the shoulder as he walked by. "No worries, J-Mac. I got your back out there." Voices from the hall spilled into the clubhouse as more players entered.

"Go get 'em," left fielder Tony Bozio said, tapping the back of James's chair.

Catcher Tyler Cavanaugh lightly bumped him on the shoulder. "Relax, J-Mac."

Over the next half hour, the rest of the team arrived, all offering a few words of reassurance, but letting him sit and stare.

Curt—fully dressed in his navy-and-white batting practice jersey, white pants, hat, and cleats—rolled a chair next to him. "Wes wants you to answer a few questions before the game. After batting practice, right here in the clubhouse. One of the local guys, I think."

James didn't blink.

"Hey, loosen up."

"What if I suck?"

"You're not going to suck. It's just like Toledo. Only more people." Curt smiled. "Lots more people. But that's it."

"But—"

"Relays and cutoffs. Are you all set on those?"

James nodded.

"Remember, tandem relays on all sure doubles. And what about Floyd, their leadoff hitter?"

"He likes to drag bunt the first pitch, so be ready to cover first."

"See? You got this."

James wrung his hands and straightened. A deep, nerve-settling breath gave life to the adrenaline, shooting a tremble down to his toes.

"Now, I've got one more thing for you to wear tonight." He dropped a light-blue wristband in James's lap. "We wear these every Father's Day."

He recognized them. Players, coaches, and umpires throughout the league donned the terry cloth wristbands, and some players used light-blue bats, too; pink wristbands and bats dominated Mother's Day games.

"But we got a little something extra on ours," Curt said.

James turned it over. Stitched through the center: *A-Mac*.

His stomach tightened, and he mustered a breathless "Wow." He slid it onto his left wrist, touched the *A-Mac*, and pictured Aaron on the mound once again.

"You see a ghost?" manager Ernie Mazarron said, leaning against James's locker. He jammed his hands in his back pockets. "I heard they gave you some Depends at Erie. You got 'em on?"

"Nice and snug."

"Good. You're battin' eighth. Get dressed, jog around the outfield, and play some catch. It'll help." In two long strides, Mazarron stood at Carl's locker and cracked up the center fielder with a muttered joke.

Curt slapped James on the knee. "I'll wait for you in the outfield."

James sat a moment longer before pushing out another hard breath. It still did nothing to calm him, but he found the strength to stand. The order from the manager helped. He had tasks: finish getting dressed, take a run, play catch. Routine.

He slid on his batting practice jersey, tucked it in, and retied his cleats three times before they felt tight enough.

As they had in the clubhouse, James's teammates left him alone on his walk through the tunnel and to the dugout, head down and glove cradled under his arm. He hopped up the half-dozen steps to the dugout, then to the field, and without looking up, continued a determined march to the middle of the infield behind the pitcher's mound. Slowly he turned in a circle, gazing at the stadium. A handful of players scattered across the diamond. Some jogged in the outfield; others stretched or played catch. Curt's mitt and a ball lay on the grass beyond third base, and groundskeepers worked on a section of wall near the tarp rolled up behind first base. The stands remained empty except for ushers.

Comerica Park no longer felt like a cathedral, no longer holy.

Now, he stood upon a stage. Opening night. Before the curtain lifted. And his lines jumbled around in his brain.

Get dressed. Jog. Play catch. Routine. Just follow your routine.

Curt whistled and waved James to the outfield behind second base, where he dropped his glove, and they stretched for several minutes before jogging side by side to the left field foul line, then down to the foul pole, along the warning track to center field, and back again. James timed his breathing with his strides, staring ahead, and neither talked. Together, they turned and ran a faster sprint back to center field. James's right leg tightened, and he stretched and shook it out.

"So when are you telling Aaron?" Curt asked while they walked back to the foul line.

"Uh . . . what?"

"Aaron. When are you gonna tell Aaron?"

"Oh. During batting practice. Skipper's got something for him."

Get dressed. Jog. Play catch.

James focused on his throwing accuracy, aiming for Curt's chest no matter the distance. As his arm loosened, he moved back after every few throws until they heaved the ball in a long-toss drill spanning two hundred feet. With a shuffle-step forward, James lined each throw on a shallow arc. He only short-hopped the ball to Curt once.

Curt pointed to the infield, where a coach popped out of the dugout, a bat on his shoulder and third baseman Cordero Ruiz alongside.

They both jogged to the second base position, and Curt fielded the first one, lobbing the ball back to Cordero. "See? Just like Toledo."

James stepped up and sank low. The ball cracked off the bat and bounced out to him soft and true. But his peripheral vision swarmed—the stands, the scoreboards, the suites, the dugouts. A thousand different things barged in; he stumbled forward but still caught the ball in his stomach, and when he stood to throw, Cordero was a speck on the horizon.

Just like Toledo, James thought. He collected himself and tossed the ball back in a simple, easy throw. Cordero caught it at his chest, and Comerica Park snapped back to its ordinary mammoth size.

But with each ground ball during the private early infield practice, the stadium shrank until only the field remained, the same as all the others he'd played on. He had no idea how it would feel when 40,000 fans packed the seats, but he pushed the thought from his brain and concentrated on one ground ball after another.

An hour later, his infield workout complete, James prepped his bat and tugged on his batting gloves, waiting behind the batting dome around home plate while others hit. He kept quiet through the chatter and joking, focusing on the ball off the batting practice pitcher's hand and how it lit up against the dark-green center field backdrop. Carl drove it deep into left field.

"We got company," Curt said, standing next to James.

Lizzie and Aaron bounded down an aisle by the third base dugout, James's parents and Emily following. "Hey, Dad!" Aaron called. He held up his forearms—covered in light-blue wristbands, from his wrists to his elbows.

James and Curt met them near the railing on the home plate side of the dugout. "They gave some to you guys, too?" James said. "Pretty neat, aren't they?"

"Not just us," Emily said.

"It's A-Mac Day!" Aaron said. "They're passing them out to *everybody* when they come in!"

James, dumbstruck again, shook his head at Curt, who laughed. "I had to have at least one more surprise for you." He slapped James on the back. "Last one, I promise."

"Well then, since it's A-Mac Day . . ." James disappeared into the dugout and returned with five white jerseys. He nodded at Aaron's shirt. "You can get rid of that piece of junk Howard jersey you're wearing. I think you'll like this one better." James held up a McConnell 51 jersey, a replica of the one he'd be wearing shortly. He passed one out to each of them but pulled Aaron closer. "I know you've wanted to see me in a Tigers jersey, but now I get to see you in one, too."

Aaron, stunned into silence, rubbed his fingers over the letters and numbers on the back and then traced the Old English *D* on the front. Then he practically leaped into James's arms. "Thanks, Dad. This is . . . Thanks." He unbuttoned the Howard 25 jersey and slipped on the McConnell 51.

James's dad's eyes sparkled as he gazed out across the field. "From Little League to here. And all the games in between." He squeezed his son's shoulder. "I can't believe I get to see you play here."

"Don't go nowhere!" Carl called from home plate. He took

his final swing, launching a line drive to the right field gap, and jogged to the fence. He rested both hands on the railing and fixed Aaron with a challenging stare. "All right, slick. Since 1962, how many times has a Tiger been named the most valuable player—" Aaron started to answer, but Carl held up a hand—"of the All-Star Game?"

"None," Aaron answered quickly.

Carl's grin hardened. "And how many people have won the All-Star MVP more than once?"

"Four."

"Who—?"

"Willie Mays, Steve Garvey, Gary Carter, and Cal Ripken Jr. each won it twice."

"Dang!" Carl said. "Kid's a genius, J-Mac." He glanced over Emily's head. "Can you get a photo?" he asked a staff photographer descending the aisle.

Carl hoisted Aaron over the railing, and for the next several minutes, as batting practice continued in the background, a procession of Tigers got their photos taken with Aaron, his grin spread ear to ear as each of his new friends knelt next to him and hung their arm around his shoulder. Finally the photographer took one of the whole McConnell family standing in the on-deck circle.

One more Tiger wanted his picture taken: manager Ernie Mazarron. He stomped up the dugout stairs, his hands behind his back and his dark eyes fixed on Aaron. Emily started to pull Lizzie back to the stands, but grinning, James told her to wait.

"How are you feeling, kiddo?" Mazarron said.

"Good."

Mazarron straightened. "Just good? We didn't put your dad through three weeks of sweaty socks and coaches yelling at him just so you could feel good."

Aaron giggled and shrank.

"Now, how do you feel?"

"Great."

"Great?"

"Awesome."

"What's that?"

"Awesome!"

"That's better. Because if you feel only 'good' or even 'great,' you can't have this." He brought one hand from behind his back and held out a brand-new baseball. "So you're sure? You're not lying to me?" Aaron reached for it, but Mazarron pulled the ball back. "Awesome? Really?"

"Yep. Awesome."

"All right, then." He handed the ball to Aaron.

"Thank you, Mr. Mazarron."

"I'm not done. Now that's a special baseball, and it's got a special purpose. Only a kiddo who feels awesome can use it. You sure you still feel awesome?" Aaron nodded. "Good. Because you'll also need this."

He brought his other hand forward. Aaron's baseball glove. The dark-tan leather mitt from Christmas. The one that had been oiled but never used. He gave it to Aaron.

Emily's eyes widened. "How—?"

James nodded to his mom.

"We've got an important job for you," Mazarron said. "Dad, would you like the honors?"

James put his hand on Aaron's shoulder. "I didn't know they were actually going to call it 'A-Mac Day' when they asked me about this, but the Tigers want you to throw out the ceremonial first pitch tonight."

One corner of Mazarron's mouth turned up in what passed for his smile.

Aaron paled to the color of his jersey.

"I'll be with you; you get to throw it right to me. It won't be a full game of catch—" James knelt next to Aaron and took both of his shoulders—"but it'll be the closest we've gotten. What do you say?"

Aaron's eyes hesitated on the ball, then the glove, then his dad.

"C'mon, pal."

The boy slid his glove on and jammed the baseball inside. He leaned into his dad's arms.

Emily hugged Aaron from behind. "Can you believe it?" she said. "This is gonna be so cool!"

"What about me?" Lizzie asked. Her McConnell jersey hung nearly to her knees.

"You think I'd forget about you, little lady?" Mazarron said. "You come see me before the game. I've got an important job that requires a beautiful young woman." He winked at Emily. "Two beautiful young women, actually. Now, let's get that picture."

After the photo, Mazarron shook James's parents' hands, and Curt tapped James on the shoulder with his bat. "Hey, J-Mac, our group's up."

James herded his family back to the fence. "All right, I gotta get some swings in. Don't want to embarrass us too much tonight." He tapped the bill of Aaron's Tigers cap and turned back to home plate.

He took only three steps when Aaron snapped out of his shock. "Wait, Dad! Remember: Mendez—"

"Yeah, I know, bud."

"No, really. He's a Tiger killer. He likes to throw the first pitch right down the middle and then work down and away, getting you to chase his slider so he can set you up for either a sinker or something hard inside."

James and Curt both laughed.

"And Floyd, their leadoff hitter—"

"Likes to drag a bunt in the first inning. I'm all ready for that, Mr. Scout." James snapped a small salute.

"He's fast, so you'll have to, like, fly to first to cover. Oh, and Giordano, their regular seventh-inning pitcher. If you get up against him, watch out for his curve. But he likes to work the inside corner, too, right where you like it, and pretty medium speed."

"That scouting job I gave him went straight to his head," Curt said.

"One step at a time," James said. "We need to get Mendez out of the game first." *And I need to still be playing.* "You guys should head out to the stands in left. Tony Bozio's hitting soon. Maybe you'll get some home run balls."

After a final round of hugs, they climbed back into the stands, and James slipped a weight on one of the bats he'd brought from Erie and looped a few practice swings. When his turn came, his family didn't race out to the left field stands; instead, they waited along the railing and cheered every line drive or fly ball, fair or foul. He spent the entire session grinning and laughing. But three pop-ups on the infield left him shaking his head.

"Hands and hips," Curt said. "You're lagging again."

The next pitch streaked right back where it came from, clanging off the metal frame of the pitching screen. No other Tiger had as boisterous of a batting practice applause.

Warm-ups and stretches and time spent with his family helped James relax for the couple of hours leading up to game time. But when he sat back in front of his locker, staring once again at his white game jersey, his stomach knotted. Most of the players were already dressed and out on the field; a few lingered in last-minute preparations or a final text to someone before heading to the dugout. As they wandered out, James found himself back where he began the day: in an empty clubhouse.

He slipped the jersey off the hanger and held it in his lap. Although it appeared the same as the ones he gave his family, this one would see action. Something Emily had said about Aaron's excitement leading up to the game, about James's entry in the *Baseball Encyclopedia*, echoed in his ear. He'd forever be known as an "ex-major leaguer."

A long-ago dream come true.

Slowly he traced the name on the jersey, wondering what new baseball memories awaited him under the bright lights of The Show.

"There he is," Wes Marco said from the hallway. He led a reporter and cameraman into the clubhouse. Curt had been wrong—it wasn't one of the local sports reporters. With the game nationally broadcast, ESPN's *Sunday Night Baseball* crew replaced the local Detroit broadcasters and sent their own reporter to ask James a couple of questions.

"James McConnell, Del Kinsky," Wes introduced.

"Sure, sure, I recognize you," James said, standing and shaking hands. Although James wasn't a giant, he still stood several inches taller than the reporter.

"Thanks for giving me a couple of minutes."

"Hope you don't mind if I finish getting dressed." James slid an arm into his jersey.

Del glanced to the cameraman and nodded to James. A red light appeared above the lens. He straightened his bright-red tie and smoothed the lapels of his navy-blue suit. "Actually, that's a good place to start. How does it feel to be putting on a major league uniform?"

James buttoned the jersey. "Pretty bizarre, actually. It's been such a wild journey getting to this point."

"And your son, Aaron, he's here tonight, correct?"

"Yep, he's in the stands. Well, he's waiting in the dugout with Curt Howard right now. He'll be throwing out the first pitch in a few minutes, so Curt took him down to let him settle his nerves."

"And what about *your* nerves?"

"Hoping they'll, uh, kinda smooth out after the first pitch."

"I know we don't have much time right now, but can you tell me how ready you feel?"

"Well, ya know, I just wanna give it my best shot, and the good Lord willing, things will work out."

Del laughed. "*Bull Durham*! I love it!"

"I'm just glad you got it," James said. "I said that to the press at Erie, and all I got were crickets. But no, seriously, the last week at Toledo, I felt like I finally smoothed the kinks out. I know it'll be different out there—" James jabbed a thumb in the general direction of the field—"but we'll see."

"All right, well, good luck out there." Del turned to the camera. "And that's James McConnell on his major league debut, the culmination of a tremendous feel-good story, playing one game for his son, Aaron. Back to you guys." The camera's red light flicked off.

Del shook hands with James again. "Really, James, good luck. And give my best to Aaron."

"I'll do that."

Wes bumped James's fist. "Go get 'em!"

James tucked in his jersey, squatted a couple times to get comfortable in suddenly tight pants, and headed for the dugout.

He found Curt and Aaron on the far end of the bench,

and while his teammates walked around him and slapped him on the back, James stood and watched.

Curt spoke to Aaron, but the boy focused on the glove in his lap. Occasionally he'd pack the ball into his mitt, but he kept his eyes down. Curt gestured to the field and smiled, his hand streaking in the arc of a relived home run. Aaron nodded but didn't smile. Tony Bozio walked by and patted Aaron on the knee. No reaction. Curt continued talking.

James's breath caught.

Aaron looked so small.

The dugout dwarfed the boy. His feet dangled off the bench, swinging back and forth. James hadn't noticed before how the sleeves of the new McConnell jersey reached past his elbows or how the navy Tigers hat pushed his ears out. He'd always seemed so much bigger in the hospital, especially during his chemo treatments, propping his feet up in the chair and clicking away on his laptop, researching stats. But here, out in the world, it seemed like everything would devour him. James glanced to the field and the section of stands he could see from the dugout. Packed. *How's he going to walk out there?* James thought.

Aaron still didn't look up.

Curt finally gave up talking and sat back, swinging his feet in time with Aaron's.

At last, the boy cracked a thin smile.

He's going to walk out there because he's stared down worse. And because I'll be with him.

Curt saw James coming, said, "Good luck, pal," and got up. James sat down on Aaron's right and draped his arm around his son.

"Seems like a good time to finally break in that glove, huh?" James said. As he figured, Aaron didn't answer. He shoved the ball into the pocket of the mitt and closed it. "Just be sure you don't throw it so hard that it breaks my hand. You do want to put some stats up on that website, after all."

Aaron gave a tiny snort of laughter. James pulled him closer.

"Listen, buddy. I haven't really thanked you for all of this." James felt his eyes brim, but he swallowed hard. "You made such a grown-up decision. You could've asked for anything from Curt, but you chose . . ." The tears threatened again, and this time James wiped them away before they leaked onto his cheek. "You chose to give it to someone else. That takes real courage, Son. And a kindness that, well . . . that people don't see too often." James rubbed Aaron's shoulder. "You're somethin' else, tough guy. Somethin' else."

The public address announcer rambled something James didn't pay attention to, but it amped up the crowd.

"What if I look stupid?" Aaron whispered.

James chuckled softly. He'd said something similar to Curt earlier in the evening.

"You're not gonna look stupid. You're gonna look like a kid who loves baseball. You know Chris Franke's pitching tonight, and I know you remember his form, right? With the leg kick and all?" Aaron nodded against his father's arm. "Well, just shut everyone out, pretend it's you and me in the living room, and try to do a Chris Franke impression. Focus on that, and focus on my mitt, and everything else will work out." James squeezed Aaron's shoulder. "It'll all work out like it's supposed to. Like it was always supposed to."

Aaron nodded again and pulled away from James. He tugged at his mitt's laces and wet his fingers, massaging them deep into the leather. Then he pulled at the laces again, stretched his fingers far inside for a good fit, and sat still.

His eyes remained on the floor.

The stadium din swelled as the PA announcer spoke again;

at the same time the players in the dugout turned to the two McConnells and started clapping.

"That's our cue," James said, and they stood. James took a step, but Aaron froze.

James reached down and took his hand. "C'mon, Aaron. Let's go do this." Together, they walked up the dugout steps.

The curtain rose on the stage of Comerica Park.

The crowd roared.

As they walked out to the dirt strip between the pitcher's mound and home plate, James squeezed Aaron's hand and leaned down. "Look around, Aaron. They're cheering for *you*." They stopped in front of the pitcher's mound, and Aaron finally lifted his head.

He didn't shrink. He didn't bury his face in his dad's side or scurry back to the dugout. He grinned. And he raised his hand in a small wave.

Now, the stadium shook, right down into James's bones.

"Before our honored guest, Aaron McConnell, throws out the ceremonial first pitch to his father, James McConnell," the PA announcer boomed, "would you please direct your attention to the scoreboard in left field for a special presentation."

James knelt and rested his arm around Aaron's waist, shocked at how quickly the crowd hushed.

A home video played: Curt Howard walked into a hospital room and presented Aaron McConnell, lying in a propped-up hospital bed, with a variety of souvenirs. The image cross-faded to Curt leaning down as Aaron whispered something in his ear, and then faded to black. A narrator's voice-over filled the stadium: "It all started when a boy made a wish."

As the footage displayed Curt and James's catch during that first visit to Comerica Park, James tightened his grip around Aaron's waist.

When James flopped face-first onto the infield at West Michigan on his very first ground ball, the crowd howled. Aaron burst with laughter and pointed at the scoreboard.

The screen showed Curt and James talking across home plate at Erie, and James trembled, remembering Curt's words: *"The only way that's going to happen is to forget you have a family. You're not a husband. You're not a dad."*

When James legged out a double at Toledo and dove head-first into second base, the narrator describing how James broke out of his slump after that conversation with Curt, the crowd cheered, and Aaron whispered, "Nice slide."

During a quiet moment in a clubhouse, James sitting on a bench in a T-shirt, his head in his hands, the stadium fell silent again, and Aaron leaned his head on his dad's shoulder.

And when the video ended with the family photo taken that night in the on-deck circle, James pulled Aaron into a hug.

He looked out at the crowd. A thousand threads of light blue wove them together. The wristbands. All with his son's name on them.

He held Aaron at arm's length. "You ready?"

Aaron pulled down his hat and rubbed the ball into his glove.

James tapped the brim of the boy's cap and jogged ten feet away down the dirt strip toward home plate, squatted down like a catcher, and smacked his fist into the palm of the mitt. Aaron stood on the leading edge of the mound.

But before he threw it, he knelt down. And in the heart of a raucous sold-out stadium, with tens of thousands of people watching and waiting, Aaron closed his eyes and gently brushed his hand overtop the grass.

James's heart swelled. *His first real baseball memory. In the middle of all this.*

He reached his hand out and did the same thing. *And now it's my best one.*

Aaron jumped up and stared at his dad, leaning in and pretending to get the sign from the catcher, his lips drawn and his eyes squinting. He stepped back and flung his arms over his head like Chris Franke, kicked his left leg as high as he could like Chris Franke, and tried to throw ninety-seven miles an hour like Chris Franke.

The ball, on a soft arc, bounced in front of James's feet.

He scooped it cleanly and popped up, holding his glove high to the crowd, which thundered once again. He jogged back to Aaron and picked him up, and together they waved to every part of the stadium. As they trotted off the field, the Tigers surrounded them, high-fiving and fist-bumping Aaron; even the Minnesota Twins, all standing in front of the dugout or on the steps, clapped, and James tipped his cap to them.

The players dispersed—some jogged back into the outfield for some last stretches; others ducked inside the dugout for more bubble gum or sunflower seeds; a few milled around the on-deck circle, adjusting their wristbands or pants or caps. Aaron and James remained on the grass outside the dugout, chatting with players and coaches before Emily and Lizzie ran out of the dugout and group-hugged Aaron.

"You did amazing!" Emily said.

"That was *so loud*!" Lizzie yelled.

The PA announcer's voice once again reverberated through the park, asking everyone to rise for the national anthem. The two kids stood between their parents. James removed his hat and held it over his heart, but Aaron hesitated. James tapped his chest with his hat. "It's okay. Stand tall," he said. Aaron slowly removed his hat. James clasped his hand, and Aaron straightened, his bald head glowing in a mixture of fading sunlight and stadium lights. He held his chin high toward the flag behind center field.

After the crowd drowned the last words of the singer's crystal clear voice, a few players drifted back toward the dugout and signed some more autographs. Curt and James led Aaron toward the gate behind home plate, where a Tigers staff member waited. "Remember, give it all you got," Curt said. Aaron slapped him a high five and disappeared into the dark tunnel.

Back in front of the dugout, Emily held a fidgeting Lizzie by the shoulders. The Minnesota Twins lineup, announced in a low, monotone, purposefully unenthusiastic voice, drew several "Who cares?" from the stands at the mention of each name.

"Think he'll do okay?" Emily asked, slipping an arm around James's waist.

"Curt told him to give it all he's got, so we'll see what happens."

After a few minutes, the announcer returned. "And now, ladies and gentlemen, it is our pleasure to have our honored guest Aaron McConnell announce tonight's starting lineup for your Detroit Tigers!"

The first three names quavered with Aaron's nervousness but strengthened at the mention of Tony Bozio batting fourth. The fans' mad cheering for their favorites loosened him up, and he got into it. He tried to roll his tongue through Alejandro Santana, called Curt Howard "Howie," and jazzed up the *o*'s in third baseman Cordero Ruiz's name, just like the PA announcer would normally do.

But then he paused. The scoreboard showed James smiling at the camera, a bat on his shoulder, and then it flashed to his turning a double play with the Mud Hens.

"And now . . . making his major league debut," Aaron said, his voice soft but growing stronger as the crowd noise intensified, "batting eighth and playing second base . . . number 51 . . . my dad . . . J-Mac . . . James MaaaaaaacConnnnnnnelllllllllllllll!"

No one in the stadium heard that catcher Tyler Cavanaugh batted ninth.

"Well done, young man," the PA announcer said. "Now, delivering our lineup card to home plate and the game ball to the mound this evening, please welcome Emily and Elizabeth McConnell!"

"Go for it, Lizard!" James said.

Lizzie wasn't shy. As soon as she stepped toward home plate, she waved like a queen in a parade. Manager Ernie Mazarron laughed as he accompanied them, and Emily handed the card to the home plate umpire, receiving handshakes from the Twins manager and the umpiring crew. The home plate ump presented a ball to Lizzie and pointed at the mound. She scampered down the dirt strip and placed it gently on the rubber, waving again to all parts of the stadium. The crowd ate it up.

As was custom on Father's Day, a child, most of them other players' kids, ran out to each position on the infield and awaited the Tigers. Aaron's stilted jog left him far behind the other kids, but glove in hand, still holding the ball from the first pitch, he ambled all the way to second base.

James watched from the dugout, his chest thudding until Aaron stopped and turned around. Almost before he knew what happened, the starting lineup loped from the dugout to their positions, and the stadium rumbled.

Curt swatted him on the back. "Let's go, rook."

James couldn't breathe, but he kept his eyes on Aaron. The boy even gave a slight wave to James, beckoning him. James bounced up the dugout steps and, shoulder to shoulder with Curt, jogged onto the infield.

Once he reached Aaron, he knelt down. Around the field,

players hugged their kids or signed a baseball the child had brought out. James pulled the ball out of Aaron's mitt and took a pen from his pocket. "This was the ball you used for the first pitch, right?"

"Yeah."

"Well, I'm not sure you need my autograph," James said, "so I'll write this instead." He scrawled a message and handed it to Aaron.

Aaron's bottom lip trembled when he read it:

You are my wish come true.

He threw his arms around his dad's neck.

"Don't forget this moment, Son. And don't forget how much I love you."

Aaron wiped his eyes when he let James go. "Remember, be ready for the leadoff bunt."

They slapped gloves, and Aaron trotted back to the dugout with the youngster who had been at first base.

James didn't move until he got a final wave from his son at the edge of the dugout, and after whispering a prayer that he wouldn't screw up, he met Curt behind second base and took in the magnitude of humanity surrounding him.

"Time to get busy, J-Mac," Curt said.

"If I can breathe." A practice grounder bounced out to him. His hands hardened into stone. He managed to hide the fact that he almost booted it and made a nice easy throw to first base. *Just playing catch . . . just playing catch . . .*

Just playing catch in front of 40,000 people. Perfectly normal.

13

THE GAME BALL ZIPPED AROUND THE INFIELD and
ended back in Chris Franke's hands. James jogged to his position. He tried spitting into the palm of his mitt, but nothing
came out. Sweat worked just as well, so he rubbed his clammy
throwing hand into the leather and pounded a fist into the
palm, senselessly pulling at a few of the laces, hoping it made
him appear like any other ballplayer. He blasted out a couple of
short, sharp breaths and pulled his cap down tighter. It helped
shut out the sea of people around him, and he zeroed in on the
plate, the only place he felt he could look without suddenly
forgetting everything he'd learned.

The short, speedy Nathan Floyd strolled from the on-deck
circle and sliced sharp practice swings a step outside of the
left-handed batter's box. He settled at the plate, swished his
bat twice more, and bounced up and down at the knee, his
bat waggling behind his head, ready for the first pitch. Chris
Franke stood on the mound as tall and straight and still as a
gunslinger about to draw, glove out front and steady at his

chin. Catcher Tyler Cavanaugh flashed the sign for an outside fastball.

All of the scouting reports, including his son's, screamed in James's mind.

"Here we go," he muttered.

At the delivery, James stepped forward and down into his ready position, but he cheated a step toward first base to be ready for the bunt everyone told him was coming.

But Floyd didn't bunt. He didn't stick a quick, level, stationary bat out over the plate at the first pitch. Instead, he slashed a flat, slapping swing at the fastball.

The line drive streaked like a white laser to James's right. He took one crossover step and dove, his eyes on the ball, closing what he thought at first to be an impossible distance. With a jolt like a boxer's punch, the ball smacked surely into his mitt.

And then for James, everything stopped—his momentum, the noise, his breathing. For an excruciating, blissful eternity, he simply hung above the ground, completely outstretched. No more scouting reports to worry about, no more pregame jitters . . . no more agonizing over Aaron's health. Just him, suspended in flight, bathed in frozen camera flashes and the stadium's glow and a soft evening sunlight, a baseball snug in his glove.

Then he fell.

The reddish infield dirt wasn't as soft as he had hoped, and what little air remained in his lungs blew out in a grunt. Yet the ball remained in place.

The noise returned.

Still not breathing, James first held up his glove to show the umpire he'd caught it, then rose to his knees, his brand-new white jersey streaked with Comerica Park dirt as if a grounds-keeper had taken a paint roller to his chest. He flipped the ball in the air, caught it in his throwing hand, and snapped it to Curt Howard. When James stood, he brushed his glove once over his chest, sending a plume of dust eddying around him, and took to inspecting his mitt again, rubbing it, tugging the laces, and pounding the pocket once more, all while his chest constricted in a vacuum.

He flashed a one-out sign to Curt and then to Carl in center field. Chris Franke took an extra walk around the mound to give James a chance to reclaim his wind. The pitcher bounced the rosin bag in his palm and, through the puff of white dust, pointed at James—"Nice play, rookie," the gesture said. James pointed back a silent thanks. A massive breath suddenly flooded his lungs, but he controlled the inhale through his nose and let it slowly leak back out.

He braved a glance around the stadium, and the 40,000 roaring people faded away. Only the world between the lines existed. Only the game remained.

His game.

The next batter struck out looking at a knee-buckling curve that broke into the heart of the plate, but the number three batter, after a lengthy at bat, yanked a base hit in the hole between Curt and third baseman Cordero Ruiz. James didn't have to worry about the base runner long—Chris jammed the cleanup hitter on the first pitch, splintering his bat with a harmless bouncer to the first baseman. Dawson Frey scooped it up, waved off the pitcher racing to cover the bag, and made the out himself.

And just like that, faster than James thought possible, his first half-inning in the major league was in the scorebook.

James walked the length of the dugout, high-fiving the other ballplayers. The celebration for his fine play culminated when manager Ernie Mazarron patted him on the butt. Then, back to business. James removed his cap, set it on top of his glove, and sat on the bench. The trainer brought him a cup of Gatorade, which he gulped, icing his parched throat.

Curt sat next to him. "Unbelievable! For a second, I didn't think you were ever going to land." They gazed out at the game, where Ramon Mendez lived up to his reputation as a Tiger killer. Carl, the Tigers' leadoff hitter, jammed his bat into the ground, having struck out on four pitches.

James didn't care. His eyes still saw the line drive shooting off the bat, and his hand still felt the thump of it popping into his glove. If Mazarron came down right then and there and told him his cup of coffee was over, it wouldn't have mattered one bit.

The Tigers went down easily in the bottom of the first, but back in the dugout after a routine top of the second inning, James's hands tingled. If a couple of the next batters reached base, he'd be up to bat. One at bat to give him a complete *Baseball Encyclopedia* entry for Aaron.

Aaron.

James didn't push him out of his mind. He let the images surround him—of Aaron's grin, his Tigers hat, the McConnell jersey; of the boy bending down in the center of the national spotlight to close his eyes and feel the grass and capture his first true baseball memory.

He wanted to see him, all of his family, and as Mendez finished the last of his warm-up pitches, James jumped up to the field and scanned the suite section. He found them sitting in the stadium chairs outside the suite, and he waved like a fool. Several fans between him and them waved back, but Aaron, Emily, Lizzie, and his parents didn't notice.

Tony Bozio flied out to lead off the inning—a stadium full of "Boz! Boz! Boz!" chants couldn't provide the extra oomph needed to lift it over the fence—but the Tigers' designated hitter, Alejandro Santana, reached base on a long single. As Curt Howard marched to the plate, James walked to the fencing in front of the dugout, yelling, "C'mon, Howie, get us started!" And he did start something—an inning-ending, around-the-horn double play with a sharp one-hopper to third base. James collected Curt's hat and glove and ran it out to the shortstop.

The anticipation of batting in the bottom half of the inning rattled him. He botched his first warm-up grounder from Dawson and made it worse by flicking the ball in the dirt. He tried to short-hop the throw down from catcher Tyler Cavanaugh to end the warm-ups, but it skipped off his glove and trickled behind the bag. Tremors shot through his hands. Distracted and tightening with apprehension, James did the one thing he wished he hadn't: he looked around at the stadium.

The 40,000 people returned. Mesmerizing. Their cheers settled upon him like a smothering blanket; sweat seeped from his temples, and his throwing hand immediately clammed. But he couldn't wipe it dry. He froze, staring in the direction of the suites where his family sat, unable to see them. Only people, a mass of people, an ocean of people, a planetful of people. And he suddenly felt so very, very far away from the most important game of his life.

He never crouched into his ready position on Chris's first pitch. Fortunately the catcher called for a time-out and waved for the middle infielders to join him on the mound. It didn't register with James until Curt hollered for him.

"What do you want?" Chris snapped, flustered at having his rhythm broken.

"I thought you'd want a second baseman behind you," Tyler said, his mask pushed up to the top of his helmet. He turned to James. "You feel like joining us tonight, J-Mac?"

Embarrassed and ticked off, James said, "Sorry, guys. Yeah, I'm here. Thanks for the kick in the pants." Curt followed up the verbal kick with a glove slap on the butt.

The umpire began his approach from home plate to break up the conference.

"Bust him inside on the next one," Tyler said as he pulled his mask down. "Then, J-Mac, be ready for a nice, easy ground ball."

Curt and James both tapped Chris with their gloves and jogged back to their positions, James cursing himself the whole way.

The Twins hitter broke his bat on the tight fastball, fouling it off, and as he retrieved another bat, Tyler nodded to James. He squatted behind the plate and, when everyone came set again, signaled for an outside fastball. The right-handed hitter lunged at the pitch, cueing it off the end of his bat but with enough power to bounce it out to the Tigers' rookie second baseman.

Back home, James had always instructed his high schoolers that the second they started thinking about a ground ball as it raced toward them, they might as well just stand up and let it roll right on by. Dropping down into fielding position too soon brought out every detail of the moment: inconsistencies in the grass, pebbles in the dirt, the lightning speed of the runner, the gusting wind ready to blow the throw over the first baseman and into the dugout. The ball became a Medusa, turning hands into stone, locking knees, and making an infielder aim his glove. The successful infielder never aimed. He trusted his training and instinct and muscle memory. He let his body naturally center itself, charged lightly on his feet, and then he'd "point and shoot"—drop down immediately, snatch the ball, cushion it up into his gut, stand, and throw. All in one motion. Graceful.

James thought about this one. Just like he had on almost

every ground ball at West Michigan and for half the week at Erie. He thought about how the stadium lights illuminated the ball like a white firefly. He thought about how each bounce on the pristine grass did nothing to change its direction. He thought about how much speed scrubbed off after each hop. He thought about how the ball seemed to skip once it hit the dirt. He thought that maybe he played too far back and that he should charge. He thought that maybe his pants would split when he dropped down low to field it. He thought he heard a million video cameras whir to life to capture the next viral YouTube sensation of a routine ground ball smacking a major leaguer right in the nose.

He thought about a big fat *E4* up on Aaron's website—error, second baseman.

He froze.

Someone—he guessed Curt, maybe Tyler—shouted, "One!" and James stopped thinking. He rose back up briefly, shuffled forward a few steps, and in one graceful motion, dropped down, his right hand above the heel of his glove, gobbled up the ball, cushioned it to his chest, rose, and snapped a throw to Dawson at first. The runner was out by twelve steps. James tried his best to nonchalant the customary throw around the infield and flash of one out to the outfield.

This has got to stop, he thought. *You're in Comerica Park, you're wearing a Tigers uniform, and you're really playing in a major league game. Get over it. Settle down, focus on the game, and just play.*

He zoned in on home plate.

The number nine hitter laced a single to right field, and a walk to the leadoff hitter, Floyd, put runners at first and second with one out. Curt waggled two fingers between himself and James and pointed to second base, saying, "Let's turn it."

A hard, perfectly routine double-play grounder shot to

Curt. James broke for the bag, his eyes on the shortstop, his glove at his chest. His feet timed perfectly, James caught the flip from Curt while sweeping across the bag, planted, and heaved a throw to first.

He never saw Floyd bearing down on him. The speed-ster had burst out of the gates from first base to break up the double play, slid hard into James, and a tangle of arms and legs and dirt rolled over second base.

The cheers told James they had completed the double play; he never saw it. Floyd unknotted his legs from James's body. "Hey, you okay, man?"

"Nice takeout," James said. Floyd cackled. "Had to give me some scars to remember today, didn't you?" They clasped hands and pulled each other to their feet, and then both patted the other on the butt.

Curt jogged with him back to the dugout. "You all right?"

James didn't answer. At the moment, everything hurt, but he didn't have time for the pain; batting second in the inning, he had to grab a helmet and a bat and get in the on-deck circle. The trainer met him in front of the dugout, but James waved him off.

Cordero Ruiz, a methodical hitter, gave James a little time to shake off the collision, but his generosity turned obnoxious. After every pitch, he'd step out, fasten and refasten his batting gloves, wave two slow swings, step back, hold a hand up to the umpire, then settle in.

James looped some dry swings while in the on-deck circle, and his legs, screaming a moment ago, numbed with adrena-line. He willed Cordero to speed it up.

Foul ball.

The crowd groaned, and so did James.

The batting glove adjustment. The swings. The hand to the ump.

Another foul ball.

More groans.

James gritted his teeth, slid a weight onto the barrel of the bat, and chopped two full-speed swings.

Ball one.

With nothing else to do to calm himself, he knelt down, knocked the weight off, and leaned the bat against his shoulder.

Ball two.

James closed his eyes.

Foul tip.

You've got to be kidding me!

The batting glove adjustment. The swings. The hand to the ump.

Hurry it up, Cord!

Finally a solid crack. The crowd swelled, but the fly ball fell harmlessly into the left fielder's glove, sending the fans back into their seats.

And then they began cheering again.

Whenever a Tiger walked to the plate, the loudspeakers blared the player's theme song. Some had Latin music, others hip-hop; Tyler Cavanaugh marched from the on-deck circle to Hank Williams Jr.'s "A Country Boy Can Survive." In all of the hoopla surrounding the night, James had completely forgotten to pick out a song for his at bats.

But his teammates remembered.

The Whitecaps made him run around the field like a cheerleader carrying a flag. The SeaWolves newspapered his locker. The Mud Hens put him on trial in Kangaroo Court.

And now "Dancing Queen" blared over the loudspeakers.

James looked at his cleats and shook his head. "Wonderful," he mumbled.

The crowd loved it, and his teammates stood on the top

steps of the dugout laughing and pointing and dancing. Even Ernie Mazarron's red cheeks rose in a mischievous grin.

The music cut off when James stepped onto the dirt sur-rounding home plate. He squeezed the bat handle and swung some more, praying each cut would calm him down. Every swing just made his stomach flop. He couldn't stall any longer.

"Hey, no softball stuff now," James said to the Twins catcher. "I want the real deal."

The catcher snorted. "Don't worry, rookie."

He dug in his right foot at the back edge of the batter's box and spread his feet wide. He pushed out one long breath, jabbed the bat at the pitcher, and shifted his weight back, lev-eling his bat. He only had to slash it forward on a level plane through the strike zone.

Mendez, tall on the mound, leaned in, nodded, and smiled. *Crap.*

James never saw the first pitch. He only heard the pop of the catcher's mitt and the ump bellowing, "Hiiiike!"

He stepped out and looked at his bat. A toothpick. A nearly three-foot-long toothpick. Trying to hit an aspirin. He glanced at the dugout, and Curt stood on the top step, his hands out, palms to the ground. He pushed them down. *Calm down,* Curt mouthed. *Relax.* He jabbed two fingers at his eyes. *See it.* He pretended to hold a bat. *Hit it.*

James pushed his helmet down—it didn't make him feel any more secure—and stepped back in.

When the next pitch left Mendez's hand, James knew instantly it wouldn't be anywhere near the plate. The catcher short-hopped it out of the dirt. He let another pitch go by, this one above the strike zone. The dugout chattered.

The next fastball streaked for the heart of the plate, and James's eyes lit up. His hands shot forward, too late by a fraction. The ball clipped the handle, lifted a few inches, and streaked into the screen behind home plate for a foul ball and strike two. Making contact with a major league fastball, however, surged his confidence, and the bat thickened in his hands.

The next pitch, a curveball, shattered that confidence.

His hitter's eye judged it clipping the outside part of the plate. If he let it go, it'd be a called third strike, yet it wasn't a good pitch to hit.

A curveball. Life had been a curveball for James. Ever since Aaron's first diagnosis. One curve after another. From treatment to setbacks to remission to relapses.

Curveball.

His son's tooth-filled grin filled his mind.

James knew what to do with the pitch.

He threw his hands out front and leaned into it, the barrel of the bat trailing behind to punch the ball to the opposite field. The contact rattled his hands, having missed the bat's sweet spot by a few inches, but it wasn't a worthless ground ball, either; that much he felt in the *thud*. And maybe, if the stars were aligned . . . just maybe . . .

He dropped the bat and sprinted for first.

The thunderous cheer told him what his eyes didn't see.

A base hit.

By the time he rounded first, the second baseman picked himself up from diving on the outfield grass and caught the ball from the right fielder. The umpire held up his hands in a time-out, and the ball, with no fanfare, rolled toward the Tigers' dugout to be saved—a brief blink-and-you'll-miss-it nod of congratulations from the opposing team of a rookie's first big league hit.

All through Tyler Cavanaugh's at bat, the crowd didn't stop cheering. And when James trotted off the field after being forced out at second on Tyler's ground ball to third, the fans behind the dugout gave him a standing ovation.

No one moved, however, in the dugout. No sound, no clapping; no one glanced in his direction. He slid his helmet into the rack and tried to "no-big-deal" his way down to the other end of the dugout; the other players continued carrying on their own conversations, ignoring him. Until he reached the middle. Then they yelled and pounced, the silent treatment gag exploding, and roughed him up in their congratulations. Curt took James's head in both of his hands and tousled his hair.

When James trotted out in the next inning, he felt the roller coaster of emotions level out. With his first at bat in the scorebook, the sold-out crowd melted away again, and this time, they stayed away.

Boz put the Tigers on the scoreboard in the bottom of the fourth inning with a long, two-run home run to left field, but the Twins struck back the next inning, scoring two runs of their own during an atypical shaky inning from the Tigers' ace pitcher. The bleeding finally stopped when a hard one-hopper streaked at James, who didn't have time to even lower into his fielding position. The ball jumped straight up into his gut; pure instinct took over, and he swiveled on his hips, sidearmed the ball to Curt at second, and the shortstop threw a dart to first. The double play squashed any chance at a rally.

Chris Franke slammed his glove onto the bench, swigged half a cup of Gatorade, and threw the rest at the wall. He stomped down to the end of the dugout where James secured his batting gloves and pushed on his helmet, and he slapped the rookie on the shoulder. "Let's go, J-Mac. Get me another run. That's all I need; then we'll finish it for Aaron."

James, again the second batter of the inning, watched from the on-deck circle as Cordero laced a two-balls, no-strikes fastball base hit to left field. Before he stepped into the batter's box, he studied the blur of meaningless arm swipes, nose taps, and chest brushes from the third base coach. The first curveball jelly-legged him and smacked into the catcher's mitt with a bellowing strike call from the ump. He backed out again, watched another series of pointless signs, and relaxed at the next pitch, low right out of the pitcher's hand. Too low. It skipped in front of the plate, scooting by the catcher. Cordero darted to second on the wild pitch.

James spotted the third base coach's bunt sign buried amid a dozen other throwaways. The Twins shifted into a bunt defense, but he squared to the low fastball and caught it with his bat, deadening the ball; it bounced a half-dozen times down the third base line. He didn't slow up until the first baseman caught it and bounced off the bag.

The first base coach slapped James's hand as he jogged by on his way back to the dugout, and his teammates congratulated him on the sacrifice bunt as if he had knocked in a run. Tyler Cavanaugh's sharp single to center did just that, pushing the Tigers back into the lead.

It didn't stop there. Right as James sat down on the bench, they all rose again, swarming around Tyler, who scored on Carl Peters's stand-up triple into Comerica Park's cavernous right-center field gap. A batter later, Carl didn't even have to slide into home on Shawn Janneson's sacrifice fly. Reputed Tiger killer Ramon Mendez didn't come back to pitch the sixth inning.

The Twins, however, refused to go quietly, stinging Chris for back-to-back hits to lead off the seventh and scoring a run to make it 5 to 3. Mazarron allowed Chris one more batter, a ground ball to Curt, before he bounced out of the dugout. He covered the distance from the dugout to the mound in a handful of strides, his hands in his back pockets and his eyes on the ground. Without a word, he held his hand out for the game ball.

Curt and James met behind second base during the pitching change. "How you holding up?" Curt asked.

"Can't believe it's the seventh already. You were right. It flies by."

"So what else was Aaron doing tonight?" Curt looked in the direction of his suite, where the McConnells sat.

"He's getting an inning each in the radio and TV booths. And then one with the official scorekeeper, which I know he'll love."

"You think he's enjoying himself?"

"Honestly, I haven't tried to think of it."

"Well, try to soak it up. If they tie this thing up . . ." Curt shook his head, unsure of what the manager might do.

"I know; I might get yanked. Skip still wants to win, after all. I do, too."

During relief pitcher Glenn Olsen's last warm-up pitches, James walked to the grass on the infield and lifted his chin to the lights. The energy of the crowd seeped into his skin. Then he squatted a few steps in front of second base. He didn't care if he looked foolish. He wanted to savor this one moment, perhaps the last one he'd spend on a major league field.

And out on the field, in front of cameras and tens of thousands watching, he wanted to send a sign to one person.

He cupped his hand at the brim of his cap, shielding the lights, and scanned the suites. Faintly, he thought he spotted someone waving from where his family sat. It didn't matter who it was. He waved back. And while still looking up, he brushed his hand over the grass. When he stood, he held his glove on his heart and waved again.

His mind drifted between the game and the suite for the rest of the inning.

While the crowd sang "Take Me Out to the Ball Game," "God Bless America," and one verse of "YMCA" in the seventh-inning stretch, James's shoulders sank at the sight of two new outfielders for the Twins, defensive substitutions to counter the upcoming relief pitchers the Tigers would trot to the mound. Now, in the later innings, baseball's chess match began, and with the Tigers in second place in the Central division, he knew Mazarron wouldn't get cute managing. He felt like a pawn about to be sacrificed.

For the moment, however, he still led off the bottom half of the seventh inning, and he marched toward the helmet and bat rack at the far end of the dugout. He nearly walked into Ernie Mazarron. The skipper wasn't about to move.

"Well, Jimmy, whaddayathink?" A flurry of sunflower seed shards exploded from the manager's mouth. He stuffed in another handful, and they bulged his cheek. "You ready to turn into a pumpkin?"

"You're asking me?"

"It's been known to happen."

With his stay of baseball execution, James surveyed the field. Vincente Giordano had taken the mound for the Twins. "Well . . . Aaron read up on Giordano—" he flicked his head toward the field—"and he thinks I can pound his fastball. And I've only got one night under the lights. So if it's all the same to you, I'll take my chances."

The players overheard, and they hooted, "Put 'im in the book, J-Mac! Put 'im in the book!"

Mazarron smiled, nodded once, and returned to his place at the base of the dugout steps.

After the first pitch, a strike at the belt, James knew Aaron was right. He held off on two close pitches—both nasty curves that ended up just outside the strike zone—and with the count in his favor at two balls and one strike, he shifted his weight back, ready for the fastball on the inside part of the plate.

It came. His hands darted inside on a straight path, his hips snapped open, and he extended through the hitting zone.

The feel of the ball hitting the bat's sweet spot was almost no feeling at all, as if he had disintegrated the ball, "knocked the cover off of it," just like one of his childhood movie heroes, Roy Hobbs.

It streaked like a bolt of lightning into the night sky, up toward the lights, higher and farther than he'd ever hit a base-ball in his life, a smoking vapor trail, a jet into the heavens. He felt a thousand feet tall. Invincible.

He flicked the bat aside, watching the ball laser skyward, the crowd's cheers billowing to a crescendo, and he trotted. No reason to sprint. He knew. As he approached first base, camera flashes rippled through the stadium.

He followed the ball all the way down until it settled softly in the left fielder's glove for out number one. The crowd groaned.

In that instant, James realized that a part of the perception of professional baseball players he had before this whole saga began was true after all—these guys *were* superheroes. At least the ones who could slug home runs.

The next three batters for the Tigers rode the buzz James created with his long fly ball and added another run before the inning ended. James never moved more than a few feet from his position during the top of the eighth inning, and when the ninth inning rolled around, closer Carlos Espinoza stomped to the mound looking for his fifteenth save.

James hesitated, his foot on the dugout's top step, and savored one more moment: the sweat on his lips and the dryness in his mouth. The body odor and leather and bubblegum and wet sunflower seeds and nasty chewing tobacco. The skin of dust coating his arms and cheeks. The people, all around him, cheering for a handful of men playing a game. His anxiety leading up to this night had almost prevented him from absorbing all of the wonderment as he focused on his performance. But now, watching his teammates take their positions for the final three outs, knowing that one of those positions sat waiting for him, that they looked to *him* to help finish out the game . . .

For a moment, he felt as if he were living—and *had* lived—a different life.

The life he had walked away from.

Absently, he adjusted his glove and the light-blue wristband above it. The stitched *A-Mac* stared back at him.

This wasn't a different life. This was *his* life. The life God had given him. The one in which he met and fell in love with the girl of his dreams. The one in which he held his newborn children as they cried in his arms. The one that he believed, with every piece of tragic news or triumphant moment, he'd been called to live.

The one in which he stood by his son's side through their worst nightmares.

The one in which he made his son's wish come true.

He touched Aaron's name on the wristband. This life had brought him to this moment, when more than 40,000 people carried his son's name on their wrists.

"Hey, Cinderella, the clock ain't struck twelve yet," the skipper called from the other end of the dugout.

James grinned, tipped his cap, and sprinted for his position.

Carlos fanned the first two batters on six straight pitches, and with the crowd on their feet, their clapping to each and every pitch thudding deep in James's chest, the last batter

grounded weakly to Curt at short. Through the PA system,
a victorious tiger's roar split the stadium.

James and Curt met at second base for a handshake and high-
fived the outfielders as they jogged in. Some jumped and
knocked bodies with each other; a few performed carefully
choreographed handshakes. A line formed to meet the other
Tigers—reserve players and coaches streaming from the dugout, each one with a smile or a shove for James. Usually both.

There seemed to be a gap in the line approaching James,
at least from what he could tell by the tops of their heads, and
Aaron jumped at his dad, slapping his hand and diving into his
arms. James knelt and gathered him into a hug.

"You did it!" Aaron yelled. "That was amazing!"

The rest of the Tigers abandoned the line and closed a
boisterous circle around the two McConnells near the mound,
jumping up and down and screaming, careful not to trample
the boy.

Tony Bozio pulled Aaron away, and the mob broke up
when Boz lifted Aaron onto his shoulders and jogged around
in front of the third base dugout, waving and cheering at the
crowd. While the other players patted James or pushed him
around again on their way to the dugout, Tony set Aaron down
near Del Kinsky, the reporter who interviewed James before
the game. Del waved him over. The applause from the crowd
behind the dugout soared as he neared.

Del raised the microphone and glanced from the camera
to James. "And here's the man of the hour, the rookie, James
McConnell. By the sounds of it, you'd think you won the game
on a walk-off home run!" He thrust the microphone in front of
James, who draped an arm around Aaron's shoulder. The boy
looked from his dad to the reporter to the camera.

"I know, pretty crazy, right?" James said.

"You told me before the game that you hoped your nerves would settle down after the first pitch. And then, on the very first pitch, you dive for a line drive and catch it! Unbelievable! Did that help calm you down?"

"As soon as I started breathing again."

"And now that it's all done, what are your thoughts?"

James pushed his hat back. "What a ride. It's been a whirlwind. We can't thank the Tigers enough, and all the minor league teams, the players, and coaches. Early on, at West Michigan, it didn't look too good, being worried about this guy and all." He shook Aaron. "But things worked out, and tonight . . . I tell ya, with everything that happened before the game and getting to catch Aaron's first pitch? That would've been fine for me if it had ended right there."

"But it didn't end there. James McConnell and his son, Aaron, joining me on the field tonight, the one and only A-Mac for tonight's special game." He leaned down to Aaron. "I hear you have a website for your dad, for his major league stats."

"Yep." Aaron's cheeks reddened.

"And throwing out the first pitch, how was that?"

"Scary."

"Now, I also heard that the guys up in the booth couldn't stump you tonight with their stats questions; is that right?"

Aaron shook his head, his smile spread wide.

"Well, I'm not gonna try. So what did you think of your dad out there tonight? Did he do okay? He got a hit, made some nice plays . . ."

Aaron's grin grew, if possible, even wider. He cocked his head up at James. "He did awesome."

The reporter stood. "James, let me ask you: how is—?"

A pair of shaving cream pies appeared from behind and smashed into James's and Aaron's faces, interrupting Del mid-sentence; some even splattered onto his bright-red tie and navy-blue suit. Aaron coughed and laughed. James wiped thick globs out of his eyes and flicked them to the ground, then smeared some off of Aaron's face. Through the haze, he thought he spotted Carl Peters running away.

"If you can get the celebratory shaving cream out of your mouth," Del continued, "I'm sure folks want to know the latest on Aaron's progress."

"He's doing great. We think we'll be able to be on our way home soon to continue his treatment there. We're still hoping for a bone marrow transplant, though, so to everyone who's listening—" he looked directly at the camera—"get on the registry. Lots of people, not just Aaron, could use it. We still have a lot of work ahead of us to get this guy all the way healthy."

"And there are a lot of people who I'm sure will keep you in their thoughts and prayers."

James pulled Aaron closer and nodded his thanks.

"But can I ask you one more thing? This taste of professional baseball—you're still young, you held your own tonight, and the guys in the booth were talking about your college stats. Have you thought about working out this off-season and doing some tryout camps next year?"

James laughed and wiped more shaving cream off his face. "Honestly, it never crossed my mind. I've been so focused on just getting to today."

"How about if someone gives you an invitation to spring training? Think you'd give it another shot? It had to be your lifelong dream, and now maybe a door's been opened."

James laughed again, but not as heartily as before.

A lifelong dream.

Maybe at one time. And maybe at various times through the years after walking away. During the what-ifs and second-guessing.

But now, under these stadium lights, in front of this camera . . . not anymore. For what he felt the moment he ran onto the field in a Detroit Tigers uniform paled against the thrill in his heart as he pictured his real dream, his true wish.

Aaron leaned into his leg, and James squeezed the boy's shoulder.

"You know, it would be awfully nice if someone did that, but really, right now, on the field with my son . . . this is a pretty good place to announce my 'retirement.' Next spring is going to be busy."

"Why's that?"

"I've got this young man to play catch with."

14

AS HE SAT IN THE PASSENGER SEAT of Curt Howard's SUV, James only heard the sounds.

Aaron announcing his name in the starting lineup.

The roar of a tiger over the stadium loudspeakers at the final out.

The wild cheer of a group of sweaty grown men surrounding him and Aaron after the game.

They mingled together in a great choir, yet each retained its distinctive voice. The images had dissolved into blurs of a night—of three weeks, really—that had been the fastest of his life. He knew these blurs would someday sharpen into snapshots, but for right now, they gelled together into an amorphous collage of colors that pulsated to the sounds of his son's voice and a tiger roar and a happy bunch of ballplayers.

He leaned his head back, and his glassy stare took in the dark landscape rushing by, the vehicle's headlights illuminating only a bit of the expressway's shoulder. After an evening underneath Comerica Park's stadium lights, the darkness soothed his eyes. Together with the physical and mental exhaustion, he felt himself sink into the leather seat.

They talked some about the Tigers' upcoming road trip, about James getting "officially released" by the Tigers after the game, about staying in touch through the coming months. Curt teased him about the parade of national interviews Wes had lined up for the morning. "Now you *really* hit the big time. Nervous? You're probably nervous. I'd be nervous."

Chitchat, all of it.

Each dark mile took him one more step away from baseball and back to the hospital. The small talk occupied James, but not enough to completely mask the blossoming fear of what would happen if Aaron never achieved a remission. Or if he did, what the prognosis would be if he relapsed again. If Curt picked up on James's anxiety, he didn't mention it; he simply stopped talking and let the hiss of the tires fill the car.

His eyes continued to find their way back to staring out the passenger window and the pitch-black forest alongside Mount Hope Road leading to the hospital. Emily talked about going home; he even said the same during the on-field interview after the game. But like the last time they dealt with Aaron's leukemia, home—even the mention of it—felt like just another hotel. And consciously or not, James couldn't allow himself to really *feel* the warmth and comfort of home. Now that the lights had blinked out on his baseball career, his old mind-set seeped back in, the one that believed every hope begged to be jinxed. Believing in home simply invited tragedy.

The Place had let him have a little vacation. Now, the struggle against its despairing call returned.

Curt pulled up to the drop-off entrance at Bertoia Building and helped James unload two heaping bags of Tigers souvenirs out of the backseat—and the bottle of champagne Chris Franke had placed in his locker. The good-bye wasn't really a good-bye, not with a new friendship sealed, and James wished him luck, reminding him to drive his hips through the hitting zone. Curt laughed. "Man, one day in The Show and now you're ready to manage. Tell Aaron I'll drop him an e-mail to check in every once in a while. And with some new stats questions he can look up." They shook hands again, and James entered the hospital, his arms stretched tight by the souvenir-laden bags.

No colorful streamers greeted him this time when he entered. Just the steady breathing of blissful sleep from two utterly exhausted children. James quietly set the heavy bags down. The light from a three-quarter moon spilled in the window, casting a blue glow along the fold-out couch and Lizzie's spread arms and open mouth. He kissed her on the cheek, and she rolled to her side and curled up like a pill bug. The thumb she used to suck right up until last year gradually moved to her mouth but stopped short. James tugged the light bedsheet to her waist and kissed her again.

Aaron lay splayed in his sleep, as always. Maybe it was a trick of the moonlight or how the boy carried himself all night, but he looked strong, even as he slept. *Maybe he really is getting close to remission.* James imagined all of those black, gnarly cancer cells, the ones he used to picture bouncing through Aaron's bloodstream and devouring him from the inside, now hiding in the corners. Their teeth chattered at their impending doom, their eyes wide in terror as the medicine performed seek-and-destroy missions.

But in some of the shadows, a few of those gremlins still grinned, their teeth telling James that he'd never be rid of them, that they'd hide out and wait, always wait, until the right moment. Until Aaron would be theirs.

He shivered.

He pushed Aaron's legs back under the covers, pulled the sheet up to his waist, and kissed him on the cheek. Aaron's eyes fluttered open; recognition flickered across them, and he smiled. "See you in the morning, pal," James whispered. Aaron turned to his side, slid his hands underneath his pillow, and nestled in.

In their bedroom, Emily snored. James slipped into the bathroom to change and didn't turn on the light until he shut the door.

Weary brown eyes stared back at him. He set his hands on the sink and leaned closer to the mirror.

The baseball player was gone.

The cancer patient father was back.

He clicked off the light and tried to open the door as quietly as he'd closed it, but Emily stirred and rose up on one elbow. "Hey there, Mr. Professional Athlete."

"That's Mr. *Retired* Professional Athlete. I made it official after the game." James leaned against the bathroom's doorframe. "You were snoring."

"I don't snore. I breathe deeply."

"You were breathing deeply with a lot of noise."

Emily flopped back on the bed. "So Wes gave me the schedule for the interviews tomorrow." She glanced at the clock. "Sorry, today. He said he got calls all during the game. It starts early."

"I know. Not even sure why I'm going to bed. Except for the whole total exhaustion thing."

"We're all worn-out."

James sat on the edge of the bed, facing away from her. Moonlight cascaded into their room and cast long shadows along the foot of the bed. A soft breeze rose from the air-conditioning vent underneath the window and fluttered the drapes. Their shadows danced.

He sat there awhile, watching the shadows.

Emily rose up again on her elbow and put a hand on his back. "What's the matter, hon?"

James didn't answer.

"James, what's wrong?"

"I know—" James stopped and rubbed his eyes. A deep breath calmed his sudden trembling. "I know that, ultimately, God's still in control here, but . . ." He couldn't finish, and another breath didn't settle him this time. "Do you think we'll ever be done fighting this battle?" he finally asked.

"He's really close to remission. You'll feel better when you talk to Dr. Barna tomorrow. He's already sent North Mercy the plans for the next treatment phase. We can go home, James. *Home.*"

"I know." He sat silent through another flurry of shadow dancing. "But do you?"

From behind, Emily wrapped him in a hug and laid her chin on his shoulder. James felt her open her mouth as if to say something, but she didn't. She just took a deep breath against his body and shook her head.

"It's just a deep-down fear, isn't it?" James asked.

Emily nodded.

"Yeah. Me too."

"Only it's not really deep down, is it?"

"No. I guess not. It's right there. Front and center."

Without a word, he stretched out on his back, and Emily pressed tight against him, her head in the pocket of his shoulder. James stared at the ceiling.

Aaron's announcer voice faded.

The tiger roar faded.

The cheering ballplayers faded.

All that remained was silence.

15

"NOW LISTEN," James said, kneeling in front of Aaron. "They're going to put some little earpieces on us so we can hear them, and we'll be able to see them on a TV screen, but we have to look at the camera when we talk, okay?"

Aaron nodded. He appeared more nervous than before throwing out the first pitch the previous night. James knew how he felt.

"Are they going to ask me some stats questions?"

"Probably not, bud, but you never know. You'll be ready if they do."

"And are you ready for all of the other questions?" Emily asked her husband.

James stood. "I think so. Wes called this morning to go over some things, and I checked with Dr. Barna to make sure I said everything right." He took a calming breath. "I knew last night this was a big opportunity, but I guess it didn't hit me how big until this morning. This could be our chance. This could be *his* chance."

"Hon, don't . . . ," Emily started to say, but she shook her head. Her hands trembled.

A young man wearing a headset, a microphone angling in front of his mouth, joined them in the hall outside the hospital conference room. "Mr. McConnell? Mrs. McConnell? Kids? We're ready." He extended his arm inside. Four chairs sat two by two, bathed in lights.

Brighter than the lights of Comerica Park.

James pushed out another hard breath, but he couldn't move. A memory popped into his head—freezing in the dugout back in Comerica Park, unable to walk onto the field to see it up close for himself. Aaron gave him the strength to go forward that day, gently grabbing his hand and urging him on.

Now Emily squeezed his hand. "C'mon," she whispered. "You can do this."

Four hours later, back in room 716, the procession of national morning show interviews over for some time, James listened from the bedroom to the sounds of everyday life. The TV blared cartoons. Emily asked sternly for someone to turn the volume down so she could make a call.

Lizzie whined, "Aaaaaronnnn!" when he changed the channel.

Aaron retorted a grumpy "Fine," and flipped it back to a high-pitched, bubbly Doc McStuffins.

No announcer, no tiger roar, no thunderous cheering from 40,000 people, no crack of the bat or smack of a baseball in a mitt. Life. Normal life. Home. A hotel, a hospital, or the house they had owned for a dozen years . . . It didn't matter. *Home* was these sounds, these people, this love.

He could have listened to it all day. But Aaron wrecked the reverie, shrieking, "Guys!" James darted into the room, expecting disaster. Instead, he found the boy's face knotted in shock, excitement, and confusion. "We're on Yahoo!"

The word *Yahoo!* didn't register anywhere on the list of things James thought he'd hear after Aaron's alarming call. His eyes blank, his mouth open, he only mumbled, "Yahoo?"

Aaron turned his laptop around. "The Internet? The interview from this morning? It's up on the front page of Yahoo!"

Lizzie walked over. "Hey, there's me! And you, Mommy!"

Emily and James moved behind the couch to see. The third story in a line of rotating features showed a screen capture from one of the morning's interviews. Aaron clicked on the blurb beneath it, and the page displayed their *Good Morning America* interview. A video box filled the top of the page, and the article continued beneath it.

"They picked it up already?" Emily whispered. "James, this means . . ." She put a hand to her mouth, unable to finish.

"It means it worked."

She threw her arms around his neck.

Aaron clicked the box. The video began with a short narration from one of the three morning hosts who interviewed the family, then showed clips of the video that played on the left field scoreboard prior to the game. Next, highlights of James in a Tigers uniform: his diving stop on the first pitch of the game—"I can't believe you caught that!" Aaron shouted—the collision at second base in a double play; his first hit; the long fly ball that brought the crowd to their feet; and at the final out, the Tigers' celebratory scrum on the field, Aaron in the center.

The video switched to the interview completed that morning, beginning with James answering the first question about his reaction to Aaron's wish.

James recoiled. "Oh, my word, did I really say *um* that much?" Emily shushed him.

Whenever he could during the interview, James turned the conversation away from baseball and to their current focus, their current battle: finding a bone marrow match for Aaron. He lost track of how many times he said either "National Marrow Donor Program" or "BeTheMatch.org."

Behind the couch, Emily grabbed his hand and pointed to the text below the video box. BeTheMatch.org, as well as a number of other cancer research organizations and foundations, displayed in blue, linking to their websites.

"Guys, this is gonna, like, go viral or something," Aaron said. "*Everyone's* gonna see this."

"I had a lot of help making Aaron's wish come true," James was saying on the video. "But we need some more help making one more wish come true. And there are thousands of kids out there who could live long, healthy lives if they had a bone marrow transplant. It only takes a cheek swab to start the process, and if you sign up on BeTheMatch.org, they'll even mail you the kit."

"Dad, how many people do you think will sign up?" Aaron said over his shoulder. On the computer, one of the hosts asked Emily a question; her answer played over footage of Aaron throwing out the first pitch, then James and Aaron hugging near the mound.

James gave his son's shoulder a squeeze. "I hope all of them."

"Do you think we'll finally find a match for me?"

James kissed his head. "That's the plan."

"Last night was great," James said in the interview, "but it'll end up being just one night if nobody does anything to help these kids who are sick right now."

The hosts thanked them for their time, and after the McConnell family said good-bye, the three people at the desk talked among themselves. Laughing, they shared one more photo from the night before: James and Aaron, huge smiles at the camera, arms around each other, and shaving cream covering their faces.

"What a brave little boy," one of the anchors said.

"And James did pretty well for his first ever game in the majors."

"That's BeTheMatch.org, everyone. Check it out, and sign up if you're able. Who knows, you just might 'be the match' for Aaron McConnell."

"Wait, guys, look at this!" Aaron said. He scrolled down a little. "They put the link to my website!" Aaron clicked on it.

Four amateur photos of James showed him in three different minor league uniforms. In other pictures, Aaron sat in the suite keeping score, posed with the TV broadcasters in the press box, and leaned into a microphone announcing the starting lineup.

James's stats, added a couple of hours ago by Aaron, scrolled in a crude animation across the middle of the page: *1 game played . . . 3 total at bats . . . 2 official at bats . . . 1 hit (single) . . . 1 sacrifice bunt . . . .500 batting average . . . 0 runs scored . . . 0 runs batted in . . . 0 errors.*

"When are the official photos from the Tigers coming?" Aaron asked.

"Later today, I think," James said.

"James . . ." Emily grabbed his wrist and pointed to the bottom of the screen.

He leaned closer. "Aaron, scroll down."

In a banner near the bottom: BeTheMatch.org. The website page counter below that already numbered over 25,000.

"Maria must've just added that banner," Emily said.

Aaron scrolled up and down on his page a couple of times before backing up to the interview and replaying it.

James pulled Emily tight. "This is going to work," he whispered. "This *has* to work."

One week after James played for the Tigers, Dr. Barna interrupted a Sunday afternoon game on TV—the Tigers and the Tampa Bay Rays. James muted the game; Aaron, lying on the couch, whined, but James wasn't interested. Not when Dr. Barna couldn't stop smiling.

He held up his iPad. "We have the latest results!"

"And?" Emily said.

"It is official. Aaron, you are in remission. Your blast count is less than 5 percent, and your peripheral blood counts are near normal."

Emily smothered Aaron in a hug. "So . . . home?" she asked.

"We can go home?" Lizzie said, perking up from her coloring book.

"Yes, ma'ams. Home." Emily and Lizzie clapped and cheered, but Dr. Barna stopped them. "But not right away. I want to begin the consolidation phase and keep him here for another few weeks." Lizzie groaned. "Maybe less. I would like to make sure the remission holds." Dr. Barna patted Aaron's shoulder. "What do you think, young man?"

"Sounds cool." Aaron looked up at the doctor, then back down quickly. "Any bone marrow matches yet?"

James, about to ask the same thing, bit his lip.

"Not yet," Dr. Barna replied. "But we needed you in remission first anyway."

"So what do you guys want to do to celebrate?" Emily asked.

"Actually, we have taken care of that already," Dr. Barna said. "Teri has reserved the Home Kitchen for you tonight." The Home Kitchen, on the far side of the hospital complex, was one of three restaurant alternatives to the several cafeterias scattered throughout St. Francis. "Arrive at six o'clock, and you can go right into the kitchen and pick out anything you want to eat. If you want to help cook, you can help cook. Our chef will show you all of his secrets. It is a wonderful family activity."

Dr. Barna walked in front of the couch and sat on the coffee table, facing Aaron. "I will keep searching the registry; you have my word. Your story has brought many new people to the registry already. I am sure we will find a match very soon."

Two weeks later, they still waited. But the remission held, and Dr. Barna, satisfied at how the second phase of treatment began, brought the discharge forms to their room after dinner.

"After tomorrow afternoon, young man, you will not have to look at me for some time." He performed a last, cursory checkup, and with an exaggerated flourish, signed the documents. "I am very proud of you." He shook Aaron's hand like a grown man and left the McConnells to start packing.

The next morning, James and Emily dawdled through their final in-room breakfast until a text message beeped on Emily's phone. "Hey, guys, what do you say we take one last walk through the gardens?" she said.

James stood. "Sounds great! Let's go."

"But Paige was gonna come over this morning," Lizzie said.

"On your feet, Lizard," Emily said. "It's gorgeous outside. You'll see her before we leave."

Aaron fiddled with his pancake.

"Get a move on, Mr. Remission," James said, slowly sliding Aaron's plate away until he crammed in the last three bites.

The gardens shimmered with color, but not simply from the flowers. Balloons floated everywhere, whipping spastically in a steady wind, held by nurses, doctors, therapists, counselors, other patients and their families, anyone who had connected with the McConnells over the past two months. They formed a spiraling line on the path to the garden's central stone paddock. Lizzie immediately ran to Paige when she spotted her by one of the small ponds, clutching three red balloons.

James and Emily led Aaron to the paddock, and the line processed. People wished him luck, said how much they'd miss his smile, or chatted a few minutes about the Tigers. For the parents of some patients, their brimming eyes expressed an unspoken envy, wondering when it would be their turn for a going-home garden party, or if there would be one at all. James took an extra moment with them.

Emily took each person's balloon and tied it to the back of a wrought-iron bench. "Mom, what are you doing?" Aaron asked between visitors.

"Just cleaning up." She winked. Aaron rolled his eyes.

"Yeah, I know; she's a terrible liar," James said.

Lizzie ran ahead of two approaching balloons—blue and orange—hiding the faces of the people carrying them. "Mom! Dad! Look who's here!" The balloons whipped to the side, and Aaron leaped into Curt Howard's arms. Kara joined the hug.

"I can't believe you made it!" Emily said.

"One more road trip before the All-Star break," Curt said. "It'll be nice to have a few days off."

"I still think you shoulda made the team," Aaron said. "You're in the top five for batting average of shortstops in the league, and you've only made six errors all season!"

"Couldn't beat out the big boys this year, I'm afraid," Curt replied. "Besides, the rest will be nice."

"Rest? What rest?" Kara turned to Emily. "He wants to go to Scotland to play golf at St Andrews this year. I swear, I think sometimes he wants to retire early so he can try to make the PGA Tour."

"Oh, like you're not going to enjoy London," Curt said.

"Mmm . . . London," Emily said. "I went there once for a conference when I was in graduate school."

"While I stayed back and tried to find us a place to live," James said.

"You said before that she's got the looks *and* the brains in the family," Curt pointed out.

"I s'pose I did, didn't I?"

"Hey, can we talk to you guys for a minute?" Curt asked. Kara pulled closer so that they all huddled together.

"You got some more stats questions?" Aaron said.

Curt held up his hands. "Uncle, okay? I learned my lesson. But I do have something for you. For all of you."

James draped his arm around Lizzie and pulled her against his leg.

"We watched your interviews the day after the game," Kara said, "and everyone we know has seen the story and video on the Internet. A lot of the other players did, too, and we're all really touched by what you said at the end, about that night being just one night unless people do something to help. In particular, Carl Peters was moved by it. He had an idea, and he and Curt talked."

"Is Dad gonna get to play in more games?" Aaron asked. His smile showed every single tooth.

Curt laughed but shook his head. "No, no, sorry 'bout that." Aaron's shoulders drooped. "Your dad caused so much trouble in the clubhouse, once was enough."

"He has been known to cause a ruckus," Emily said.

"Carl is the team's representative to the players' union," Kara said, "and he and Curt came up with something they could do. For the bone marrow registry."

Emily took James's hand.

"We talked to Lou Schelling, he spoke to the other GMs, and we met with our union chief, too," Curt explained. "Right now, we're putting something in the works with some of the national cancer foundations to get all of the major and minor league ballplayers on the registry, and we're also approaching other teams to hold their own A-Mac Day at their parks this summer. It's like you said: thousands of kids need a match."

Emily put a hand to her mouth; James's eyes instantly welled.

"Not only will we pass out information on the registry, but each stadium will have its own bone marrow drive. They'll work with a local hospital to set up kiosks toward the end of July and through August where people can take a cheek swab and sign up for the registry right there."

"Someone said we should wait until September, which is National Childhood Cancer Awareness Month," Kara said. "But attendance is usually higher in July and August."

"And then each team is going to donate a portion of ticket sales to make sure those swab results get on the registry. Guys, each ballpark puts through several hundred thousand people in August."

James's mouth dropped. "That's millions of people." He managed only a whisper.

"And I'd be thrilled if one percent of them sign up," Curt said. "Sound okay?"

James answered by hugging Curt like a brother, lifting him off his feet; then he kissed Kara on the cheek. And while Emily cried against Curt's shoulder, James leaned down to his son. "You hear that? Tons of new people on the registry!"

Aaron looked to the ground, then off toward one of the fountains.

"Hey, did you hear Curt?" James said. "All of baseball's going to help!"

Aaron glanced up at his dad and smiled. It looked weak. Forced. "Yeah, that's cool," he said. He accepted another hug from Curt and Kara, then stared at the colorful mass of balloons tied to the bench.

Curt poked Aaron in the chest. "So you let me know when you want to come down for another game, okay?"

"Uh, we'll see about that," Emily said, wiping her eyes. "We've all got some readjusting to do, especially Aaron, and he still has more treatment."

Curt waved her away and made a silent *call-me* signal to Aaron, who smiled, faintly. James decided that maybe Aaron's smile wasn't necessarily weak after all. Maybe contented. Relieved. Quiet strength. He rubbed Aaron's scalp and hugged the Howards again.

James scanned the gardens. "I think that's all the balloons," he told Emily. "You ready?" She nodded, and James stuck his thumb and middle finger in his lips and cut a piercing whistle to call everyone's attention.

Emily stood on the bench holding the balloons. "Thank you all for coming to Aaron's going-home party. And thank you all for the support you gave us while James was away." She looked at James, her eyes still red. He gave her a thumbs-up. "So, you all brought a balloon when you came to see Aaron, and now—" she turned and batted them with her hand—"here they are. Sixty-four balloons. One for each day Aaron has been here at St. Francis. And we thought a wonderful way to say good-bye would be for Aaron to let them go."

The crowd in the gardens applauded when James held a pair of scissors high over his head. Emily grabbed the strings while James cut them loose from the bench. Keeping a firm grasp, she held the colorful bouquet out to Aaron.

But he didn't take them. Instead, he motioned to Lizzie.

"Can you help me, Lizard?" She bounced up to him, her eyes wide, and she held out both hands. "You guys, too," Aaron said to his parents.

Emily pressed her lips together to keep her composure, but tears rimmed her eyes. She didn't let go of the balloons. Instead, Lizzie, Aaron, and James joined her so that they all held tight to the strings.

They counted together.

"One . . . two . . . three!"

A blossoming cloud of color rose into the summer sky.

The four of them stood together in silence and watched them race off in the wind.

The party—and the hospital odyssey—officially ended later that afternoon. With suitcases loaded, the McConnells played one more game of Uno Attack! while waiting for the discharge wheelchair ride. Aaron, wearing his McConnell Tigers jersey, made a few silly mistakes that led to Lizzie's winning, again. That contented, relieved expression never really left his face, and even when they talked about what they looked forward to at home, Aaron only casually said, "Yeah, that'd be fun. Can't wait."

Maybe, James thought, it wasn't contentment after all. Maybe it was fear—fear of trying to get back to a regular routine at home, fear of never finding a bone marrow match. While the girls made a last sweep of the room, James took him aside.

He bent down and peered into his son's blue eyes.

Aaron's eyes searched his in return.

"I know, Son," James whispered. "I'm scared, too."

Aaron finally looked away. "Let's go home, Dad."

Teri brought the wheelchair and held Lizzie's hand walking down the hall while another nurse pushed Aaron. James and

Emily lingered by the door and gazed back in at the room. So quiet now. Empty. No more posters and pennants on the walls, no clothes heaped in the corner or magazines and coloring books and markers littering the tables. Just like back in May, when they checked in, so much unknown lying before them. Aaron might not be leaving cancer-free, but still God had worked miracles here.

And now, the next step in their fight, so much more unknown again before them, this time outside of room 716, outside of St. Francis.

Emily leaned her head on his shoulder, and he kissed her.

They stopped in the hall. The picture of all of them standing in Comerica Park's on-deck circle now hung on the wall's sunrise mural, across the door from their room, among the seventh floor's other "guardian angels." James touched the photo and read the few words he wrote, remembering the difficulty he had coming up with them: *Every day together is a wish come true.*

"C'mon," he said. "Home's waitin' for us." He pulled her away.

Dr. Barna met them by the visitors' entrance. He hugged everyone and received a kiss from Emily. James tried to ask him again about the next phase of treatment, but Dr. Barna cut him off. "Just go home. There is no treatment today. Your appointment schedule is in your discharge packet, and Dr. Adams will be at North Mercy to conduct Aaron's first examination. But for right now, enjoy your ride home." He gave Aaron a final handshake and promised to keep following the Tigers. Teri's good-byes mingled with tears, and she and Lizzie hugged an extra minute. Lizzie gave her one more coloring page—a pink toad with a purple smile—and Teri said it would look marvelous at the nurses' station.

In the rearview mirror, James saw that the doctor and nurse stood side by side and watched them drive away. Before he turned onto the hospital access road, he stuck his hand out the window and waved a final time.

Within ten minutes of leaving, Aaron fell asleep. Lizzie passed the time with a video game on Emily's phone.

"He's been so quiet ever since the party," Emily whispered.

"This is a big step for him. Like you said, he's got a lot of readjusting to do."

"I hope you're right."

"Once he's back in his own room, you'll see. We need to hit the beach a lot this summer. I bet the sun will do him good. And who knows, maybe in a few weeks, if he's feeling strong enough . . ."

"Now don't go pushing him." Emily wrung her hands and glanced to the backseat. "But hopefully . . . this time . . ."

James saw she didn't believe it, that—just as he imagined—she probably pictured driving down this very road again in the opposite direction, going back to the hospital, no matter how big their story became or how many people walked through the ticket gate of a major league ballpark and joined the registry. James rubbed her knee and clasped her hand. "We've got him right now, Em. And he's better. And we're going home. Let's think about that." She squeezed his hand, met his eyes, and smiled.

Within minutes, his three passengers slept soundly. Only the road in front kept him company. The road and his thoughts, morphing from stadium lights to black gremlins to fireballing pitchers to a rainbow cloud of balloons to a boy's empty bedroom at home covered with dust.

He set the cruise control and stared down the highway.

16

THE McCONNELL HOUSE GLITTERED with color in
the evening sunshine—balloons, streamers, lights woven
through the deck's pergola, a mammoth blinking Welcome
Home sign on the side of the garage. Friends, families from
school, and James's parents waited in the front yard amid a
patch of Congratulations signs, and the party, while lively,
didn't last long. Kids raced and dove on a Slip 'N Slide
and sat in the grass to eat their slices of the giant chocolate
baseball cake. Although he'd been in the car for more than
three hours during the drive home, Aaron only wanted to sit
some more. But he looked much more comfortable in the
reclining deck chair, dappled in sunlight from the trees and
pergola, than in the backseat of the family SUV. Or *anyplace*
in the hospital.

People streamed across the deck throughout the evening
to talk to Aaron, but James noticed they only stayed long
enough for a few welcoming words and a smile. Judging
by his soft laughs and giggles, home appeared to calm him,

dimming the fear James thought he saw back at St. Francis.
I bet he's just worn-out, James finally decided.

When twilight's blues and purples tickled the treetops and
the pergola lights cast a Christmas tree–like glow over the deck,
the last of the partygoers said good-bye. By that time, Aaron
lay on the couch, ready for *Baseball Tonight* on ESPN. James
carried him to bed after ten minutes.

He pulled Aaron's Detroit Tigers covers up to his waist and
tucked him into his own bed. One of life's greatest pleasures.

James sat on the floor and rested a hand on Aaron's back. The
sleep machine whispered a rainstorm. In a crack of light from the
other room, he saw Aaron's mitt back in line on the bookshelf.
An official major league baseball sat snugly in the pocket.

James returned to the insurance agency the next week, after
Aaron's first round of treatment in the North Mercy outpatient
center. He thought he could handle the transition. He'd spent
so much time away from his family on his tour through professional baseball, but this felt different. Arduous. The suit, the
office, the meetings . . . He didn't realize how much readjusting
he needed to do himself. It took him three days to go through
his messages and e-mails, even though assistants had monitored
them for the last couple of months. Finally, by Friday, he felt
caught up.

That evening, like all the others that first week, James found
Aaron on the couch. A book replaced the video game from the
day before, and as on the other evenings, James's suggestions to
do something outside together drew only a shrug.

"That's okay, Dad. I know you had a long day."

"It wasn't that long."

Aaron shrugged again but nestled deeper into the couch and
turned the page in his paperback.

"It's not like I'm asking you to run a marathon. Just a walk around the subdivision."

"Maybe tomorrow," Aaron said. "Before the chemo."

But he slept in instead, and the concoction of at-home chemo pills struck hard and left him on the couch. The ball game in the afternoon kept him occupied. A bowl on the end table kept him company.

By the following weekend, James and Emily's concern bloomed into distress. Dr. Adams's tests at North Mercy showed the chemo working as expected, but she couldn't explain his lethargy. "Every patient responds differently," she said. "Take charge and get him out of the house. He needs to build up his strength."

So on Sunday after church, James and Emily danced around the lunch table. "Beach day! Beach day!" they sang. "Finish up and get dressed. We're wasting sun!"

Lizzie squealed and scampered upstairs to put on her bathing suit. Aaron tried a list of excuses, but James and Emily simply smiled and chirped, "Not buying it!" after each one.

"But we'll miss the Tigers game! They start in an hour!"

"I'll set the DVR," James said. "We're going to the beach."

Aaron growled and stamped downstairs to his bedroom to change.

On the beach, a short chair inches off the sand replaced the couch. Aaron stretched out, wiggling while Emily lathered him with sunscreen, then pulled his Tigers hat down and dug his toes in the sand. The sun and the breeze and the Great Lake's Caribbean-blue water soothed the entire family, but Aaron remained listless. He braved the always-frigid lake but ventured in only as far as his shins before scurrying back to his chair.

"Pretty awesome out here, isn't it?" James said, dragging

his chair next to Aaron's. Down the shore, Emily and Lizzie combed the sand, filling a pail with rocks.

"The water's freezing," Aaron said. He shoved his feet deeper into the sand. "But yeah, the sun feels good."

James studied Aaron gazing across the water. "Have you been feeling okay? Other than being tired, I mean. And the chemo."

"Yeah," Aaron said. "It's great being home, but kinda weird."

"Yeah, work's the same way. Is Franke pitching today?"

"No. At least—" Aaron cocked his head, thinking—"I don't think he's pitching today." He shook his head. "No, he's not. Harrison goes today."

"Hey, boys!" Emily called. She waved them over.

"C'mon, let's take a walk," James said. "The sand will feel good."

"But—"

"We won't go far."

Aaron slumped his shoulders, but James grabbed his hand and pulled him up.

The next week brought more of the same for Aaron—sluggishness during the day, a couch potato in the evening. James managed to get him out for a walk in the neighborhood, but Aaron only made it as far as the driveway two houses down.

James simmered. "I don't get it," he told Emily after the kids went to bed. "They say the chemo's working, but he's got no energy at all. Or motivation. Is he having a side effect to the new drugs?"

"They test for that each time," Emily said.

"Is he getting anemic again?"

"They test for that, too." She took a sip of her white wine. On TV, the Tigers' Tony Bozio struck out to lead off the seventh inning.

"Is it because they haven't found a bone marrow match yet?"

"He's told me he's not depressed."

"Then what is it?" James said, too loudly. "It's like he's afraid of something. Or like he doesn't have any fight in him anymore."

"It can get exhausting, hon. Even if 'fighting' is deciding to be happy. Choosing to live and have fun and just . . . be better, you know?"

"But he *seems* okay. It's like he's . . . lazy almost. But not . . ." James rubbed his forehead. "I don't know how to explain it, I guess. He just doesn't seem himself. It's like he's content to breathe in and breathe out, and if something bad happens, that's fine, and if something great happens, that's fine, too. Does that sound totally nuts?"

"You said that he might be afraid of something. Maybe he's scared of pushing himself too hard, that it'll somehow cause another relapse."

"That's ridiculous."

"I know that and you know that, but he's nine, James."

"Why wouldn't he say anything to us if that's it?"

"Again. Nine."

On TV, Curt Howard hit a long fly ball to the warning track in left field for an out. The camera caught him in a close-up as he removed his helmet and batting gloves.

"I think he should talk to someone," James said. He nodded at the TV. "And I don't mean Curt Howard."

"I've been thinking the same thing."

When the therapist told them his conclusions—that other than maybe more trouble readjusting than they had anticipated, Aaron seemed fine—James hit the roof. He slammed cupboard doors, barked at everyone, and spent his nights on the computer digging through medical websites hoping to uncover a magic bullet. Throughout the week, he ranted to his parents on the phone, got in a blistering argument with Emily over their medical bills, and brooded while he and Aaron watched a ball game. He watched his son more than the game.

Before the bottom of the fourth inning, the broadcasters put up their Tiger Trivia question, and the play-by-play announcer read it: "Of the six player statues in Comerica Park, can you name the one whose nickname also appears on his Hall of Fame plaque?"

As the color man said the name and nickname of each of the Tigers who had their jersey retired, the camera zoomed in on the stainless steel statues standing beyond the left field wall: Willie Horton, Willie the Wonder, with one hand on his bat on his follow-through; Ty Cobb, the Georgia Peach, sliding, his cleats up; Charlie Gehringer, the Mechanical Man, leaping and throwing on a double play; Hank Greenberg, Hammerin' Hank, a baseball soaring off his bat at the moment of contact; Hal Newhouser, Prince Hal, rearing back in a high leg kick, about to fire a pitch; and Al Kaline, Mr. Tiger, leaping high for a catch in the outfield.

Aaron stared at the screen and remained silent.

"Well? Which is it?" James asked.

Aaron shrugged.

"Oh, c'mon; you know this one."

"No, I don't."

"Aaron, I depend on you for knowing these things and teaching me." James laughed; no response. He sat up straighter in the recliner. "Okay, you just heard their nicknames."

"Yeah?"

"So Mr. Tiger. Al Kaline."

"Yeah?"

"On his plaque in the Hall of Fame, does it say 'Mr. Tiger' on it?"

Aaron shrugged again.

James clenched his teeth. "Aaron, you know *everything* about the Tigers who are in the Hall of Fame. How many home runs did Hammerin' Hank hit?"

Shrug.

"How many wins did Hal Newhouser have?"

Shrug.

"How many hits did Ty Cobb have?"

"Four thousand and . . . something?"

"It's 4,191," James said. His heart raced.

"Oh yeah. Right."

"Buster, you and me need to talk," James said quietly. And sternly. He muted the game, and when Aaron wouldn't look at him, he paused it. He shifted forward on the chair and faced his son, elbows on his knees. "What's going on?"

"What do you mean?"

"I mean you. What's going on? Why don't you want to do anything? Every time I come home, you're either on the couch or in your room, doing . . . I don't know—nothing. How come you don't want to do anything outside?"

Aaron shrugged again.

"Stop shrugging at everything!" James yelled. Aaron jumped, his eyes wide. "Every time we say something to you, it's met with this . . . this indifference, this flippant, casual, 'I don't really care' attitude. It's driving your mother and me bonkers."

Aaron snickered at the word *bonkers*.

"It's not funny, Aaron. I mean it. What's going on? Do your legs hurt? Does your head hurt? Your back? Your arms? Your eyes? Your stomach? What? Something has got to be wrong! Didn't talking to that therapist help at all?"

Aaron started to shrug but caught himself. Instead, he nodded. Sort of.

"I don't know how to help you if you don't talk to me. We can talk about baseball, about the Tigers, and you're fine. At least I thought you were. Four thousand and something? Aaron, you don't miss a stats question like that."

Still no response.

"You don't want to take a bike ride; we have to drag you to the beach; you don't want to play . . ." James softened with a breath. "Are you scared about something? Are you afraid of relapsing again when the treatment's done? Are you angry we haven't found a match yet?"

Aaron's eyes darted to the TV.

"Buddy, all of the parks are starting their bone marrow drives this month. Millions of people are going through the stadiums, and you know a lot of them are going to get on the registry. It's only a matter of time before we find a match."

"I know. I guess. It just feels like we'll never . . ." Out of reflex, he shrugged. "I'm not really scared. Or angry."

"Then what is it?" James yelled again. "Aaron, you've come through so much. You're a *cancer survivor*! You beat it once, and you'll beat it again."

Aaron's blue eyes rimmed with tears, but his face softened. "No, Dad, that's just it. I'm not a survivor. I'm just . . . surviving." He pulled his knees to his chest and sank into the corner of the couch. "Everything's . . . everything's fine. My life, my wish . . ." He glanced at his hands in his lap, then back at James. A gentle smile creased his lips. "You're right, Dad—4,191. I knew that. I was testing you." He nestled into the couch and stared at the frozen game on TV.

Sure, James thought, trying to comprehend everything. He settled back into the recliner and resumed the game.

A week later, on an early August morning, Aaron lacked the energy to get up—and when he did, he only went to the bathroom, crawling right back into bed. James and Emily called Dr. Adams. She listened, reviewed all the tests she herself performed since Aaron's return home in July, and said she'd talk to Dr. Barna, again.

Two hours later, when Aaron, finally on the couch, asked for lunch in the groggy, somewhat-slurred speech of someone drifting off to sleep, James's cell phone rang.

"I think it is time for a road trip," Dr. Barna said on the other end. "Can you be down here tomorrow?"

It rained hard enough on the expressway that James needed the intermittent windshield wipers. The pause between swipes gave the rain time to blur the road as the drops ran together into rivulets that streaked down the glass. Blurry, then clear. Blurry, then clear.

Like his mind.

Whenever the windshield cleared, a new, sharp memory from the previous month at home popped into his head. At first the images appeared random: the missed stats question, the welcome home party, the night after night sitting on the couch, the beach. The disorganization frustrated him, and he wrung the steering wheel.

Raindrops pelted the windshield.

He reached into his head and plucked out his earliest memory since their arrival home, then withdrew others one at a time, reviewing them in chronological order, hoping to see something he'd missed. Something that might tell him what was happening.

Blurry. Clear. Blurry. Clear.

The windshield wipers continued. He ticked up their speed

to keep up with the strengthening rain. Emily in the passenger seat and Aaron in the back both dozed. His thoughts drifted to Lizzie, at his parents' house. Once again. Until they figured this out.

"I'm his father," he said to the silent car. "I should know what's wrong. I should *know*." The miles peeled away as he recalled everything again. But this time, the memories remained blurred. Tears mixed with the rain to leave him totally lost. And empty.

The green highway sign for exit 150 shone through the misty gray day like a beacon, and he guided the car onto the ramp and turned left onto Mount Hope Road. In the opposite direction from a month ago.

He still had several miles to go to reach St. Francis hospital, still time to try to figure things out. Still time to pray.

17

DR. BARNA AND TERI waited for them at the entrance to
Bertoia Building East, in the same spot where in early July
they had said good-bye. Aaron sat down in the wheelchair Teri
drove. "Well, it ain't nice to see ya, darlin'."

"Gee, thanks," Aaron said. Teri laughed and playfully
rubbed his shoulders in a quick massage.

"I went to a Detroit Tigers game the other day," Dr. Barna
said, squatting down by the wheelchair.

"Really? Did you like it?"

"The food is expensive."

"Who did they play?"

"The Tampa Bay Mariners."

Aaron snickered. "There isn't a Tampa Bay Mariners. It's
Tampa Bay Rays or Seattle Mariners."

"Oh. Well, I am certain it was the Mariners. But the Tigers
lost."

"They've been doing that a lot lately."

Dr. Barna winked. "Perhaps they need your father to play
again."

"All right, Doctor, let's get this trouper checked in," Teri said, turning him around and starting inside.

Emily followed, but James pulled Dr. Barna aside. "So what's your plan?"

"We will run all of the tests and blood samples again," Dr. Barna explained. "And we will make sure the chemotherapy is still working."

"But that's what they've been doing up north," James snapped. "They just keep testing and testing. But he's still—"

"James, I know. I know." He stuffed his hands in the pockets of his doctor's coat. "Did you bring your things with you? This might take a couple of days."

James nodded.

"Good. Then let us settle in and get started." They followed the others several steps behind.

"I'm not sure if it's the physical causing the mental or the other way around," James said when the double doors ahead parted. "You said before that what's good for the mind is good for the body. Something's making his mind not good."

"Well, every patient is different in how they respond to chemotherapy, especially after a relapse."

"Yeah, I know. That's what everyone keeps telling us. Look, just . . . just figure it out."

"That is why you are here."

The nurses welcomed Aaron back up to the seventh floor again, though not to room 716. They made a point, like Teri, of saying they weren't too pleased to see him. Maria, their child life counselor, spent most of the day with them; she had as much luck as the others in discovering a root cause of the problem.

During that first day of tests, James glowered and bombarded anyone he saw with questions. On the second day, the questions continued, but now he demanded answers. On the third day, Emily couldn't stand to be in the same room with him, banishing him to the lobby or the cafeteria or anywhere else until he calmed down. Aaron tried extra hard to cheer him up, to watch the game or talk about the Tigers, but now James was the one who didn't want to do anything, other than search the Internet for clues and grill doctors and nurses about why they failed to do this or that.

The morning of the fourth day, Dr. Barna entered wearing the same look he had since they arrived, the look of no answers. James didn't care that Aaron lay in bed two feet away. "So what's next, Doc? Exploratory surgery? See if the batteries need changing?"

"James!" Emily gasped. Aaron slunk down in bed, and she pulled him into a shielding embrace.

Dr. Barna tried a smile to defuse the situation, holding his hands out for James to settle down. "We are doing everything—"

"I don't think you are." James stood and paced in front of the doctor like a caged tiger. "I think you're looking for a needle in a haystack. Why haven't you brought in other specialists? Where are they?"

"They are consulting and fully aware. I sent Aaron's case around the globe."

"And?" Still pacing in his cage.

"They are reviewing his case, his previous treatment protocols, and the details of his relapse and current treatment." He looked at Aaron and tried to smile.

James clenched his fists and visibly shook. Still, he paced. "Why doesn't he have a bone marrow match yet? I bet other people have found matches from the drives done in *his name*. Where's the one for him?"

"James, you know he has a rare HLA tissue type. They continue searching."

"And?"

"I do not know what else you would like me to say."

The door to the cage opened, and he pounced. "I want you to say you know what's wrong with him!"

"Every patient reacts dif—"

"I do not accept that!"

"Now, James, please, not in front of Aaron."

"Not in front of Aaron?" James yelled. "Not in front of Aaron? This has *all* been in front of Aaron! Every needle, every poke, every pill, every IV, every scan—this has *all* been about him!"

"No, now I think you are making this about you."

"Me? *Me?*" James's cheeks flushed. Another roar boiled.

"Yes, Mr. McConnell, you. You cannot control this, and that scares you."

"Of course I'm scared!"

Dr. Barna's voice remained calm. "I am scared, too. And we are trying everything we know to try. I came in here to talk to you about another blood transfusion, to see if that would put some energy back into Aaron. Would you like to discuss it calmly? Or do you want to keep shouting?"

"What I want—"

"Dad?" Aaron's soft squeak stopped him cold. He was crying. "Dad, it's okay."

James felt his face tighten and twist. "Aaron, it's *not* okay!"

"It is, Dad. Really. Everything that's happening . . . it's okay."

"Then why are we losing you?" He buried his face in Aaron's chest and wept.

In his mind, the black gremlins grinned.

What have you done to him? James screamed. *What have you done to us?*

One of them opened its mouth: *You'll never know.*
Emily wrapped them both up and cried with them.

James apologized to Dr. Barna later that day after the blood
transfusion got Aaron up and walking around the hallways.
Not long after, however, Aaron asked to go back to bed, completely winded, crushing James's short flirt with hope. The next
day of tests, accompanied by a great deal of encouragement and
smiles from Aaron and a few stern reminders from Emily, he
choked down the words that kept bubbling up and reacted as
best he could: stoically.

He spent much of the following day alone in the hospital's
chapel. He sat in silence, knelt in prayer, begged for a sign.
He shouted in his mind at God. He offered himself in Aaron's
place. He pleaded for a bone marrow match. Prayer had always
helped him before. Now, he only felt cold.

James's spirits lifted a day later when, after a round of
chemo pills, Aaron didn't feel like he needed a nap. He wanted
to go for a walk in the gardens. "It looks pretty nice out, Dad."

"You sure?"

"Yeah. I think I'd like to go outside."

"How about I push you instead?"

"That'd probably be better."

They moved slowly down the spiral path, soaking up the
August sunshine. Bird calls and voices and laughter drifted
through the gardens on a humid breeze. James lifted his face
to the sky that once welcomed a cloud of balloons in a family's
good-bye. The sun felt good on his arms and legs and cheeks,
sapping some of the anger and tension and depression. It left
him weary.

James pushed Aaron over the grass to a wooden bench
that sat snug against a pond in the shade of a plum tree's

dark-purple leaves. Rising from the middle of the pond, a fountain—a gigantic frog poised on one leg like a ballerina, its head
raised—spit water out of its mouth in a continuous stream.
Bright-orange fish swarmed underneath scattered lily pads, and
the sound of splashing water cooled James as much as the shade.

He parked Aaron's wheelchair perpendicular to the bench
and plopped down. Aaron absently rubbed a baseball in his
hands, the same one his father signed the night of the Tigers
game, the one that said, *You are my wish come true.* They didn't
talk for some time, just listened to the breeze through the
leaves and the splashing water.

James studied his son. He didn't look like such a boy anymore.

"What are you thinking about?" he asked.

Aaron fiddled with the ball, at first shy to speak, but then
he leaned back in his wheelchair. Something settled over him,
and he changed. He matured before James's eyes. "What do
you think heaven's like?"

Swaying branches fluttered shadows across their laps, and
for a long, heavy minute, James didn't answer. He continued to
stare at his son. His eyes hadn't deceived him.

He gazed into the blue sky. *Is it up there somewhere?* "Sort of
a *Field of Dreams* question, isn't it?" James asked.

Aaron smiled. "'It's Iowa,'" he quoted from the movie.

"I guess, for me, I always go back to the 'many mansions'
verse in the Bible. You know the one: 'In My Father's house
there are many mansions. . . . I go to prepare a place for you.'"

"Oh yeah, I've heard that before."

"Well, I take that to mean that the place prepared for each
of us is full of the things we loved when we were here. It's not
something untouchable or something we can't understand."
James held out his hand for the baseball, and Aaron gently
placed it in his open palm. "God's there, of course. Which,

I suppose, is really what makes it heaven. But also the things we love to do, the people we love—I think our individual mansions in heaven are filled with those. Grandparents, friends, family, pets—"

"Hot dogs," Aaron said.

James laughed. "You bet. With loads of mustard and onions."

"And baseball. On that awesome grass."

"Well, yeah, of course baseball. Every day. In your very own stadium." His voice lowered. "But each mansion—your mansion, my mansion . . . It's both unlike anything we can imagine, and yet it's precisely what we can imagine. Does that make sense?"

Aaron stared at the fountain. "I think that maybe this is heaven."

"Back to *Field of Dreams* again, huh?" James smiled, handed the ball to Aaron, and leaned back on the bench.

But Aaron didn't blink, serious. "It's just . . . how you described it. That's, like, *now*, isn't it?"

"Aaron, this most certainly isn't heaven. Having to fight cancer, twice, is not heaven."

"I don't mean that. I mean . . . *this*. What we've done together, what we've seen, my wish coming true, and that whole experience. Dad, I've had it all. And God's always with us . . ." He looked at his father, that grown-up, mature understanding of life painted plainly in his blue eyes and on his tender skin. "Why would this *not* be heaven?"

James turned to the gardens to keep his son from seeing his brimming eyes. He stood and kissed him on the head and sat back down. "You're a wise young man, Aaron McConnell." His words trembled.

They sat awhile longer. There was nothing for James to

argue about or rage against, nothing to throw in anger or to wallow in. Only the gardens and the water and the sun and the breeze. And Aaron.

"What we've done together, what we've seen, my wish coming true . . . Dad, I've had it all. . . . Why would this not be heaven?"

Something inside James diminished, weakened, and then simply vanished.

And again, Aaron looked different. Whatever he thought he'd seen over the last month and a half—contentment, laziness, relief, lethargy, or even a moment ago, maturity—he could not mistake what he saw now. The smile on Aaron's lips as he gazed at the flowers and the pond and the fountain and the sky, his fingers still twiddling the baseball, was beautiful. Not beaming or exuberant, but angelic, almost. Comfortable.

Peace.

Pure. Simple.

Peace.

James watched the sun sparkle off the pond, reminding him of Lake Michigan and a bank of Comerica Park lights at the same time. When the shimmering faded and disappeared after a time, he pushed Aaron onto the paved path. They didn't say a word the whole way back.

That evening, when Aaron crawled into bed, he closed his brilliant-blue eyes. He didn't open them the next day, even while awake and carrying on conversations or listening to the evening ball game on TV. Emily took charge of catering to him; James sat vigilant by his bed, offering only his presence and commentary on the game. Although Aaron didn't sleep, he lay suspended somewhere between consciousness and dreams, alternately restless and then unusually calm and still.

After nine o'clock, James stood staring out the seventh-floor window down at the gardens. The solar-powered path lights again glowed like stars.

"Dad?" Aaron said in a faraway voice.

James turned off the TV and sat by the bed. "Right here, bud. You having trouble going to sleep?"

"Dad, tell me the story again. Tell me about the grass."

Out of habit, James blurted, "Aaron, I told you back then, and—" He caught the next words before they came out of his mouth. After their conversation in the gardens, they took on new meaning. "You'll get your own ball field someday."

"Just tell me. Tell me about the grass."

He held Aaron's hand and spoke slowly, almost in a whisper, his voice a calm, tranquil, lilting lullaby that eventually put Aaron to sleep.

"The grass . . . the grass . . . You're in the middle of the infield, and you squat down and run your hand over the blades, as green as emeralds but as soft as feathers. The green is so bright that it has its own smell, like tart apples and trees and all the smells of summer. You bounce when you step on the grass; it's so soft, and all you want to do is stretch out and lie down and fall asleep. Just . . . fall asleep. But you stand up, and the stadium towers are all around you. It's like standing in the middle of a cathedral, and everything melts away until it's just you on that beautiful field . . . standing on that soft grass.

"But you have a game to play. The lights are brighter than the sun, and the crowd . . . the crowd sounds like an ocean wave rolling onto shore, wave . . . after wave . . . after wave. The crack of the bat echoes through the stadium, and you dive for a line drive, stretch out in the air, diving, flying, and the ball pops into your mitt and stings your hand. And it's the most wonderful sting in the world, the sting of catching a ball solidly in your glove. Then you're up to bat, and you hear the ball hiss when it's pitched to you. But your bat is quicker, and it comes through the zone, and the contact is so solid that you barely feel it. And you know you crushed it. And it soars, higher and higher into the night, up into the lights; you swear you see it burning up, arcing through the sky like a shooting star, farther . . . and farther . . . into the night, over the fence, over the stands, over the stadium . . . farther and farther . . . soaring . . . soaring . . . soaring . . ."

James told the same story for the next three nights. It was the only thing Aaron asked for. After that third night, he didn't regain consciousness. Doctors and nurses swarmed around him, trying to figure out the cause of the coma, wheeling him out for tests, scans, and exams. Emily and James remained with him the whole time. They stood along the wall and watched silently as the doctors worked, and when the doctors left, they sat by his bed and cooed to him and prayed. And James kept telling the story of the grass.

Each night, Emily grappled him out of bed and carried him to a rocking chair she pulled close so he could stay hooked up to the monitors. His arms curled underneath his body, and his gangly legs hung down nearly to the floor. She rocked him and sang "Sleep Sound in Jesus," the only lullaby he ever asked her to sing when he was little. James watched her, his eyes stinging, and when her words choked, he gathered Aaron from her and lifted him back into bed.

In the morning, Dr. Barna showed up alone—no iPad, no team of nurses or other doctors. He motioned to the coffee table. "I do not know what else to do, except . . ." He sighed, pushed up his glasses, and rubbed his eyes.

"Except what?" James said.

"Except send you home. If you want to go. It is your

decision to make. There are not any more tests for us to do that cannot be performed at North Mercy. And there is no reason for him to stay in a hospital. They can perform the tests and take any necessary samples right at home."

"So you mean . . . hospice." James barely got the word out.

"No, at-home care."

"Is there a difference?"

Dr. Barna didn't answer.

James and Emily held hands.

"I am sorry," Dr. Barna whispered. "I am so very sorry I let you all down." At Aaron's bed, he squeezed the boy's toes and walked out.

While Emily tried to get something into her stomach in the cafeteria, James sat by the bed. The muted monitors blipped weak, yet stable, vital signs. Teri came in and leaned against the wall near James.

"He's so still," James whispered. "It's so quiet."

"*It* is quiet."

"What do you mean?"

"Dyin's loud. Monitors and machines beepin', nurses and doctors barkin' orders. Parents—"

"Acting like idiots and getting in the way," James interrupted.

Teri patted him on the shoulder. "Wantin' the best for their children. The pain . . . that's all so loud, so . . ." She shook her head. "But death . . . death is quiet. Some people say they want peace and quiet. But peace *is* quiet."

"So death is peace, then."

"For some of these kids . . . yeah."

"Not for the parents."

"Nope. Not for the parents."

"For Aaron?"

Teri squeezed his shoulder. "I don't know, honey. I really don't know."

James leaned forward and clasped his hands in front of his face. So tired. Utterly beat up. Punched in the gut and kicked in the ribs. Nothing left in him, nothing left to offer Aaron. Except himself.

"I think it's time to take him home," he said.

James had no more tears. His journey to this moment began during their talk in the gardens, when he decided that whatever was taking his son could be met with a struggle and anger and yelling, or it could be done in Aaron's way. With maturity. And understanding. And peace.

"I want to take him home today."

Late that afternoon, the McConnells waited to leave Bertoia Building East again, their bags packed and loaded in the car. Aaron, his breathing steady but shallow, lay stretched out on a gurney, and a procession of nurses and doctors flowed through the room to say good-bye. Dr. Barna walked them down to the ambulance port underneath Bertoia Building, and he grasped Aaron's hand and cupped his comatose cheek. "I will come up and see you myself next week, young man. Sleep well."

Emily rubbed Dr. Barna's shoulders and shed a few tears into his doctor's coat, the one that said *Kick Me!* surrounded by colorful handprints, including Aaron's. Teri kissed the boy one last time, and they stood by silently as the staff loaded the gurney into the patient-transport ambulance. James kissed his wife and helped her inside. A paramedic slammed the door closed and whacked it with his palm. The vehicle slowly pulled away.

James followed in the SUV. He tried the radio, but the sports talk shows argued about stupid, meaningless things. They were all meaningless now.

He shut everything off and existed in the loneliness.

In The Place.

No escape this time.

A mile from the expressway, his world exploded.

The ambulance's dormant lights burst to life like a fire-work, and the sirens screamed. James yanked the wheel so quickly that he almost put the car in the ditch. The ambulance jolted through a three-point turn and tore back down the road toward St. Francis.

James duplicated the turn while fumbling for his cell phone. *Oh, God, no! Not now! Not in the ambulance! Not while I'm here! I need to be there! I need to be there! I need—*

His cell phone rang in his hand. Emily.

"What happened? What happened?" he yelled.

She was crying.

And laughing.

"They found a match! They found a match! They just called, and they found a match!"

18

THE AMBULANCE PEELED OFF into an emergency entrance on the far side of the circular hospital complex, its lights flashing and the siren burping a few more times. James veered off right behind, his emergency flashers blinking, but fell victim to a uniformed security officer waving him down. The officer dashed in behind the ambulance as it stopped in front of a building James hadn't entered before: the Heintz Memorial Transplant Center. His eyes darted from the guard to the team of people hurrying from the entrance.

James rolled down the window. "That's my son in there!" he shouted.

The guard jogged over, holding up his hand. "I know, sir, but you can't park here. Over there, please." He pointed to a line of angled parking spots across from the entry; James zipped into a slot, jumped out, and sprinted for the ambulance.

James caught up to the cluster of medical personnel in pale-blue scrubs wheeling Aaron toward sliding double doors. "Are you sure? They really found a match?"

Emily, her eyes red and swollen, tried to hold it in; her body heaved through a clenched sob. James clasped her hand while they jogged alongside the gurney. "Do you think he knows?"

Emily took a big breath and pushed it out slowly. A tear-bubbling laugh followed, producing more, yet controlled, tears. "I screamed it loud enough. He *had* to hear me." She rubbed Aaron's hand gently at first but then more vigorously, as if shaking him awake. "I *know* he heard me."

Dr. Barna waited in the lobby, his fingers flying across his iPad, and he hustled to the team guiding Aaron's gurney. They pulled it to a stop and wired him to the vital signs monitors. Almost too happy to speak, Dr. Barna managed to tell James and Emily that these new doctors and nurses, the transplant team, needed to take Aaron away to begin an intensive series of tests. The McConnells didn't understand at first what he meant until Dr. Barna held a hand out for them to go in the opposite direction of the rolling gurney. Emily recoiled and jogged after Aaron, but James caught her, wrapping his arms around her waist from behind. "They'll bring him right back, Em," he said. "They've got work to do. He's been through tests before. He'll be fine."

"But what if he wakes up and we're not there?" She strained against him, but James tightened his embrace. The swarm of medical personnel, the gurney, and their little boy disappeared behind two doors that closed slowly on electronic hinges. She sank back against him.

"Then they'll tell him the good news."

Another jolt of emotions seized Emily, but James turned her around and led her back to Dr. Barna. He took them to a brightly lit family meeting room.

"I am glad that we caught you before you got on the highway," Dr. Barna said. He motioned them to a plush love seat and sat down on the edge of a matching chair.

"What happened?" James asked.

"We found Aaron a match." Dr. Barna leaned his elbows on his knees and rubbed his hands together. "It is not a perfect match, but . . ." He trailed off, shaking his head, clearly thrilled.

"Will it be good enough?"

"It will have to be. We cannot delay this any longer hoping for something better. But yes, James, this will be good enough," he said when he saw that James didn't like his first answer. "Now, do you want to hear the really wonderful news?"

"There's something better?" Emily said. She composed herself through some stuttering breaths while wiping her eyes with a tissue.

Dr. Barna's grin spread, and he rubbed his hands again. "This match was found through a private marrow donor collection entity."

"Private?" James asked. "By who?"

"The entity hired by the Major League Baseball Players Association." It bounced off of James and Emily. "This means that Aaron's bone marrow donation will come from a major league baseball player," Dr. Barna said.

"But how? I mean, I didn't think they'd tell us who—"

"If the collection is made for a specific patient, the donor can request to be notified if he matches. This donor wanted to know. And he said that it was okay for you to know who he is, too. It seems that most of the baseball players who agreed to be typed made this request."

"So who is he?" James asked.

"A Mr. Trent Matthews. He plays for the Texas . . . uh . . . Texas . . ."

"Rangers."

Dr. Barna snapped his fingers. "Yes, the Rangers. I swear, by the end of summer, I will know all of the teams. Yes, the Texas Rangers. We are placing calls to him and other people at his team right now. Technically, we do not know if he will agree to it, but I find it difficult to believe that he would not make a donation."

James drew Emily into his arms when she started silently crying again, and he felt himself joining. But he pushed the emotions back down in order to ask the question that had unsettled him ever since receiving the phone call from Emily, the one thing that could render all of this happy news pointless. But it had to be asked.

"Will he be strong enough to get through this?" James asked. "I mean, we've read enough about bone marrow transplants . . . They're going to up his chemo, and probably radiation this time, to prepare his body, right?"

Dr. Barna brought his clasped hands to his mouth, nodded, and his smile vanished.

"Can he take all of that? Can he even survive the preparation?"

Dr. Barna swallowed and took each of their hands. "I have never tried to pretend good news for the sake of good news, and I will not begin now. Yes. The preparatory regimen will be very difficult. And he could even have a reaction during the infusion process that would make it fail. And posttransplant carries significant risks for rejection and graft-versus-host disease. But we must take one step at a time. Aaron needs this transplant. We crossed the first bridge and got him into remission, and it is good that he is still there. If we can get him conscious again, that would be even better. And we have crossed the next bridge, too: there is a match for your son. Now it is time to cross another one."

Dr. Barna spoke of bridges. James thought only of curveballs.

The hospital assigned a new family counselor to the McConnells, who led them through the towers of paperwork in a conference room. They skimmed and signed any form put in front of them, authorizing every test the transplant team deemed necessary. James asked, only half-sarcastically, if one all-empowering form existed to allow them to do whatever they needed to do to make this transplant happen, but the counselor apologized and said that each one needed to be discussed.

The evening passed in a haze of phone calls to family and the details of the tests to come: echocardiograms and lumbar punctures and dental exams and blood tests and bone marrow biopsies and pulmonary function tests and, of course, more chemotherapy and total body irradiation to eliminate any last hiding cancer blast cells. The counselor stressed that Aaron might not require all of them, but that the process would be smoother if they had the necessary forms on file just in case. Each time they finished a handful of papers, the counselor passed the documents off to a nurse, who whisked them away to the transplant team.

After eight o'clock, they reunited with Aaron in their new room, more confining than the hotel-like suite of Bertoia Building. Rigorous sterilization of the room itself and anything or anyone prior to entering left them, essentially, isolated. James and Emily methodically washed their hands and faces before hovering over his bed, holding his hand and kissing his face and whispering into his ear how proud they were. Still unconscious and now with a central line protruding from his chest, Aaron looked like he'd just come from surgery.

As in so many of the hospital rooms they stayed in over the years, sleeping arrangements consisted of a cot and a chair alongside the bed. Emily flopped on the cot and rested her hand on Aaron's arm while she stretched out. Pummeled by the violent jarring from one emotion to the next, she fell asleep almost instantly. In minutes, she matched Aaron's deep, steady breaths.

James had seen her in that position too many times. But now, with the news that this Trent Matthews agreed to the donation . . . now, with a transplant on the horizon . . . *This is really happening,* James thought. *This is all really happening.*

The black cancer gremlins didn't grin anymore. They knew. James imagined the marrow as maple syrup, a syrup that absorbed into Aaron's spongy bones and transformed them into living factories for new, healthy, potent blood. The gremlins would be overwhelmed, drowned, and evaporate into wisps of smoke.

But for some reason, when he saw them disappear, he only saw Aaron all alone.

James scooted his chair closer and rubbed Aaron's arm with one hand and his forehead with the other. "I'm right here, kiddo. I'm right here. I'm not going to let you go, okay? You're stuck with me. I think maybe . . . before . . . if you thought it was time to go, I think I could've let you. I think I could've said good-bye. It would've been awful—" he didn't bother to wipe his face—"but I think I could've done it. But not now. Not now.

"You've got to get to that ball field. We've got to play catch.

"That's my wish, Aaron. I made yours come true. Now it's your turn."

James continued stroking the boy's forehead. With each touch, something passed between them. Love? Energy? Peace? Strength? Life?

Maybe all of them.

"I take that back. That's not right. That's not my wish. It was, all this time. But now . . . now I just wish you were here.

"I need you here, Son."

He thought of the dugout at Comerica Park. *"C'mon, Dad. . . . Let's go see it,"* he heard Aaron say, feeling again the squeeze of his hand. He thought of pressing Aaron's fingers down into the infield grass behind the pitcher's mound. He thought of his whispered *"Please"* when James resisted the overtures from the Tigers' front office to make Aaron's wish come true. He thought of the excitement in Aaron's voice when he told James about the website. He thought of the ceremonial first pitch and heard Aaron announce his name. He thought of the smile on his face during happy visits to the beach, staring out over the expanse of blue water and sky. He thought of the gardens. *"What do you think heaven's like?"* He thought of the peace.

And then he saw him in a chair getting chemo. He saw him grit his teeth and dig in during a tantrum. He saw him hold still but sob during a lumbar puncture. He saw him watching the bag of blood drain into his arm during a transfusion. He saw him gulp pills and spit them out and pick them up again and, crying, choke them back down. He saw his blank stares out the window at a brilliant summer sun.

"You are the strongest young—" James swallowed. "You are the strongest man I know. A superhero. I thought guys who could hit home runs were heroes. But they met you. And you're their hero. You're my hero, Son. And I can't let you go.

"I can't let you go."

He laid his head on Aaron's bed and didn't dream.

James startled awake after an hour, pushing himself up and rubbing his eyes. Neither Aaron nor Emily had moved. Cold water from the bathroom and a cup of coffee from the nurses' station doused the last shreds of his impromptu nap. He checked the clock—10:32. Dr. Barna said Trent Matthews would call around eleven, and James wanted to put a face with the voice. He opened Aaron's laptop, updated Aaron's Facebook care page, and zipped off an e-mail to close friends and family. Then he searched for a photo of Trent on the Rangers website—young man, wavy blond hair flowing out from underneath his red Rangers cap, and a wide, openmouthed smile.

Nearing eleven o'clock, his cell phone vibrated; the caller ID displayed *Texas*. He ducked into the bathroom and shut the door. "Hello?"

"This Mr. McConnell?" said a voice dripping Texas.

"Yes, sir, Mr. Matthews. It's so great of you to call," James said.

"Not a problem, not a problem. Did I wake ya?"

"No, no. Too keyed up to sleep."

"So how's things goin'?"

James started to say something, but his voice caught. It finally hit him. Of all the nurses and doctors and specialists and therapists and counselors who had worked with Aaron, this man—*this man*—in all the world was the one who would save his son's life.

"Ya there, Mr. McConnell? Did I lose ya?"

"No, sir, I'm here," James said through a sniff. "And please, call me James."

"Well, yer a ballplayer. Thought I could call ya J-Mac."

"For what you're doing, you can call me anything you want."

The Texas accent even infected the man's cackling laughter. "So how's he doin'?"

"He's okay. Tests started today," James explained, "and so far everything's looking good. But he's been unconscious for a few days now. Doctors are . . . well, they're a little worried."

"Don't you sweat it, J-Mac. Once he gets a drip of Texas in 'im, he'll be a new man."

"Mr. Matthews, we—"

"Please. Trent."

"Trent. We can't thank you enough for what you're doing. It's . . . it's an answered prayer for us. A wish come true."

"Don't mention it," Trent said. "I told them nice ladies when they swabbed my cheek that if I matched A-Mac, I wanted to know. We had a good turnout at the stadium for our A-Mac Day."

"You do know what the procedure's like, right?" James asked.

"They filled me in, yeah. They take it outta the hip, right?"

"That's one way. The painful way. Big needle. It won't hurt going in, but you'll feel it for a few days. The other way, the more common way, is through a blood stem cell donation."

"Yeah, yeah, they mentioned that, too. What's that involve again?"

"Drugs for a few days, and then it's just like donating blood."

Trent snorted. "So do I get a vote?"

James laughed. "Afraid not. That'll be up to Aaron's doctor."

"So the other way, the painful way . . . will it put me on the disabled list?"

"Not likely, but there's a chance."

"Well, way I figure it, if I was fixin' to win the battin' title, I might be a little pickier." He paused, obviously waiting for James to laugh. "I'm kiddin', J-Mac. Wouldn't matter if we were headin' into game seven. This is bigger than baseball, man."

James choked up again, and this time, Trent let the conversation linger in silence until James cleared his throat.

"So when's this all happenin'?"

"Probably about a week, as long as Aaron stays strong during the tests," James said. "Plenty of time to heal up before the play-offs."

"If they do it with that big needle, ya mean."

"Well . . ."

"My luck they'll use that big needle," Trent muttered. "Hey, who knows; maybe this'll bring me outta this slump!" They both shared a laugh this time. "You tell that boy a' yours to get ready for this shot of Texas in his bones. It packs a kick like hot sauce." Trent said he wanted to be the first to know how it came out, and James promised. "I'll hold ya to it. And trust me: you don't wanna break a promise to a Texan."

After another week of preparation, August 22 arrived like every other day. Like the day they found out Aaron, then five years old, had leukemia. Like the day he finished his treatment right before Christmas, a few months from turning nine. Like the day he suffered his anemic bout and relapsed. Like the day James played in a professional baseball game for the Detroit Tigers. Like the day a father and son shared a very adult conversation about heaven.

This was Transplant Day, but it arrived like any other.

But in just about every way possible, it was Day Zero. The day everything would change, one way or the other.

James and Emily intended to bury themselves in menial tasks, but that lasted only as long as a shower and a half cup of coffee. The parish priest from their church back home called and, over the phone, led them in an Our Father, Hail Mary, and Glory Be. He added his personal prayer asking for healing, skill for the doctors and nurses, and strength for Aaron, Lizzie, Emily, and James. Afterward, they called Lizzie, still with James's parents, and she asked in an oddly mousy voice if she could say something to her brother. Though Aaron still lay comatose, James held the phone up to Aaron's ear. He leaned in to listen.

"Hi, Aaron. Good luck on the transplant. I know you'll do great. We'll play Monopoly when you get home, and you can even start with whatever properties you want. I love you. Miss you."

Tears sprang from James's eyes, and he had to hand the phone to his wife.

Ten o'clock neared. James and Emily witnessed the passage of time in silence, lost in their own thoughts. For James, prayer mixed with a reflection on his time in professional baseball, hope for playing catch with Aaron, and morbidly, picturing how many people would be at the funeral. Whenever those images popped into his brain, he tried to quash them with more prayers and more pictures of bright-white baseballs streaking through a sunshine-drenched backyard.

Emily sat on his lap. She leaned her head down on top of his, and he wrapped his arms around her waist, clasping his hands together to hold her tight.

"This is all we got. You know that, right?" he said.

She nodded against his head.

"So what are we supposed to do then?"

"What do you mean?" she whispered.

"What are you so good at saying? What do you tell me, right when I need to hear it?"

"That this is the path before us right now. We can sit on the sidelines and let this . . . this cancer tell us how to act—"

"Or we can move forward with life and living. For whatever time we have left with him," James finished. "We just have to make the choice."

Her next breath shuddered. "I see what you mean now, though. Finally. About it not being so easy to make that choice."

"But you're right. You've always been right."

Someone knocked at the door. Dr. Barna and Teri entered with the transplant team. "Good morning, McConnells," Dr. Barna said. "We have a special delivery from Texas." He stopped inside the door when he saw them cuddled on the chair. "How are you folks doing?"

"Hanging in there," James said.

"I believe you will enjoy seeing . . . this," Dr. Barna said. One of the transplant nurses handed him an IV bag filled with a reddish fluid.

"Is that it?" Emily said, rising from James's lap.

"This is it. The peripheral blood stem cell donation from Mr. Matthews."

So much pain. So much heartache. So many prayers and drives and nationwide searches. All for the liquid contained in that one little bag.

"Do you need to take him somewhere?" Emily asked.

"No. We will perform the infusion right here. The entire process takes about an hour. It is a very simple procedure."

James didn't hear the word *simple*. He only heard Dr. Barna say that Aaron could have a rare, serious reaction during the infusion, causing it to be aborted. The hour would never end.

Emily pulled James to his feet, and they stood on either side of the bed to whisper good luck. Emily rubbed Aaron's face and kissed his cheeks. The monitors continued to beep the signs of life, even if his body didn't show them.

James had dreamed of this moment, prayed and begged for this moment, ever since hearing, the very first time, that his son had leukemia. But he suddenly didn't want Dr. Barna to begin. He huddled close to Aaron, protective, a shield.

He didn't want it to fail.

He didn't know what he'd do if it failed.

He clutched the bed with both hands and wouldn't let go.

Emily gasped. "James? Did you—?"

Aaron's eyes, still closed, twitched as if in a dream.

"There!"

James saw it.

"Aaron, you there?" he shouted. "Can you hear me? Open your eyes if you can hear me!"

I need to see his eyes. I don't know why, but I need to see his eyes. He has to wake up now. The donation, the transplant . . . He has to wake up. Please wake him up, Lord. Please—

"James," Dr. Barna said, "patients in comas sometimes—"

He shook Aaron's arm. "C'mon, pal; those new cells are here! Just open those blue eyes and look at me for a second!"

If he doesn't wake up right now . . .

"James . . . ," Teri said quietly.

"Aaron, it's Dad. Tigers play a big game in Minnesota tonight. They really need their biggest fan. C'mon, Aaron; open your eyes!"

If he doesn't wake up right now, this will fail. He'll have a reaction, and this will all fail.

"Honey . . . ," Emily said.

"Aaron!" James yelled.

The boy's eyes twitched again and then opened into slits. His lips moved.

James lowered his ear.

And he smiled and cried at the same time.

"He said to stop shouting," James said. Emily's head fell to Aaron's shoulder, and she sobbed. James rubbed both her back and Aaron's arm as the boy returned to his dreams.

"That is a wonderful sign, my friends," Dr. Barna said. "So let us complete this phase of the journey, shall we?"

With only nods to show they were ready, James and

Emily backed away and held each other while the infusion started.

James sat again in the chair and leaned forward, his hands clasped and the tears flowing freely. Emily rested her head on his shoulder and rocked him. "He woke up," she said through her tears. "He came back to us."

James didn't respond. He studied his son, just like the rest of the transplant team surrounding the bed, watching for any hint of a reaction. He didn't move for an hour.

And neither did Aaron.

When it was complete, Dr. Barna knelt in front of James and waited, silently, until their eyes met. He gripped James's clasped hands. "He did outstanding."

Near midnight, while Emily lay on the cot again, her hand once more on Aaron's bed resting on his arm, James's cell phone chirped with an incoming text message. He hadn't been sleeping. He sat and watched Aaron, still on guard for any reaction, but he imagined the bones soaking up the syrupy cells and gushing out new blood that bubbled through his body like a fountain of youth. The gremlins drowned and vanished in puffs of smoke, one by one. And then they were gone. All of them. Along with the images of his son's funeral.

All that remained was a baseball in the air that came to rest in Aaron's glove.

The text message was from Curt.

U up?

Yes. Tired but excited.

Howd it go?

Awesome. Might have new fave player.

Matthews?

300

Yes

Ouch

Howd u guys do?

Lost 5-3. 2 Ks.

Nice.

Ouch again. Nasty cutters. Head wasnt in game.

Thx. Get some sleep. Visit soon?

On long road trip. Not back in MI til Sep 10.

We will b here at SF.

C u then. I will tell Kara. Hug big guy and Em 4 me.

Get in line, pal.

Three days after receiving the donation, constant testing and observation showed no initial symptoms of infection at the beginning of the critical engraftment period. Although the more serious graft-versus-host disease wouldn't appear for a couple of weeks—if it came at all—that didn't stop James from inspecting Aaron for each and every symptom and burying his head in his hands in prayer with a repeated, muttered "Protect him . . . Protect him . . ."

By the following midnight, though, James's hope began to crack. Jubilation at news of the bone marrow match, the overwhelming relief when he talked to Trent, the giant step closer to playing catch with his hero . . . none of it compared to seeing Aaron's blue eyes for those few, brief seconds and hearing his whisper.

Yet Aaron still lay there.

His body produced new blood, cancer-free blood; James was certain. And each drop that flowed through his blood vessels spread new strength and new health and new hope.

Yet Aaron still lay there.

Doctors and nurses came and went, all smiles, checking his

vitals. They gave him a red blood cell transfusion and a platelet transfusion and pumped new drugs into his IV.

And yet . . .

No beeps from the monitors, no voices in the hall. Not even Emily's heavy breathing from the cot on the other side of the bed.

It was so silent.

James folded his hands, closed his eyes, and rested his forehead on the bed.

He felt a twitch.

Aaron's hand moved.

James jumped.

"Dad?" Aaron's eyes remained closed, but his hand rose, searching. "Dad? Are you there?"

He grabbed Aaron's hand with both of his, squeezing and kissing it. "I'm here, Son. I haven't left. I'm right here. What do you need? Do you need some water? Can I—?"

"Dad . . ."

"What is it? What do you want?" James swallowed hard. "Do you want me to tell you about the grass? Is that it? Do you want to hear about the grass again?"

"No." His thin fingers curled around James's and squeezed. "I want my glove. Do you have my glove?"

Tears poured onto the bed, and James opened the bedside stand and took out Aaron's mitt, a white baseball inside. He tucked it against the boy's leg and placed his hand on top.

"It's right here, Son."

He covered Aaron's hand with his own.

"I got it right here."

EPILOGUE

UNDER A BRILLIANT-BLUE SKY and a warm spring sun that gilded every blade of grass with a single stroke of golden light, Aaron McConnell raised his leg high, reached back, and—summoning every ounce of strength—fired a baseball across the backyard toward his father.

And when he caught it again, the ball smacking solidly in the palm of his glove, he realized his dad was right.

The sting in his hand of a ball popping into a mitt felt wonderful.

Acknowledgments

BRINGING A BOOK INTO THE WORLD IS A TEAM SPORT. And with that team come the relationships developed over the many months and years as strangers become friends and contribute their own passions to the story. A handful of paragraphs doesn't seem enough to convey my gratitude.

I am forever thankful to Karen Watson, Tyndale House's associate publisher. When she told me she saw *Wish* as "fiction with a mission," I knew immediately that she recognized and believed in the bigger purpose behind the book. I could not have asked for a more patient, tolerant go-to person than Stephanie Broene, Tyndale's senior acquisitions editor—her integrity, dedication, and tenacity carried *Wish*, from beginning to end, through the sometimes-crazy publication process. Thank you to editor Caleb Sjogren for his insightful eye and honing the manuscript with considerable care and respect, and to copy editors Erin Smith and Mary Johansen for their guidance in wrapping everything together so beautifully. I can't thank art director Dan Farrell enough for his work in capturing the story's emotion with such a dramatic cover—it's a moment every writer dreams about, seeing the cover for the first time. Finally, I am truly moved by the diligence of senior marketing manager Cheryl Kerwin, senior publicist Andrea Martin, and acquisitions assistant Shaina Turner. Each member of the

Tyndale team brings such enthusiasm to every step of the journey, and they are joined together in their mission to produce faith-filled books that make a difference. I feel so blessed to be part of the Tyndale family.

I would not have had the chance to work with the amazing people at Tyndale, however, if it weren't for my equally incredible agent, Jeff Kleinman of Folio Literary Management. In fact, this book would've gone *nowhere* without him. I will always be indebted to Jeff for believing—in the manuscript, in the larger goals of the book, in me. Editor, psychologist, negotiator, taskmaster, friend . . . the guy doesn't have an Off switch and maintains his dedication to each of his authors with amazing consistency and passion. Everyone at Folio—Michael Sterling, Melissa Sarver, Molly Jaffa, and all the others—share Jeff's tireless work ethic and commitment on behalf of those they represent, and for that I am grateful.

Those in the medical community who work with pediatric patients on a daily basis, or who further research or raise funds for the care and treatment of current and future patients, are angels, plain and simple. Dr. James Feusner, Dr. E. Donnall Thomas Jr., and Dr. Albert Cornelius all provided their expert input; and many people at various children's hospitals—among them Brad Kaufmann, Cari Tiensvu, Tammi Carr, Anna Beeman, and Anne Berluchi—offered their time, opinions, and experiences.

The heroes, however, are those kids and families who fight cancer every day, even after treatment is complete and they proudly wear the badge of *cancer survivor*—and especially when they continue to fight after a devastating loss. To Pat and Leslee Heintz and the loving memory of Katie; and Susan, Steve, Sarah, and Maria Bertoia—I am so incredibly proud to know you and am amazed at your strength, determination, and faith.

Many people—on and off the field—helped round the

baseball scenes into shape. Doug Glanville (and his fantastic memoir, *The Game from Where I Stand*) and Doug Mirabelli provided on-the-field help; and the remarkable work of Brandon Inge and his wife, Shani, at the C. S. Mott Children's Hospital in Ann Arbor, Michigan, served as quite a dose of inspiration. Scot Pett, Maggie Brookens, Ellen Hill Zeringue, and Nicole Blaszczyk of the Detroit Tigers and Mickey Graham of the West Michigan Whitecaps were sounding boards with front office matters and provided some fantastic tours.

A significant team of friends and relatives kept my confidence up during those times I wanted to bang my head against the wall. *Everyone* played a significant role, so I'm doing this alphabetically: Rebecca Avers, Autumn Brady, Jennifer Brooks, Karen Dionne, Carol Erickson, Pete Gaspeny, Tom Hitchens, Brandon Hoffman, Eric and Jenni Huffman, Jill LaCross, Chip Laughton, Andy and Michele LePere, Scott Lizenby, Michael McCatty, Katie McNulty, Deb Neuman, Melissa O'Brien, Tina and Dean Parker, Ben Ready, Matt Riley, John Roddy, Richard Smith (Bomps), Nancy Whitten, and Buz Zamarron. And a very special thanks to Lisa Maxbauer-Price and Jason F. Wright for getting this great big ball rolling in the first place.

To my eternal champions, my family. I've always believed that God makes His presence and His love known, in His purest form, through those around us. None of this is possible without your encouragement of my imagination, your love and support while I sequester myself to write, your unwavering belief in me, and your inspiring message of perseverance. Mom and Dad, Chris and Lani, Amy and Steve—you always said this would happen, and I think your saying it is what got me through many storms. And, Dad and Chris, my first and best baseball teachers—not sure where I'd be without the thousands of ground balls and double plays and one of my most precious memories of sharing a state championship with my big brother. Mom and Dad Schafer, in addition to your constant support, you guys blessed me with the greatest gift of all: your daughter.

Vickie, the love and life we share is beyond measure. Pete, Mark, and Madeline—my little inspirations for Aaron and Lizzie, and the next generation of Smith ballplayers—I couldn't imagine life without your smiles and laughter.

And that's why I'd like to ask everyone to take a minute and visit BeTheMatch.org. Join the bone marrow registry. A cheek swab, that's it, and you could save someone's life so that a family doesn't have to live without their loved one's smiles and laughter. Further, contribute to one of the many cancer research foundations or, more specifically, a children's hospital in your area. They all have foundations to support the care of patients. You can purchase "wish list" items needed for therapy and treatment, and families could sorely use help with expenses when travel is necessary. That is the real mission that this work of fiction is supporting: the care of those in hospitals right now and those who anxiously wait to receive word that there's a bone marrow match and a donor ready to give. If I can throw a few frightening statistics out there: the nonprofit CureSearch for Children's Cancer says that more than forty thousand children will undergo treatment annually; the American Childhood Cancer Organization estimates more than thirteen thousand new cases of childhood cancer (children up to nineteen years old) will be diagnosed each year; and according to the National Marrow Donor Program, someone is diagnosed with a blood cancer every four minutes, and 70 percent of patients who are in need of a bone marrow transplant must turn to nonfamily members for a match.

Each one of these people has a hope and a dream—a wish. *You* could be a wish come true for someone today.

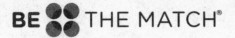

BE ⬤⬤ THE MATCH®

Be The Match®, operated by the National Marrow Donor Program® (NMDP), is a nonprofit organization that's dedicated to helping every patient get the life-saving transplant they need.

Your actions give hope for a cure:

- Join the registry as a potential marrow donor
- Make a donation to help patients find a matching donor and afford a transplant
- Volunteer your time to help spread the word

The cure for blood cancer is in the hands of ordinary people[SM].

BeTheMatch.org

About the Author

JAKE SMITH is the editor of three national, award-winning bimonthly magazines. He has also written several outdoor and dog-training books and published more than 150 articles in national outdoor magazines. A former assistant high school baseball coach and all-state high school shortstop, Jake now spends his time on the field coaching his kids' youth baseball teams.

While researching *Wish*, Jake talked with current and former major league baseball players, children's hospital administrators, pediatric oncologists, and families who fought against childhood leukemia and other illnesses. Their expertise, along with tours of C. S. Mott Children's Hospital in Ann Arbor, Michigan; Helen DeVos Children's Hospital in Grand Rapids, Michigan; and "behind the scenes" of Comerica Park (home of the Detroit Tigers) and Fifth Third Ballpark (home of the West Michigan Whitecaps), provided the basis for *Wish*. Jake hopes this novel will help support children's hospitals, patient and family foundations, and participation in the National Marrow Donor Program's bone marrow registry (BeTheMatch.org).

Jake holds both BS and MS degrees in wildlife sciences and management and lives in Traverse City, Michigan, with his wife, Vickie, their three children, and their Labrador retriever. Visit him online at www.jakesmithbooks.com.